IN THIS MOMENT

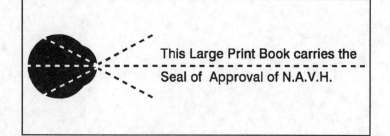

This Large Print Book carries the
Seal of Approval of N.A.V.H.

THE BAXTER FAMILY

In This Moment

Karen Kingsbury

WHEELER PUBLISHING
A part of Gale, a Cengage Company

Farmington Hills, Mich • San Francisco • New York • Waterville, Maine
Meriden, Conn • Mason, Ohio • Chicago

Copyright © 2017 by Karen Kingsbury.
Wheeler Publishing, a part of Gale, a Cengage Company.

**LIBRARY OF CONGRESS CIP DATA ON FILE.
CATALOGUING IN PUBLICATION FOR THIS BOOK
IS AVAILABLE FROM THE LIBRARY OF CONGRESS.**

ISBN-13: 978-1-4328-4434-9 (hardcover)
ISBN-10: 1-4328-4434-2 (hardcover)

Published in 2017 by arrangement with Howard Books, an imprint of Simon & Schuster, Inc.

Printed in the United States of America
1 2 3 4 5 6 7 21 20 19 18 17

To Donald:

Well . . . we are into our second year as empty-nesters. I never liked that term. And I can tell you now with all my heart that there's been nothing empty about our lives. It's been full of beautiful walks and meaningful talks, nights when we randomly jump into the car and spend an evening with Kelsey and Kyle and little Hudson. We play tennis and Ping-Pong and hang out with friends. And yes, we miss having our family all together every day. But when they come home the celebrating never ends. Yes, I've loved raising our kids with you, but now I love this season, too. God has brought us through so many pages in our story. The Baxter family came to life while we were raising our kids. When they told stories around the family dinner table, we were doing the same. And when their kids auditioned for Christian theater, our kids were singing the same songs. Our family is — and always will be — inexorably linked with the Baxters. Thank you for creating a world where our love and life and family and faith were so beautiful that I could do nothing but write about it. So that some far-off day when we're old and the voices of our many grandchildren fill the house, we can pull out books like this one and remember. Every single beautiful moment. I love you.

To Kyle:

You will always be the young man we prayed for, the one we believed God for when it came to our precious only daughter. You love Kelsey so well, Kyle. And you are such a great daddy to Hudson. You are a man of God and talented in so many ways. Thank you for bringing us so much joy. We pray that all the world will one day be changed for the better because of your music, your books, your love, and your life.

To Kelsey:

What an amazing season this has been, watching as you became the best mommy ever through all the firsts of Hudson's life. Little Hudson is such a happy two-year-old, such a miracle. His laughter rings in my heart always. What a beautiful time for us all! Hudson is strong and kind and joyful, with a depth that defies his age. God is going to use him in powerful ways. And God will continue to use you, also, Kelsey. You and Kyle and Hudson — and whatever other kids God might bring your way. Your family is a very bright light in this world . . . and I know that one day this generation will look to you all as an example of how to love well. I treasure our time together. Every moment is another best day. Love you with all my heart, honey.

To Tyler:
Watching you take wing this past year has been another of life's great joys. Long ago when I imagined you graduating from college and moving out on your own, I thought it would be with tears and sadness. The quiet in the front room where once the sound of you playing the piano filled our nights. The empty space where you once made your bedroom. But last year caught me by surprise. I was simply too happy for you to find time to be sad. You shine so brightly for Jesus — your songwriting, your singing, your screenwriting, your novel writing. The amazing group of godly friends the Lord has surrounded

you with. All of it is wonderful! God has great things ahead, and as always I am most thankful for this front-row seat. Oh, and I'm also thankful for the occasional night when you stop by for dinner and a few songs on the piano. You are a very great blessing, Ty. Love you always.

To Sean:

I'm so glad you're doing so well at Liberty University, working on your degree and growing in faith and strength as a man. You have come so far, Sean. Your dad and I are so proud of you! From the first day we held you, we knew your spirit was bright and that you were born with a beautiful kindness. You love God and people with a passion and joy that survived your first five years in Haiti. And you continue to use the heartache of those early days to lead people to Christ. Keep talking to us about your hopes and dreams. Keep asking us about romance. We are here for you always! I am convinced God has amazing plans ahead for you, Son. I love you forever.

To Josh:

Just yesterday you were that little six-year-old boy, staring up at me with those beautiful brown eyes, saying, "Hi, Mommy. I love you." How the years have flown since then. Now you're married and living in Florida with Makayla, the girl we have prayed for all these years. You're grown up and on your own! Always remember that having a relationship with Jesus is the most important gift you will ever give your family. You belong to Him, Josh. You always have. As you lead your family in the years to come, as you walk out your faith together, just know how much we love you. We believe in you. We are here for you always!

To EJ:

What a tremendous time this is for you, EJ. You are doing so well at Liberty University, so excited about the career in filmmaking you have chosen. I love how God knew — even all those years ago when you first entered our family — that you would need to be with people who loved Him and who loved each other . . . but also people who loved the power of storytelling. I'm so excited about the future, and the ways God will use your gifts to intersect with the gifts of so many others in our family. Maybe we should start our own studio — making movies that will change

the world for God. I love it! And I love you
— always.

To Austin:

I knew you would blossom at Liberty
University, and so you have. God has
been faithful, speaking to you about your
future, opening doors to your dreams. You
are a leader and an example to your
peers, and I am so proud of you. I'm grateful I can see you boys when I travel to
Liberty University to teach, so many happy
times together. So many beautiful breaks
and special family times. But even as you
are midway through your second year of
college, I still miss you in the everyday-
ness, Austin. You are still such a light in
our home, our miracle boy. Our overcomer.
You are my youngest, and no question the
hardest one to let go. The quiet here is
so . . . quiet. Even with your dad's jokes
and little Hudson's visits. So . . . while
you're at Liberty, on still nights when you
lie awake in your dorm, just know that we
have cherished every moment of raising
you. And we are still here. We always will
be. Keep putting God first, and keep following the path He has for you. Love you
forever, Aus.

And to God Almighty, the Author of Life,

who has — for now — blessed me with these.

Those who stand for nothing . . . fall for anything.

— Alexander Hamilton

1

Wendell Quinn walked into his office that September morning with a plan. But he also had a problem.

Well, truth be told, he had a bushel of problems.

As principal of Hamilton High School, situated between Haughville and the Indianapolis Motor Speedway, on the rough side of the city, Wendell's students were routinely killed in gang violence and regularly locked up for dealing drugs. They traded their futures for grand theft auto or attempted murder or a life of skipping school, and too many of them were left with the dead-end futures their choices created.

Test scores and graduation rates lay drowning in the gutter, respect for teachers was at an all-time low, teen pregnancy was epidemic and suicide was on the rise.

Wendell had tried every means possible to change the situation at Hamilton High.

15

Because of his efforts, the school used a positive incentive program, rewarding good behavior and high grades with exemption from final exams. Local businesses had donated goods and discount coupons for students on the honor roll.

He'd gotten creative with discipline, too.

Wendell had doubled suspensions and expulsions for bad behavior. Teachers used a demerit system to deter students causing the most trouble. On top of that, his team of guidance counselors had brought in a number of guest speakers.

In recent years they'd heard from a mother who lost two sons to gang violence, a college girl whose sibling was behind bars for dealing drugs, and a trio of convicts who shared stories intended to wake up the kids at Hamilton High.

If any of that worked, Wendell hadn't seen proof. Every measurable means of analyzing Hamilton and its students showed just one thing: The school was getting worse.

And Wendell Quinn was sick of it.

He set his worn black leather briefcase on his desk and opened it. On top was a presentation folder graced by a cover sheet that read: "In This Moment." It was a look inside Wendell's heart: his reasons and research behind his most risky decision yet.

16

The decision that later today Wendell would launch a Bible study program right here at Hamilton. All of it was detailed inside the folder, the result of an entire summer of reading legal documents on the topic.

Reading and prayer.

A knock at his door and Wendell turned to see the one face that caused his heart to soar. Alicia Harris, Hamilton High's favorite teacher. His favorite, too. Wendell and Alicia had been friends for several years — since the car accident that took Wendell's wife. But in the past few months his friendship with Alicia had grown into a dating relationship.

Wendell admired everything about her. The way she loved his children, her concern for her students. Her gift of inspiring students — something that couldn't be taught in college. But there was a tragic secret about Alicia that the rest of the school didn't know.

She was battling an anxiety disorder.

Not just a struggle with being anxious. Alicia was in a debilitating fight with panic attacks like nothing Wendell had ever seen. Since they'd gotten closer, Alicia had opened up about her episodes. She was a Christian with a strong faith. But on some days she considered it a miracle that she could leave her house at all. And once in a while she couldn't even do that.

Alicia and Wendell had discussed his new program. If there was one person at Hamilton High who would struggle with what was coming, it was Alicia. Which just about killed Wendell. But he had made his decision. He could pray for her and be there for her. But he couldn't let her anxiety stop him from helping the students at Hamilton High.

He gave her a weak smile and met her at his office door. "Alicia. Come in."

She closed the door behind her and turned to him. Her expression was tight, the fear in her pretty eyes tangible. She'd been this way since Wendell brought up the idea of the Bible study, and now Alicia seemed to almost hold her breath. "I feel sick."

"Hey . . ." Wendell reached for her hand. Her fingers were freezing. This wasn't the time or place for a hug, so he looked deep into her eyes. "God's got this."

Now that they were seeing each other, the two were careful to keep things professional when they were at school. Dating wasn't forbidden among the staff at Hamilton High. But they had no intention of flaunting their new relationship. A case could be made for conflict of interest.

Wendell released her hand. "This is my decision. My plan." He searched her eyes. The eyes he had come to love. "It doesn't have to affect you."

If Wendell could've found someone else to run the program, he would've. He had certainly tried. But the few students he was comfortable asking had been unable to help. Even his own son, whose faith was rock solid, hadn't felt confident leading the group. He'd asked a few of the teachers, the ones he was sure shared his beliefs. But all of them said some version of the same thing.

They couldn't afford to jeopardize their jobs over a program that, in their minds, clearly violated the Constitution's separation of church and state rule. Wendell disagreed about that much. Still, he couldn't do more than ask his staff and students — otherwise he would be at risk of an actual violation. So he was on his own. After a summer of research, he was certain a voluntary faith program that met after school was legal.

Even if he facilitated it.

It was this personal conviction, one he'd lived with, that in the end gave him the courage to move forward: Here and now at Hamilton High, Wendell was the only one who could step forward. The only one who could make a difference.

In this moment.

Wendell's tone was gentle. "You're not saying anything."

"I'm sorry." Alicia trembled and her teeth chattered. "I'm just . . . I'm so scared." She looked around, like she was searching for some way out of the situation. "Everything's about to change. It's the first day of school and I have no idea how I'm supposed to teach."

Wendell studied her. "All because you don't agree with my plan?" He hesitated. "That's it?"

Alicia looked at the folder on his desk. She was the picture of professionalism, neat black skirt and white blouse, new heels. Her black hair straightened just the way she liked it. She seemed to attempt a smile, but it became a slight nod. "I mean . . . I know the students need help. They need something . . . someone." She was clearly frustrated. "But you're the principal. Why does it have to be you?" Anxiety darkened her beautiful wide green eyes. So much anxiety. "You could be fired, Wendell. You know that. And . . . I guess I'm afraid if I stand by you . . . I'll be fired, too."

"We have rights. *Freedom* of religion, Alicia. It's a voluntary program." *Calm,* he told himself. *Stay calm.* "They won't fire us."

"They could." Her answer was quick. "I don't know what's going to happen."

"I don't, either." He had to be honest with her. "But I trust God. This is what He wants. I'm convinced."

For a long moment they were quiet. Then she drew a sharp breath. "I have class." A pause and she looked deep into his eyes again. "I'll be praying."

"Me, too." He opened the door and they stood together, staring at the words everyone saw when they entered Hamilton High School. The quote painted on the school wall, the one that had started this whole thing last May, the day school let out for the summer.

Those who stand for nothing . . . fall for anything — Alexander Hamilton.

Hamilton had spoken those words hundreds of years ago, when he was the first U.S. Secretary of the Treasury, and one of America's founding fathers. The quote was emblazoned on the hallway in letters fourteen inches high. Wendell read the lines silently, the way he read them every day when he arrived at school.

Alicia angled her head, her eyes fixed on the quote. "Alexander Hamilton was a

Christian." She turned and gave Wendell a softer look. "I know . . . he'd be cheering you on today."

"Maybe God will give him a front-row seat today."

"Maybe." Alicia hesitated for a long few seconds. "See ya, Wendell." Her smile felt genuine. But the fear was still there. The one that would certainly remain an hour from now, when Wendell's very risky plan would become a reality.

She gave him a final look and then turned and walked down the hall toward her classroom. First period was at eight o'clock. The assembly was at nine.

Wendell took the seat behind his desk and looked at the folder. He couldn't blame Alicia. She had to take care of herself. Still, her pulling away from him was the most difficult part of his decision to run the Bible study.

He ran his hand over the folder. He hadn't prepared the material inside for anyone but himself. He wanted his research all in one place. The reasons he felt justified in starting his voluntary Bible study program.

Just in case he needed to defend himself at some point.

The information was something to fall back on when that time came. And Wendell had no doubt it would. One way or another he would pay for what he was about to do. And if he paid, his four kids would pay. Alicia, too. At least she thought so.

He studied his family's photo on his desk. His kids were the joy of his life, a constant reminder of God's goodness. Jordy was seventeen, a junior, and Leah was a fourteen-year-old freshman who played trumpet in the school's marching band. Alexandria was twelve and in her seventh-grade theater club, and Darrell, the youngest, was ten.

The light in their faces, the love between them warmed Wendell's heart on the coldest of Indianapolis days. He looked at his kids one at a time. Each of them carried a part of Joanna, their mother. Jordy had her kind eyes . . . Leah, her pretty smile. Alexandria had Joanna's laugh, and Darrell, her sense of adventure.

A ripple of concern tightened around his chest. Yes, they would likely all pay for what he was about to do. Wendell could be fired. People would mock his children for having a father who dared bring God into a public school. Wendell had come across a three-year-old case where a local social services agency attempted to remove children from the home of a public educator who taught an after-school Bible study.

As if teaching the Bible at school might make someone like Wendell an unfit parent.

The educator won that case. But things were changing. A growing sector of people were vehemently against anything Christian. If Wendell and his kids suffered, then Alicia believed she would suffer, too. In her mind, the events at Hamilton would be splashed across the news and no public school in the state would ever hire her or Wendell again. Yes, as far as Alicia was concerned, the whole scenario already felt like a reality. A fait accompli, as Hamilton might've said back in the day.

Which was why Alicia was already pulling away.

The sad thing was that she was probably right. Any attention on social media meant a tsunami of scrutiny would be on all of them. Every Christian on staff. So the first cost was almost certainly going to be his relationship with the woman he loved. Wendell's heart already hurt over what was coming. But even so he had to follow through with his plan.

This was what God wanted of him. Wendell was sure. And God would see him through. He sighed. *Lord, if only I could help Alicia trust You. Really trust.*

He thought back to a recent day in mid-July when he'd made his intentions known. He had grilled burgers for her and the kids and they'd spent the day swimming at the neighborhood pool. Back at his house, once the kids were in the other room watching a movie, Alicia had hugged him. The smell of her hair and perfume had filled his senses, and Wendell had known he couldn't go another day without telling her how he felt.

He sat across from her in the living room that day and searched her eyes. "My kids love you."

"I love them." Her smile lit up her face. "I had the best day, Wendell."

"The kids aren't the only ones. *I* love you, too, Alicia." His heart pounded in his chest. "As more than a friend." It felt like Wendell's brokenhearted season since losing Joanna was finally over.

Her eyes sparkled brighter than the sunshine on the pool. "I wondered if you'd ever tell me."

The two of them laughed and stood and hugged again, and as Wendell walked her to her car that evening, he did what he'd longed to do for months.

He kissed her.

After their beautiful summer together, Wendell had planned to propose. That way they could be a family sooner than later. Which was something his kids wanted. Just a few weeks ago Alicia took Leah and Alexandria back-to-school shopping, and when the three of them came home and the girls modeled their new clothes, it was as if they'd been close to Alicia forever. Jordy and Darrell loved her, too. The boys took bike rides with Alicia and Luvie, their family dog.

But he had done more than spend time with Alicia over the summer.

Driven for some way to help the Hamilton students, Wendell had worked late at night and early in the morning poring over the Federalist Papers, written mostly by Alexander Hamilton. Wendell hadn't seen the Broadway musical about the man, but he had heard the Hamilton cast recording. A line from one of the songs stayed with Wendell.

I am not throwing away my shot . . . not throwing away my shot.

Because of his research, Wendell had come to admire Alexander Hamilton. The man's visionary ability to bring people together. His unwavering faith in God. Wendell agreed with the words of George Will, a famous politician.

Will said, "There is an elegant memorial

in Washington to Jefferson, but none to Hamilton. However, if you seek Hamilton's monument, look around. You are living in it. We honor Jefferson, but we live in Hamilton's country."

Those quotes were in Wendell's presentation folder. The details Wendell had learned or read or researched about Hamilton and the U.S. Constitution. The freedoms afforded every American citizen were highlighted in the pages of the folder in front of him. Wendell had also included a number of esteemed studies showing the academic, social and personal benefit of prayer and faith.

In addition, he'd researched his rights. What he was about to do was legal, but he had to be careful. He could alert students to the optional after-school club, but he couldn't push them to attend. And bottom line, he could be sued, because anyone could be sued for anything.

The question was whether he'd win.

Wendell had a strong sense that he could. Because it wasn't only the statistics and research on Hamilton and the Constitution that drove him to come up with the plan. It was the Bible, too. The verses in Proverbs and Psalms that spoke about training a child in the way he should go and teaching the next generation the truths of God.

The students at Hamilton High were utterly broken. How could he not share with them the truths of the Bible, the hope of God? For a year, Wendell had felt a holy calling to make this move. That's why he'd spent so much time this past summer pulling together his research, making certain he wasn't breaking any law.

Now, with his folder of research before him, Wendell felt ready. He would do this. He had to do it. He was the only one willing to take a stand.

Wendell closed his eyes and leaned back in his chair. All summer he'd been telling Alicia about his idea, how he wanted to bring the Bible back to Hamilton High. Six days ago he'd taken her to coffee and explained what his research had netted. How he felt he had the right to do something to help the students.

The bell rang out in the hallway.

Wendell blinked his eyes open but the memory remained. Alicia had nodded, but her breathing was different. Faster, filled with fear. She struggled to speak. "With all my heart . . . I want to stand by you on this, Wendell. I do." Her breathing was faster still, completely panicked. Each breath came faster and faster, and they had to hurry out of the coffeehouse. Alicia barely made it to her car, and she struggled even to talk. "My heart . . . it's racing. I . . . I can't breathe." She gasped. "I'm dying, Wendell! Help me!"

Wendell could still hear her, still see the terror in her face. He had tried to comfort her, but there was nothing he could say. For the next thirty minutes he held her hand and watched her as — between panicked gasps — she did the only thing she could do. She popped two pills and recited the same Bible verse over and over.

It was from Philippians 4.

"Do not be anxious about anything, but in every situation, by prayer and petition, with thanksgiving, present your requests to God. And the peace of God, which transcends all understanding, will guard your hearts and your minds in Christ Jesus."

Over and over and over again.

It was the first time Wendell had seen Alicia suffer a full-blown panic attack. Before then, she had downplayed her anxiety disorder. But there was no denying it now. And since then he could feel her pulling away a little more each time they talked. He was making her anxiety worse.

All because of his desire to help the students at Hamilton High.

Wendell stared out the window. *You'll get*

me through this, right, God? Not just me, but the students? He sighed. *Open their eyes and ears, Father. Help them find hope in You. Please do that.* Wendell pulled the report closer. The front of the folder included every encouraging example that had inspired Wendell to finally act. He flipped to the back. Here were the detailed reasons why Wendell couldn't wait another year. The terrible truths and statistics that defined his school.

The truth was there in black and white. Hamilton High and its students were on the brink of disaster. A total collapse. It was even possible the school board could close Hamilton for good. Late last April the members had discussed a plan where the students would be bused to other schools across town. In that case, the doors of Wendell's school would be shut forever. Until the board decided what to do with the property.

Wendell clenched his jaw. No, that would not happen. That terrible possibility was the past. This year would be different. Today was the first day of the new Hamilton High, and very soon at the assembly, Wendell would inform his students of the program. After today they would have a choice. If they wanted, they could raise the bar for their lives, their futures.

Wendell could hardly wait to tell them about it.

He closed the folder and studied the title again. "In This Moment." The words came from his old youth football coach, Les Green. "You have to ask yourself," the coach used to say, "what good can I do in this moment?"

What good can I do in this moment . . . ?

Indeed.

Wendell took a deep breath and turned to the first page. He'd written just one thing on it: the job description he'd agreed to when he was hired by the school district to serve as principal of Hamilton High. The description read:

Establish a schoolwide vision of commitment to high standards and ensure the success of all students.

The verbs spoke to him as he read the words again.

He lifted his eyes to the blue sky outside his window. *You called me to establish and ensure, Lord . . . that's why I was hired.* It was his job to establish a vision. Not just any vision, but a vision of commitment to high standards. And it was his job to ensure the success of all students.

That's what he was paid to do.

Wendell leaned forward and planted his elbows on his desk. Last year six Hamilton High students were killed in gang violence. Two committed suicide and three overdosed on drugs. Forty percent were flunking at least one class. In a school of a thousand, Wendell had failed his job and his students.

But not anymore.

Fresh air. That's what he needed. The weather outside was beautiful, cooler than usual and crisp. None of the summer humidity. Wendell opened his office window and sat back down at his desk. He turned the page in his folder and saw the words God had given him. Words that made the most sense considering his job duties. Being called to create a vision of commitment to high standards could only be summed up one way:

Raise the bar.

That's what Wendell had been hired to do. Raise the bar. Now, finally, that's what he was going to do. And so his program for Hamilton would be called Raise the Bar. It was intended to give kids hope and a reason to care, a reason to try and grow and learn and live.

Wendell stood and crossed the room to his bookcase, the one that spanned most of the far wall. The top shelf contained things that inspired him: gifts from Alicia and his kids, more family pictures, a framed photo of a student who graduated from Hamilton High and made her way into a career as a surgeon in nearby Bloomington. And there at the far end, an old grass-stained football with the message Les Green had scribbled across it.

In this moment.

Oh, Les, my friend . . . I wish you were here. Wendell took the ball in his hands. Les had been there to pick up the pieces when Wendell's father was shot and killed in a drug deal. Wendell was just seven years old.

"I got you, Wendell," Les had told him at the funeral. "God's got you. He has plans for you. Keep your eyes on the sky because these streets have nothing for you."

Les Green became the father Wendell needed, a man he clung to all his growing-up years. Les used to say, "A man is nothing without God." He'd quote Bible verses like Proverbs 16:3. *Commit your actions to the Lord whatever you do, and he will establish your plans.* It was no surprise that Wendell made his first trip to church in the passenger seat of Les Green's Chevy sedan.

Les was best man at Wendell and Joanna's wedding, and Les became Wendell's greatest confidant in the early days, when the kids came along. A year after Wendell's youngest was born, Les was raking leaves in front of his single-story, small suburban home when he dropped dead of a heart attack.

The loss left a gaping hole in Wendell's heart. A hole Wendell filled with Jesus and more Jesus. Which was exactly what Les would've done.

Wendell smiled as he set the football back on the shelf. He knew what Les Green would have told him today. *Something has to change. Get out there and tell the kids about your program. The students at Hamilton High need Jesus.* Or as Alexander Hamilton would say to him: *You need to stand for something . . . or you'll fall for anything.*

Today was the day Wendell Quinn would take a stand.

Les would be proud. Hamilton, too. Jesus most of all.

Wendell sat back down at his desk. *What good can I do in this moment? In this moment.* He repeated the words until they were etched in his heart and soul. This was his chance to make a difference. God would help him, no matter the cost.

Whatever came next, Wendell was ready.

2

Twenty minutes before the assembly, Wendell walked to the auditorium and onto the stage. He stood there in the silence and tried to imagine the student body and staff reaction later that morning.

The last hour had passed in a blur of paperwork and conversations with a number of teachers and office assistants — "How was your summer, Mr. Quinn?" "How was the lake?" "How are the kids?"

None of them had any idea what was coming.

Wendell took a deep breath. The place smelled stale, the way it always smelled after a summer behind closed doors. He filled his lungs and folded his hands. *Lord, I'm gonna need Your help. Please let me get the point across.* He looked at the empty seats. *Help them hear about this plan with fresh ears. If only they could see the possibilities.* Wendell exhaled.

His staff would think he'd lost his mind. Some of them might even complain or report him. He could be fired. Anything was possible.

Wendell felt his courage double. He had to take that chance. It wasn't illegal to tell students about a voluntary after-school program. Each student had a choice.

The bell rang and Wendell stood a little taller.

Here we go.

He stayed on the stage as the students dragged themselves in. One by one, group by group they came, backpacks flung over their shoulders, their faces etched with anger and indifference, fear and disinterest. Only a few of them talked or laughed as they took their seats.

Teachers joined them, filling the rows in the back of the room. He watched Alicia enter with two English teachers. *Please, God, give her peace.* Wendell sighed. *Ease her anxious heart.*

The second bell should've signaled a full auditorium, all the students in their seats. But Wendell could see that one in four seats were still open. The seniors, probably. Last year during the first-day-of-school assembly, half the seniors hung out in the parking lot — some openly smoking pot and drinking.

Wendell had laid down the law after that. Anyone caught missing future assemblies would have detention for a week.

But the kids didn't care.

There wasn't a single reason they would come to detention. What could Wendell do to them? They would have to care about their high school experience before they would care about detention.

Typically, Wendell wore a button-down cotton shirt, sleeves rolled to the elbow. Not today. For the unveiling of his plan, Wendell wore a suit. Gray pinstripes. Never mind that right now it felt like a straitjacket. He wanted the students to know he was serious.

Wendell took the handheld mic and made his way to the front center of the stage. "Good morning!" He kept his voice cheerful. Something he'd learned from Les Green. "This isn't any ordinary school year, people. This year everything is going to change at Hamilton High."

It was impossible not to notice the dozens of boys slumped in their seats, hoodies and baseball caps pulled low over their eyes, or the girls on their phones. There were rules against these things, but none of them seemed to care.

Wendell stayed patient. He told them

about the new bell schedule and how after-school tutoring would be available this year. "A teacher from each department will stay for one hour Monday, Wednesday and Friday in the Four Hundred Building. You can show up for help anytime you wish."

A few more announcements and it was time. The plan had to be revealed. To kick it off, Wendell had created a short film. Only four minutes long, it was a recap of everything wrong and heartbreaking about Hamilton High. Factual information, nothing more. Produced in a way that some students might actually pay attention.

"I'd like you to watch a video." Wendell pointed to the screen overhead. In the back of the room a skirmish broke out. Two male students shoved each other and then quickly wound up on the floor in a brawl.

Students all around the incident were on their feet, yelling at the two, cheering them on.

"Enough!" Wendell stared at the back row. Even with a mic, he wasn't getting their attention. "That's enough!" He looked to the nearest teacher. "Please take them to the office. Keep them there." The other students were still standing, still watching as two teachers rushed in. They broke up the fight and finally walked the kids out of the auditorium. Wendell lowered his voice. "Sit down. All of you."

Gradually, the students obeyed until everyone was seated and generally facing the stage again. "Okay." Wendell couldn't believe things were going so poorly. He needed to get the video up and running. "Take a look at the screen."

Someone lowered the house lights and pushed play. The video began with a burst of statistics. Dreary, gut-wrenching statistics. The Hamilton gang violence, the drug abuse, the suicides. The transition shot read: "Those are the statistics. These are the stories."

Using images from the yearbook and photos taken by students in Alicia's journalism class, the rest of the film was a more personal look at the losses from the previous year. Rasha Carter, a sophomore. About to walk home from school last January, killed in an exchange of gunfire between two rival gangs. She never even made it past the school parking lot before she was killed.

The footage showed Rasha alive and happy, talking about her dreams and laughing with friends. But it was followed with video coverage of her funeral. The day the girl's future was buried with her at the cemetery.

Wendell heard a few sniffles coming from somewhere in the front row. That was when he saw he had their attention. Not everyone. Still plenty of students hanging their heads, sleeping through the moment or too busy on their phones to care. But a few girls in the front were crying, and gradually students were tuning in.

The film continued with additional clips of the other students who'd died last year, followed by a montage of news headlines featuring Hamilton High's worst criminal element. The video ended with the quote from Alexander Hamilton. *Those who stand for nothing . . . fall for anything.*

Wendell waited for the lights to come on. The room was quiet. Not much, but something of an improvement. "That was the old Hamilton High School." He looked around. "Today you are sitting in the auditorium of the new Hamilton High."

He spotted Alicia. Even from so far away he could feel her support, her prayers. She wouldn't stand beside him in this season. But however afraid this made her, in her heart she would always be for him. Wendell knew that.

Determination flooded his veins and stirred his voice. "This school was named after one of our founding fathers — Alexander Hamilton. He was a man of faith and conviction. A man who did not believe in wasting his chance."

Wendell noticed a kid in the fourth row roll his eyes and whisper something to the girl next to him. Wendell pressed on. He could tell them about the club, tell them about the reason for the club. But this was where he needed to be most careful. Especially during school hours. "From now on you have the choice to be people who do not believe in wasting your chance, either." He paused. *Facts, Wendell . . . stick to the facts.* "There will be a voluntary after-school program called Raise the Bar. I want to stress that this program is voluntary. But the goal of the program is to change your life."

Wendell didn't need notes. "Raise the Bar will be a time of looking into the Bible for wisdom and direction. I will lead each session, and afterward, there will be a time of prayer." He hesitated.

There was so much more he wanted to say. If he could, he would tell them how miracles could happen if they would take their troubles to God. And how it was his belief not only as a Christian but as an educator that Hamilton High needed redemption.

But even without his saying any of that, muffled laughter came from a group of freshman boys at the right side of the auditorium.

Wendell ignored them.

He wanted to tell them how statistics showed that faith in God improves test scores and a student's outlook on life and school. Instead, he chose his words with great intention. He didn't tell them that Scripture backed those statistics. Or that God promised in the book of Jeremiah that He had great plans for the students.

Wendell looked around the auditorium. Maybe it was his imagination or his strong belief that this was what the kids needed, but suddenly the room seemed quieter. For the most part, the students were listening. At least Wendell thought so. His voice grew steady again. "If you — each of you — want to win . . . if you want a different life than what you just saw on the screen, show up at Room 422 at four-thirty today, after practices and clubs let out."

He looked around the room again. "If you don't play a sport, if you're not in a club, you can choose to stick around and do your homework. Then come to the meeting." He paused. "What do you have to lose?"

He explained how the Raise the Bar

program would never conflict with tutoring, since it was on Tuesdays and Thursdays. "We'll have free snacks for anyone who comes." Wendell noticed several kids raise their eyebrows. Free food was something for these students. A few whispered amongst themselves.

Wendell took a step closer to the edge of the stage. He wasn't finished. There was something he had to say before he could end the assembly. "Hear me loud and clear about one thing." He made eye contact with every section of students. "The Raise the Bar program is voluntary. No one is insisting you attend, and you will have no repercussions if you do not attend. This is merely an option. Raise the Bar . . . or not."

When the assembly was over, Alicia found him and gave him a quick hug. "That was perfect." His words seemed to have emboldened her some. After Alicia moved on, other teachers approached him.

One of the math teachers leaned close. "Mr. Quinn, I'm concerned." He whispered his words — as if the political correctness police might be lurking nearby. "What you're doing is illegal." He allowed a quick smile. "But I say more power to you. Nothing else is working."

Five teachers approached to tell him he

was tempting criminal charges. "You're not considering the rights of atheists in this room." His lead science teacher was furious. "No one has any right to mention God in a student assembly."

"I'm only giving students an option." Wendell was ready for this. "You want to start an Atheist Club, by all means do so. Get a proposal to me."

Lonnie Phillips, his vice principal, was one of the last to pull him aside. "You could get us all on the front page with this one." She raised her brow. "Truth is, I like the idea. But let's be honest, Wendell. I'll be surprised if one student shows up."

For the rest of the morning, Wendell worked in his office and tried to wish away the hours. Other teachers came in to share their concerns or enthusiasm for the program. Everyone was talking, for sure.

At lunchtime he walked through the cafeteria, making himself available for the students. One after another they came to him. "Mr. Quinn, does God really care if I read the Bible?" And the few angry students. "You can't talk about God in school. You know that, Mr. Quinn." Or "What are we reading in the Bible first?" And "Mr. Quinn, thank you for this morning. I'll be there." Or even the occasional "I don't believe in

God, but I'll be there. You got a lot to prove, Mr. Quinn."

Positive or negative, Wendell listened. This was his first hint that maybe — just maybe — students really had truly paid attention earlier.

Finally it was four-thirty. Wendell got caught in a meeting with a parent, explaining that her son had been arrested the day before school started. By the time Wendell carried his Bible into Room 422, he was six minutes late. He rounded the corner and saw students gathered in the hallway near the door.

What's this? Wendell hesitated, then picked up his pace. Were students protesting already? He eased his way through the crowd. Inside the classroom every desk was taken. Students lined the room, two and three deep. Among them was his son Jordy.

Chick-fil-A had provided sandwiches for the meeting, but clearly they hadn't brought enough. The group standing outside the door was not protesting. They were trying to be included.

Tears stung Wendell's eyes. He took the spot at the front of the room and struggled to find his voice. When he could speak, he prayed out loud. "Look what You've done, Lord. You brought these students here.

Now . . . please, speak to them. That this might be the first day of the rest of their lives. Good, beautiful, productive lives lived out for You."

A boy sitting up front took attendance as they got started. Fifty-eight students filled the room. Wendell couldn't believe it. This had to be Jordy's doing. His son smiled big in his direction. *Deep breath,* Wendell told himself.

He took his worn Bible and opened it. He loved this old book. The notes in the margin, the highlighted areas. The thin worn pages. His kids wanted him to get a Bible app for his phone. Wendell wouldn't hear of it. He pulled out his notes. No place to start like the beginning. He steadied his voice. First . . . "God is real. And God created the world. He created all that you see and He created you."

At the back of the room, Alicia slipped in and leaned against the wall. She stayed only ten minutes. Whatever was going through her head and her heart, Wendell would have to deal with it later. This was for the kids.

When the meeting was finished, an enthusiasm and energy filled the room. A dozen students approached him with questions about salvation and sin and forgiveness and redemption. Wendell could hardly believe it.

46

He had expected maybe a dozen students and at least one who would challenge him. But none of that happened. It had to be the Lord at work. How else could he explain it?

With God at the center of this, nothing could stop it.

After the last students left the classroom, Wendell returned to his office. Jordy had already promised to make dinner for his siblings, so Wendell could take his time getting home.

Basking in the light of all that had happened today, Wendell closed his office door. Once more he took the old football off the shelf and read Les's words.

In this moment.

Yet if the media got wind of what he was doing . . . if the school district found out and ordered him to stop, then Wendell could be forced into silence. But he had a plan for that, too. He had already looked into his options, already Googled who could help him if things fell apart.

There was a lawyer in Indianapolis who had won several religious freedom cases in the last few years. Given the very real possibility he would need to call the man, Wendell had researched the guy. A Christian with a kind but outspoken faith in God. The man was a successful litigator. Someone you'd want on your side. Wendell had memorized his name.

The lawyer was Luke Baxter.

Ashley Baxter Blake took the call ten minutes before the kids would get home from school. They'd been back for a week now. The routine was familiar again.

As soon as Ashley answered the phone, she knew something was wrong. It was her sister-in-law Reagan. She was crying. "Ashley . . . I'm so sorry. I had to call."

For an instant, Ashley felt her heart drop. The Baxter family had been through enough tragedy over the past decade. *Please, God, let everything be okay. Please.* Her prayer came even as she got the word out. "Reagan!" Ashley had been slicing apples and string cheese for the kids. She leaned against the kitchen counter. "What happened? What is it?"

"Oh, it's not anything like that." Defeat rang in Reagan's voice. She sniffed a few times and regained some control. "It's Luke and me. It's us."

Oh no. Ashley hung her head. Reagan and Luke had struggled before. This wasn't a car accident or an illness. But it was bad, all the same. "Tell me."

"It's his work. He's never home. I'm just

so tired of it." Reagan sounded like her heart was breaking. "He spends more time at the office every month." She sniffed a few times. "First it was Monday nights. Then it was a few nights a week." A shaky sigh came from her. "Now it's every day except Sunday." A sob cut her off before she seemed to find her words again. "I know he's important. He's a big-time religious freedom fighter. People need him. I get that." She sniffed again. "But the kids and I . . . We need him, too." She hesitated. "I'm not sure how much more I can take, Ash."

"Awww, I hear you, Reagan. I do." Ashley felt the urgency. "Have you talked to Luke? Told him how you feel?"

"I've tried." Defeat filled her tone. "He's too busy to listen." She started crying again. "I had to call."

"I'm glad you did." Ashley wished she and Reagan could talk in person. But her brother lived nearly an hour away, and even now she could see Devin, Amy and Janessa walking up the driveway. "Let's do this. I'll call you back in half an hour and we can make a plan."

Reagan agreed, and by the time Ashley called her back Reagan sounded more in control. "What you asked me before made me think. If I tell him it's important, he'll listen to me. I know Luke."

Relief took the edge off. Ashley smiled. "That's what I think."

"I'll call him now." A new determination came from Reagan. "Maybe he and I can talk tonight."

"Yes. Good plan." Ashley paused. "I'll pray that it'll be a breakthrough. Then maybe call me later. Let me know how it goes."

"I will." Reagan's voice held the beginning of a smile. "It'll be okay. God will give me the words."

"There you go!" Ashley had taken the call outside, in case it needed to be private. Now that it was over, she headed inside. The kids were doing homework at the kitchen table. Amy looked up, her eyes tinged with fear. "Is everything okay?"

"Yes, honey." Ashley's answer was quick on purpose. She smiled at her niece. "Aunt Reagan and I were just catching up."

"Okay." Worry lingered in the girl's eyes for a few beats. Then she returned to her schoolwork.

Ashley felt for the girl. Poor Amy. More than any of the kids, Ashley's young niece was very aware of potential bad news. And of course. After losing her parents and sisters in the terrible car accident years ago,

Amy was bound to be sensitive. Ashley walked closer and put her hands on Amy's shoulders. "Math today?"

Amy nodded. "First test tomorrow."

"Well, if it's like your other math tests, you'll ace it no problem."

Amy grinned up at her. "You think so?"

Ashley kissed the top of Amy's head. "Absolutely."

She made her way around the table. Devin was working on flash cards for a science exam. "You and Dad can quiz me later." He grinned at Ashley. "I feel good about it. But still . . ."

"Flash cards are our favorite." Ashley loved that Devin had his older brother Cole's confidence. They were different in many ways. Cole was more of a leader. But Devin was learning, and in moments like this there was no denying they were siblings.

"Look at my work, Mommy." Janessa waved Ashley to her end of the table. "I'm coloring a picture for you."

Once a week Janessa had spelling homework. But Ashley's heart soared over the fact that her little girl still had plenty of time to color. Like Ashley, Janessa loved to create. Ashley pulled up a chair and studied her artwork. "Tell me about it."

"Well." Janessa drew a long dramatic

51

breath, like her explanation was coming to life in that very moment. "The blue trees are because the sky is shining on them." She lifted her eyes to Ashley. "That's pretty, right?"

"So pretty."

A half hour later Ashley was still at the kitchen table with the kids when Cole and Landon got home. Dinner and laughter and details about everyone's days came next. In between the moments she didn't want to miss, Ashley did as she'd said she would.

She prayed.

God, please open Luke's heart. Help him to see the changes he needs to make for Reagan and the kids. Yes, he was working for his faith. But if he won cases at the expense of his family, the wins would all end up as one big irredeemable loss.

Nothing more.

Janessa was in bed and the others were playing badminton with Landon out back when Reagan finally called back.

"Ashley!" Her voice was lighter than air. "You were right! I should've talked to him sooner."

"What did he say?" Ashley loved that her sister-in-law trusted her. Luke was one of Ashley's best friends. From the beginning Ashley could say that about Reagan also. A soft laugh came from Reagan. "Well, let's just say he's *very* sorry. He's going to work less and the two of us are going to date more." Her tone grew more serious. "Really, Ash. He had tears in his eyes. He's going to change. I believe it."

The conversation lasted another few minutes, before Ashley hung up and joined Landon and the kids. She was grateful Luke had so easily come to see things Reagan's way. It was Luke's nature to give everything to his job. The balance he was promising Reagan now was exactly what he needed.

Ashley could only pray that over time Luke wouldn't forget his promise.

3

Anger had long been Cami Nelson's constant companion. So it was that — and no other reason — that caused her to be one of the first students through the door of Room 422. Not because she was curious about God or because she wanted to know about the praying Principal Quinn had talked about at the assembly. Or even because she had the slightest belief something hopeful might come from attending.

No, Cami was angry. Angry that Principal Quinn was starting something so ridiculous, and angry that some of her classmates were actually interested in the program. Angry for a hundred other reasons.

As if God could possibly make a difference for any of them at Hamilton High.

Besides, Cami was on Facebook. She watched the news. It was illegal to talk about God at school — or in any public place, for that matter. If Principal Quinn thought he was going to get away with this, he was wrong. Cami would call the police herself.

Raise the Bar. Ludicrous. If they were going to raise the bar at Hamilton High, Principal Quinn would have to personally put the families of a thousand kids back together. All the kids Cami knew at Hamilton were like her. Too angry to care about homework or whether they might get pregnant or overdose on drugs. At least those things made you feel alive. School certainly didn't. And God wouldn't, either.

Cami didn't believe God was real. He had stopped being real a long time ago. This was her junior year at Hamilton High, nearly two years since Cami came home one afternoon and found her mother's note.

I've moved on. You deserve better.

What her mom meant was that she'd taken up with some married guy from their church twenty minutes east of Indianapolis, a guy she'd met during a midweek Bible class. Church girl on Sundays, home wrecker on Wednesdays. That's what Cami's dad said.

Cami knew the note also meant her mother, Audrey Nelson, was tired of sneaking around, hiding and tricking people into thinking she was a good little church member. Tired of lying that she was at the gym or the grocery store or the library every Monday. That was Cami's favorite one. The library. As if her mother had been spending her days reading books.

That day her mother must've been tired of it all, so she wrote the note and she left. And that was that. Cami and her twin sisters, Ensley and Ellie, hadn't seen their mother since. Their father saw her a few times at court during the divorce and custody hearing. From what Cami understood it wasn't much of an ordeal.

Cami's mother signed away her rights and left the courtroom without saying goodbye. At least that's what her father reported. Left with no regret, no remorse. No message for the girls. Just signed the papers and left. When Cami and her sisters came home from school their father blurted out the news.

"We're done with your mother." He grabbed a beer from the refrigerator, popped the top and drank down half of it.

Cami would always remember how her heart pounded, how she couldn't take her eyes off the aluminum can. She had never seen her father drink in all her life. Not until then.

That day her dad's eyes stayed on the beer, not on Cami and her sisters. "None of you will ever see her again." He sounded like a zombie. "That's how she wants it." Their father slammed the can on the counter. "I say good riddance."

Anger became Cami's constant companion that day and it never left. Never gave Cami a day off or any time to herself. Because what sort of mother leaves her three girls? Even at her school, where families were broken to pieces, Cami didn't know any other kids with moms like that. They had moms who were desperate because they were doing all the work and raising kids. Or moms who were too high to care. Some of her friends had mamas with different men at the house every week.

But at least they stayed.

Cami was the only one with a mom who just left. Who didn't like her children enough to stay.

So yeah, Cami was angry. Of course she was.

She woke up angry and went to school angry. When Cami sat down to take a test in English literature, anger sat down beside her and whispered into her ear from the first to the last question. *It doesn't matter,* anger would hiss. *Don't try. Whatever grade you get, it won't make your mother come home. You'll never be anything, anyway. Otherwise your mother wouldn't have left.*

And when Cami sat down in her next class, anger would bombard her with the same words all over again.

Cami wasn't sure how the last two years had made her younger sisters feel. Ensley and Ellie were still in middle school, and they didn't look much like her. For all Cami knew, her dad and the twins' dad were different guys. Given her mom's track record. It was something she thought about asking her dad, but she hadn't, for one reason.

If Cami was angry, her father was furious.

He worked as a mechanic at the airport, and even though he acted like he didn't care that his wife had moved on, that day after the court hearing, something changed. For one thing, after that first time Cami saw a beer in his hand, her dad was never without one. Before her mom left, Dad used to keep his blond hair short and his face smooth. And on the weekends he would constantly be thinking up adventures for the family.

Something in their budget, he would say. A peanut-butter-and-jelly picnic at the park. They'd pack a bag of sandwiches and oranges and spend half the day on the swings or kicking around a soccer ball and eating PB&Js. Other times they'd head to the lake and build sand castles.

But after their mother left, a part of her dad died. That must have been it, because he never again suggested an adventure for the weekends. Instead he stayed home, anchored to ESPN and drinking beer.

"Do your own homework," he would tell the girls. "Make your own sandwiches." "Take your own trips to the park." It became pretty obvious to Cami and her sisters that they hadn't only lost their mother the day she left.

They lost their father, too.

All this time later, Cami's dad wasn't the same person. He didn't act the same or talk the same. He didn't even look the same. His hair was long and straggly. Oily, maybe. Like some of the airplane grease must've gotten mixed into it. He cut it every once in a while, but never shorter than his jawline.

He looked like someone trying to hide himself. Because all that hair made it impossible to see his face unless he looked straight at her. And Cami's father rarely looked straight at any of his girls. It was like he was living in his own world and just happened to share a house with Cami and her sisters.

Like he was a stranger.

And that wasn't all. Her dad had gotten a tattoo. Which was fine for other dads. But her dad used to brag about being the only mechanic at the airport without a tattoo. "Don't want to be like everyone else," he would tell Cami and her sisters. Not that it mattered. Cami sort of liked tattoos. But her dad didn't. That was the thing.

After her mom left, everything changed.

The weird thing was, Cami caught her mom drinking alcohol before she ever saw her dad have that first beer. A year prior to her mom moving out, Cami found her in the laundry room pouring herself a glass of wine.

"Mom!" Cami had stared at her. "What are you doing?"

Her mother had quickly opened the cupboard above the washing machine and set the bottle on the shelf. She held up the glass and tried to laugh. "This?" She looked like she was grabbing words from thin air. "Sometimes Mother needs a little help to get through the afternoon." She laughed again and set the glass on top of the machine. "You'll understand someday."

Cami didn't know what to say. But she did know one thing for sure. The wine her mother was drinking wasn't "once in a while." Because late that night Cami checked. The cupboard where her mother stashed the bottle held four others just like it.

Her mother never mentioned the wine again, but Cami felt weird about it. Why would her mom need to drink while she did the laundry? Cami knew the kids at her school drank because it gave them all the feels they didn't get at home. When they were lonely, drinking made them feel included, and when they were ignored, drinking made them feel accepted. Bigger than life. Like they mattered.

But why did her mom have to drink? And why did she hide it?

Cami had tried drinking, but she didn't like it much. And after that day in the laundry room, Cami never drank with her friends again. The image of her mom pouring herself a glass of wine, surrounded by dirty clothes, between folding towels, was too surreal. Cami had no idea what she was going to do with her life or how she'd even make it out of Hamilton High.

But she knew one thing for sure. When she was older she didn't want to be sneaking glasses of wine next to the washing machine.

A year later, after her mother left, Cami

understood the wine a little better. Her mother needed alcohol the way the kids at Hamilton needed it. So that the reality of life wouldn't kill them. For her mom, it was her own fault. Her own actions that had been driving her crazy.

Sitting in the front row at church Sunday morning . . . cheating with someone the rest of the week. Which meant all that time they were pretending to be a family, Cami's mother was living a lie.

No wonder she drank in the laundry room.

Before her mom left, there were times Cami would think about God. Her mom had even starting taking Cami and her two sisters to church. Sometimes Cami would give Him credit for putting her in this family. For giving her a mom and dad and sisters. Like, they had to come from someone. So maybe they were a gift from God. After all, her family seemed pretty happy back then. No, they didn't have much money. Her mom had worked part-time at a temp agency. One day a secretary, one day a filing clerk.

"There's too much to do around the house for me to get a full-time job," she used to say.

So they went to the movies here and there and took their adventures to the park. No big deal. And yes, every so often Cami would think about God.

But now that her mother was gone, now that Cami knew the truth about how her mom spent her off days, Cami's view on God had changed. A lot. The part she couldn't get past was the fact that the man who had destroyed their family was a Christian. Or at least he claimed to be.

Cami settled into the back corner of Room 422 and pulled her long blond hair into a ponytail. The first Raise the Bar meeting was set to start in five minutes, and already the place was packed. She wanted to walk to the front of the room and scream at everyone.

Were they kidding? Did they honestly think God was real or that He cared about their terrible, empty lives? Did they believe He was all-knowing and all-seeing, but He couldn't make a mother stay with her children? Anger was right there beside her, chuckling under his breath. He was whispering at Cami again. *Glad you're not stupid enough to believe there's a God.*

Of course she wasn't that stupid.

Cami pulled a spiral-bound notebook from her backpack and opened it to the first page. It was blank. She hadn't taken notes in class today. She was too mad about this

Raise the Bar club thing. After all the kids at Hamilton High had to deal with, now Principal Quinn was going to lie to them and tell them there was a God?

She wasn't having it. She would take notes, and tomorrow she would call the police. They didn't need to arrest Principal Quinn. Just make him drop the ridiculous idea of teaching students about God and the Bible. Cami shook her head and waited.

So stupid.

Sure, if some kids were blind enough to believe in God, let them start a program. But why the principal? Mr. Quinn was using his position to practically force students to come. *Free food. The nerve of him.* Cami wasn't going to take it. The whole thing was illegal and she knew it.

Mr. Quinn needed to be shut down.

She took in the situation around her. Most of the kids were young. Just one other junior, and no seniors. That was because most of the upperclassmen were meeting a dealer across the street in the overflow parking lot. The guy was a regular at Hamilton. Pot. Cocaine. Opioids. Ecstasy. Whatever drug the kids wanted. The juniors and seniors would get high and then go hide in their bedrooms and pretend they were doing homework. All so they could fall asleep and repeat the whole routine tomorrow.

Cami didn't like pot, and she was too afraid to try other drugs. Pot made her feel dizzy and out of breath. Like she was dying. The one time she tried it she thought the walls were closing in on her. So this year she'd already resigned herself to staying clean. Which meant being alone at Hamilton High. Just her and anger, hanging out. She had no other friends, no one to take her on a date, and no idea what she was going to do next year when high school was over.

Cami studied the students in the room. The only other junior was Jordy Quinn, the principal's son. The kid everyone liked and no one wanted to hang out with. He was a goody-good. Cami stared at Jordy for a long moment. He was at one of the desks up front, smiling and talking to another football player beside him.

In fact, half the guys here were football players. Jordy had probably convinced them to come. Because while most kids at Hamilton pretty much didn't believe in God, Jordy was the exception, and everyone knew it.

The Quinn family not only believed in God. They acted like it. When school let out for a break, Jordy Quinn and his two sisters and brother went with their dad to places like Haiti or Kenya. Last year Jordy sat next to Cami in biology and he showed her pictures on his phone. Him and his siblings teaching village kids about Jesus, feeding them from a gigantic pot of chili. Teaching them how to swim.

That sort of thing.

Strange about Jordy. If anyone else had a reason to be angry with God, he did. Jordy's mother was one of the nicest people Cami had ever known. When they were in fifth grade, she used to come every Monday with fresh-baked chocolate chip cookies and help the kids in Jordy's class with their writing projects.

That was the year everyone made an actual book. Something the school helped them get bound and printed. A great accomplishment, their teacher had said. And Jordy's mother was right there giving her time, walking around the room and complimenting kids she didn't even know.

Jordy's mother was half black, half white. His sisters and brother looked like their dad. But Jordy had his mom's features and long eyelashes. Cami thought of Jordy's mother every time she looked at him.

There was another time, a field day back in middle school. Jordy's mother came dressed as a referee. Black-and-white striped shirt, long curly hair pulled back in a ponytail. And smiling. Cami didn't have a single memory of Jordy's mother not smiling.

But then the accident happened.

A few weeks after field day, Mrs. Quinn was coming home from the grocery store when a kid from Cathedral High crossed the double yellow line. Everyone said the guy tried to veer off the road altogether before hitting the Quinns' car. He almost made it, too. But instead he drove his car straight into the front driver's seat. Jordy's mom was dead before the paramedics arrived at the scene.

Certainly Jordy had no reason to believe in God, no reason to be at the Raise the Bar meeting today. He should be as angry as Cami. More, maybe. Cami stared at him, at the way he was still smiling, still talking to the guy beside him. *You should be so mad, Jordy. If there is a God, He let you down the same way He let me down.* Cami thought about that. *No, not the same way.* Her mother made a decision to leave. She was a terrible mother.

Jordy's mother was the best mom anyone could have.

And God took both of their mothers, all

the same.

The kids at Hamilton High didn't know how angry she was. They thought she was shy. Pretty much she was invisible to everyone around her. Everyone except Jordy Quinn.

Jordy was the best-looking guy at school. Sometimes Cami would catch herself watching him at lunch or when he was practicing football out on the Hamilton field. Not just because he was so cute. But because for the life of her, Cami couldn't understand him. Couldn't understand why he could still smile.

Just then Jordy looked over his shoulder straight at Cami. His eyes were kind, as if he could tell Cami was thinking about him. But then again, Jordy was nice to everyone. Cami gave him a quick nod and then stared at her hands.

Six minutes after the bell, Principal Quinn walked into the room. His suit coat was gone, and he had rolled up his sleeves. His forehead was shiny with sweat, as if he'd rushed across the school to get here. Cami watched him raise his brow and look around.

She did the same thing, and that's when she realized how full the room had gotten. Every desk was taken, and kids were squished along the back and sides of the classroom. They were even gathered at the door and spilling into the hallway.

Cami wrinkled her face. What the heck were all these kids doing? Didn't they know this whole Bible club thing was illegal? Were they all here for the free food? She took a pen from her backpack. Whatever their reason, she knew why she was here. After she turned Principal Quinn in to the authorities, Jordy would no doubt stop smiling at her.

But it didn't matter.

Jordy Quinn would never like her, anyway. He liked the popular girls, the ones on the cheerleading squad. Cami was a skinny blonde, a reporter for the school paper with a messed-up home. Cami was surprised Jordy even knew she was alive.

Principal Quinn cleared his throat and looked at the students. At each of them, as if they were his own kids. "You're here because you want to be here, is that right?"

Cami rolled her eyes. Did he really think that question would make him innocent? If she had her way this would be the first *and* last meeting. Period.

The kids nodded. A few leaned forward in their seats, like they couldn't wait to hear what Principal Quinn was going to say next.

"Okay, then." He folded his hands. "Bow your heads, and let's pray." He paused a moment. "God in heaven, You are real and You are here."

He's not real, anger whispered to Cami. *He's not real and He's not here.* She watched a few of her peers. They were following Principal Quinn's directions. They were actually *praying* in school! She grabbed her phone from her backpack. She could film this, and it would go viral in an hour.

A principal praying with his students. The whole country would come against him.

"We confess that the life of our student body at Hamilton High has not been pleasing to You, and we ask You to come into our midst now. Your Holy Spirit is welcome here, God. We love You, and we ask for Your changing power in this place. Speak to us through Your Word. In Jesus' name, amen."

Cami uttered the quietest gasp. She didn't believe the words, couldn't make sense of them. Some kind of holy talk. Still, something had happened inside her while Principal Quinn was praying. Something she hadn't expected. A shiver ran along Cami's spine and down her arms. Whatever was happening to her, it continued while Principal Quinn opened his Bible and read Jeremiah 29:11: *"For I know the plans I have for*

70

you," declares the LORD, "plans to prosper you and not to harm you, plans to give you hope and a future." Followed by John 3:16: For God so loved the world that He gave His one and only Son, that whoever believes in Him shall not perish but have eternal life.

It happened while Principal Quinn assured the students that the words were true. And the strange sensation continued as the Chick-fil-A sandwiches were handed out. Then there was something that hadn't happened to Cami in forever.

The angry voice beside her didn't say a word. And another thing. Her notebook was empty. She hadn't written down a single thing to report about Principal Quinn.

When the meeting was over, Cami felt different. More free somehow. Jordy came up to her and put his hand on her shoulder. "Glad you were here." His eyes shone with kindness. "Better than being in the parking lot across the street."

She nodded, feeling the heat in her cheeks. "I'm . . . I'm glad I came."

Which was crazy. Because it wasn't only something to say to the cutest boy in school. Her words were actually true. She *was* glad she came. Glad anger had stopped yelling at her for a full hour, and glad she'd heard two things today. Whether God was real and

71

the words in the Bible were true or not, she wasn't ready to turn in Principal Quinn just yet. She couldn't resist the idea that God had good plans for her.

And God loved her. Because one thing was sure.

That was more than Cami could say for her parents.

4

Alicia showed up at Wendell's office door just as the sun was setting. At first Wendell's heart filled with possibility. They hadn't gotten to talk after school and he could hardly wait to share the news about the success of the first Raise the Bar meeting. Maybe the program wouldn't cause her additional panic attacks after all. But as soon as Wendell ushered her into his office his enthusiasm died.

Her eyes were red and her makeup was all but worn off.

She shut the door behind her and searched his face. "Hold me, Wendell. Please."

Wendell's heart pounded in his chest. He didn't say a word, just drew her close. Was this the breakup he'd been expecting? He closed his eyes briefly and ran his hand along the back of her head. "I'm here."

For a while neither of them said anything. Then Alicia drew back and studied him.

"You were brilliant. At the meeting today."

Where was this going? He chose his words carefully. "You only stayed ten minutes."

"That's all it took." Fresh tears filled her eyes. "Every word you said . . . the students loved it. They loved you." She smiled, and despite her tears the joy on her face seemed genuine. "It's going to be a huge success, Wendell." Her smile dimmed. "Until someone stops you, it'll make a tremendous impact."

"But . . . you didn't stay."

"I couldn't." Her eyes looked closed off. More of the fear from earlier today. She took a step back, distancing herself. "My heart started racing. I couldn't catch my breath." She hesitated. "I thought . . . I was going to die. For real this time."

"Alicia . . ." He hated this. If only he could help her. "You won't die. Please . . ."

"No." She shook her head, her voice as broken as it was tender. "I'm not like you, Wendell. I told you, I'm not strong. And I need my job. As wonderful as this will be for the kids, it's against the law. You know it is."

Be gentle, he told himself. He drew a slow breath. "That's your fear speaking, Alicia. Listen to yourself." He kept his voice soft, his tone kind. "God will get us through this.

Whatever happens. It's not wrong to hold a voluntary club. I've been very careful in my research. Don't you believe that?"

"Wendell, you're not a lawyer." Alicia wiped at her tears and shook her head, her eyes locked on the floor between them. "I need to think about things. About us. I need time."

Time. There it was. Her way of stepping back. Ending things with him. The actual breakup was just a matter of days now. Wendell drew a slow breath. "Alicia, look at me."

She lifted her eyes and there it was. Already she was pulling away from him.

Wendell brushed her hair back from her face. "You don't have to be afraid. We can get through this together." He hesitated. "Remember? You feel safe with me."

"I did." This time her expression told him she had all but made up her mind. "I don't want to lose you . . . or the kids. But my doctor told me to avoid triggers." She paced a few steps and then turned to him again. "Do you know how much it hurts me that you're a *trigger*?" Tears spilled onto her cheeks.

"I'm not a trigger, Alicia." Wendell held his hand out to her. "I love you."

Her breathing was fast again, the way it

75

was when he first watched her have a panic attack.

"No, baby." Wendell reached for her hands. "Don't do this. God's here. He's with us."

"I can't." She took another step back, clearly working to maintain control. She closed her eyes, and a series of slow, full breaths followed. A coping mechanism, she'd told him before. Her tone was calm when she continued. "If I can't . . . stand by you . . . it's wrong for me to stay." She paused. "I'm broken, Wendell. You need someone whole."

Be gentle, he told himself.

There were a hundred things Wendell could tell her, ways he could remind her about why she had fallen in love with him in the first place, and how beautiful their summer together had been. But in the end he said nothing. This had to be her decision.

He took a step back. "I'm sorry, Alicia. Whatever you decide . . . I respect that."

She reached for his hand and squeezed it. Like it about killed her to let him go. But when she left his office she went without looking back. Wendell moved to the window and watched her walk to her car and drive off.

Suddenly the years melted away and he could see the way Alicia had looked when Wendell first knew something was wrong. Back when they were merely co-workers. Wendell would catch a glimpse of fear in her eyes, even in her happiest moments as a teacher.

He knew now that her fear had a name. A man who had stalked her and terrorized her, loved her and dated her off and on for the past few years. A man she hadn't quite escaped until recently.

A man named Jack Renton.

Wendell returned to his desk and opened the top drawer. Just inside was a list of phone numbers for law enforcement. People he could call at a moment's notice if Alicia needed his help. If Jack ever showed up at Hamilton High. The phone number of a buddy who worked for the FBI, and the number for the police chief of the precinct that included Hamilton. Also the number to the courthouse where she could file a restraining order against Jack if ever it came to that.

For today Jack was out of her life. But the man was never far away. Even now.

Wendell pulled a photo from his desk drawer, the one that sat next to the list of phone numbers. It was a picture of Alicia and Wendell the first time they went to dinner. Taken the evening the line between friendship and attraction dissolved like sugar in her iced tea.

The waiter had taken the photo. "Celebrating an anniversary?" he had asked.

Wendell and Alicia had laughed and Wendell spoke first. "More like a first date."

Surprise had filled the waiter's eyes. "Could've fooled me." He had winked at Wendell. "You two look like you've been together for years. Like you were made for each other."

Made for each other. Wendell looked at the photograph for a long while. She was pulling away. *How can I help her, God?*

Another memory came. One from longer back, a year at least. The first time Wendell had figured out what was sucking the life out of Alicia Harris. Wendell had been working late when Alicia hurried back into the school from the parking lot.

She had knocked on his office door, her face stricken.

Immediately, Wendell went to her. "Alicia, what's wrong?" He searched her eyes. "Is someone hurt?"

"No." The word sounded like her mouth was dry, and Wendell could see her heartbeat at the base of her throat. She seemed breathless as she continued. "It's just . . . my tire's flat. And my cell phone's dead. Could I . . . could I call for a tow truck from your office?"

Wendell knew one thing immediately.

The panic in her voice meant something else was bothering her. Something more grave than just a flat tire.

"You can use my phone." Wendell took off his jacket and rolled up his sleeves. "I'll take a look at your tire."

"No!" Her answer came too quickly. "I . . . I'll call for help. I don't want to bother you."

Wendell uttered a confused laugh. "Alicia, I know how to change a tire. Do you have a spare?"

"I'm not . . . sure."

Wendell looked intently at the woman. Alicia had always been happy, full of light. But she had changed. Lately she was as distant as she was beautiful. And on that particular day, Alicia was clearly terrified. She looked over her shoulder and then out Wendell's window and back at him.

Finally she agreed to have Wendell look at her tire. He followed her out to her car and stooped down to examine the problem. That's when he got his first hint at the secret life Alicia Harris had been living.

Her tire wasn't only flat. It had been slashed.

Wendell could still remember how he had stood up and looked at her. The fear in her eyes was eclipsed by a raw embarrassment. She hung her head and a few tears fell onto the parking lot asphalt. It was early fall and not that cold. But it might as well have been snowing for how Alicia shivered.

For a long while they just stood there, the truth hanging between them. Something was deeply wrong. After a few seconds Alicia brought her hands to her face and her tears came in earnest. "I'm . . . sorry. I didn't want you to find out."

"Who did this?" Wendell touched her shoulder. "Alicia . . . please. Tell me."

"I can't." She stepped back from him and glanced toward the road in front of the school. "I'm . . . so afraid."

The moment might have happened a year ago, but Wendell could still feel the way his heart had melted for her. "Come here." He held out his arms and despite her reluctance, she closed the gap between them. The smell of her perfume filled his senses and for a moment her trembling stopped.

But right when she had seemed comfortable in his arms, when Wendell was thinking this might just be where she actually

80

belonged, Alicia pulled away. "I'm sorry." She looked at him. "He might come by."

"Who?"

She was shaking harder than before. "Can . . . we go inside?"

"Of course." Wendell wanted to put his arm around her or take her by the hand. Anything to make her feel safer. Warmer. But she was clearly afraid of being seen with him. The two walked back inside and into his office. Wendell closed the blinds and motioned for Alicia to take the seat opposite him.

That's when he heard the story. Every sad detail.

For the past few years Alicia had been dating Jack Renton. He was a well-bred accountant on the right side of the city. Alicia explained how at first things had gone well. Jack had money and connections and a Princeton education. He liked fine food and he had a penchant for extravagant nights on the town.

But then, according to Alicia, one morning she walked out of her house to find Jack sitting on the curb in front of her house. Right next to her car. He accused Alicia of staying out late and cheating on him — none of which was true. After that the man became increasingly possessive and threatening.

The slashed tire was another of Jack's abusive ways. His attempt at punishing her for imagined offenses.

Wendell had listened to her story that day, and suddenly so much about Alicia Harris had become clearer. Wendell looked at her for a long moment. "Alicia . . . why are you still dating him?" Even if he couldn't believe it, Wendell had to ask. "Is it because you're afraid he'll hurt you if you stop?"

Alicia tilted her chin, as if she was trying to save what little pride she had left. "He has his good days, Wendell. It's just . . . he thinks I'm cheating on him. He watches me all the time." She hesitated for a long moment. "Last night he took my cell phone. So he could check it."

Wendell had been shocked. A year later the memory still surprised him. So that had been the reason Alicia couldn't call for roadside assistance. Because Jack Renton had her phone. And her tire was slashed because whatever he'd seen on her phone had made him angry. Clearly.

That day, when Alicia's troubles fully came to light, Wendell had looked her square in the face and told her the truth. "He's a dangerous guy. You should end things. Immediately."

For a long while she only stared at her hands. Her shoulders still shook. When she finally lifted her eyes to Wendell, she nodded. Her expression was dark with fear. "You're right. It has to end." She started to cry. "He'll kill me. I know he will."

Wendell couldn't believe she was actually afraid Jack would kill her. Then Alicia admitted that Jack's threatening behavior had been going on for two years. Wendell remembered being sick to his stomach. No wonder the light in Alicia's eyes had grown dim.

And there in that moment Wendell's sense of protection and attraction had come together in a rush of emotion greater than anything he had experienced in years.

Not since he'd lost Joanna.

He stood and walked to the other side of his desk. Then he reached out his hand. When she took it, when their fingers touched, Wendell wondered if he might spend the rest of his days loving Alicia Harris.

He drew her onto her feet and into his arms, and for the longest time he held her, running his hand along the back of her head. Her tears stopped and she let herself relax against him. This time she didn't pull away. "I feel safe here, Wendell. With you."

And like that Wendell was hooked.

Forever Wendell would remember the way it felt to hold her that day. He would do whatever he could to protect her and treat her the way she deserved to be treated. Alicia felt safe with him. She still did.

That day in his office had only been the beginning. Over the next few weeks Wendell met with Alicia after school. He would talk about God and the Bible, especially the verses that spoke of life's battles. "God wants to fight those battles for you, Alicia. Do you believe that?"

She told him she did believe. But her faith had been stymied by two years of living in fear. Two years of letting Jack Renton dictate her actions and feelings and emotions. "It's like I forgot God was there at all," she had told Wendell one afternoon.

Wendell looked forward to their times together like nothing in all his life. This was different than his love for Joanna. He and Joanna had been confident in their relationship, comfortable with life and each other. Joanna didn't need special protection.

Alicia did.

And that only intensified Wendell's feelings for her.

Back then, after three weeks of meeting

with Wendell, Alicia had been ready to break things off with Jack. Wendell prayed with her about the outcome, then she went home and called Jack. He had worked late that day, otherwise he would've been waiting for her at her house. The way he usually did.

Wendell had known this was Alicia's one chance. He had even given her the words to say. *I'm done. I want out. If you come here tonight, Jack, or any other time, I will call the police.*

At first it seemed the plan had worked. Jack understood things were over, and he agreed to stay away. But nothing about Jack Renton was ever that simple. Jack was a master manipulator. Alicia was his target.

In the week that followed Jack sent her a series of messages apologizing and begging her to come back. He talked about the early days and how he had let stress from his job affect the way he treated her. He was sorry about being so intense, sorry about not trusting her and sorry she felt the need to move on.

Alicia took Jack's apologies as proof that she was supposed to get back together with him.

And so began a roller coaster of events and emotions for Alicia. It was also the start of Alicia's crippling panic attacks.

Wendell was there for it all — even before she'd been diagnosed with an anxiety disorder. Before he knew about her panic attacks. Wendell was there time and again when Alicia got back together with Jack, and he was there each time Jack started his creepy, obsessive behavior again.

Finally, she told Wendell the truth about her panicked heart. He had prayed with her and showed her Scriptures to ease her anxiety, including the verses from Philippians 4. Wendell thanked God when this past spring Alicia broke up with Jack for the last time. Until then Wendell had been Alicia's best friend, her confidant. The one she turned to when she was afraid. Wendell hadn't told Alicia how *he* felt about her yet. That could come later, he had told himself. After she was free and clear of Jack.

When summer started, Alicia began joining Wendell and his kids for movie nights and cookouts. At first, Jack still called her but she blocked his number. Once summer was in full swing, Alicia didn't check her phone. And the few times Jack showed up at her house she stayed inside until he left. Eventually his calls came less frequently and she didn't fear coming home.

As for Wendell and Alicia, their friendship grew stronger every day. Wendell loved having her at his house, loved watching the kind way she interacted with his children. Around Wendell and his family, Alicia laughed easily and the fear in her eyes seemed gone forever.

Until now.

Father, speak to her. Let her know how much I love her and help her feel Your perfect peace. Don't let this be the end. Please, Father.

The prayer came as easily as Wendell's next heartbeat. But when Wendell locked up his office and drove home he had an almost certain feeling that things between him and Alicia Harris were finished.

And that the price he would pay for reading the Bible at Hamilton High had just begun.

Alicia couldn't see the road through her tears that evening. Long after she got home and changed clothes, the heaviness of the decision ahead remained. Wendell was the best man she'd ever known. The kindest father, the most caring principal. He was exactly the sort of role model the kids at Hamilton needed. The sort of man Alicia needed. But this battle over faith at Hamilton was destroying what they shared.

Alicia sighed. She believed in God with

everything in her. But the panic attacks were coming more frequently now. Each one felt like certain death. She closed her eyes. Why couldn't someone else lead the Bible club? She'd already told him, praying with students was going to cost him his job. Hers, too, if she supported him.

Then what? Who would care about the kids at Hamilton once Wendell Quinn was gone? Where would she live and how would she find a job? What if the panic attacks became worse and she couldn't get out of bed?

Her heart jumped and began racing. Faster and faster until she could barely feel the beat. The muscles in her throat tightened. "No!" She spoke the word out loud. "No, please, God, no!" She bent at the waist, exerting pressure on her abdomen. Sometimes that stopped the panic. *Help me, God. Not another one!*

But it was too late. She couldn't catch her breath, couldn't slow her speeding heart. *Exhale,* she told herself. *Breathe out.* That was the only way to break free from the panic. Exhale. Her doctor had told her that.

Exhaling and Xanax.

Alicia's head was spinning and she could feel herself losing consciousness. Was she going to faint? Hit her head on the floor?

Was this how death would finally catch her? She forced her feet to move, closer toward her purse and the pills inside. One step and then another. Just a few feet away to the kitchen counter and she was there. In a burst of effort, she grabbed the Xanax bottle and managed to remove the lid.

One pill, she told herself. *Just one.*

Dizzy and sweating and gasping for breath, her heart ready to burst from her chest, she poured a glass of water and downed one of the blue tablets. Just one 1 milligram pill. That would do it. She closed her eyes tight. *Please, God, let it work.* The Bible verses flashed in her mind. Why hadn't she remembered that earlier? Reciting Philippians 4 had worked even better than the pills last time.

The words came over her, filling her heart and soul. *Rejoice in the Lord always. I will say it again: Rejoice! Let your gentleness be evident to all. The Lord is near. Do not be anxious about anything, but in every situation, by prayer and petition, with thanksgiving, present your requests to God. And the peace of God, which transcends all understanding, will guard your hearts and your minds in Christ Jesus.*

A strange peace worked its way through her veins. This was it. The way out of the madness. *Rejoice in the Lord always. I will say it again . . .*

She wasn't sure how long she stayed there, eyes closed, leaning against the counter. But gradually the Scripture and medication began to work. Another ten minutes and she could breathe normally. She moved to the sofa and for a long while she sat there not moving, exhausted.

Eventually, when the panic attack seemed far off, she stood and slowly made herself a cup of decaf coffee. She hadn't eaten, so she reheated a plate of leftover chicken in the microwave. The meal was lukewarm when she sat down to eat. Just like her lonely life. If only Wendell's Bible study program didn't make her anxiety so bad. Wendell and she might've had a beautiful life together.

Instead everything was different now.

Alicia's heartbeat felt more stable now. She finished her dinner and checked her messages. One from Jack Renton. "Hey, baby, I know it's been a while, but I'm not going anywhere. I can tell you're mad at me, but I'm here." He paused. "Always."

Alicia shuddered. Good thing she'd already taken the Xanax. Jack was always a trigger. She had blocked his number, but somehow his calls still went straight to voice mail. She would call her carrier and get that fixed. But for now . . . "Please, God," she whispered. "Make him stop calling."

No wonder she had an anxiety disorder.

She sat down in her living room again and kept the television off. She couldn't imagine being fired. But if she sided with Wendell on the Bible program, that's exactly what would happen.

And the anxiety would win. She might die in the process.

Her mind ran through the list of bills she paid every week. The mortgage on her two-bedroom condo, the utilities, her car payment. Two credit cards. Her debt wasn't something she'd shared with Wendell. Another reason she was suffering from anxiety.

It had happened during the years she dated Jack. He had plenty of money, so he convinced her to live high. Don't just drive a car; drive an Audi. Why rent when she could buy a condominium in a new development? New shoes and clothes for black-tie benefit dinners.

Alicia had willingly taken on the debt as part of her effort to impress Jack, to keep up with him. Now she had to work to keep him out of her life, and even harder to pay off her debt. All of which meant one thing.

She needed her paycheck. Every penny of it.

A familiar sting filled Alicia's eyes as she looked around the quiet living room. Empty nights like this were about to be the norm. Already she missed Wendell with every anxious breath. She closed her eyes and pictured him. So good and true. Of course he had to do this for the students at Hamilton.

Who else would risk everything to help them?

But right now, Alicia only wished she had Wendell's help. So she would know what to do about Jack's incessant calls. Maybe it was time to call the police, file a restraining order against him. That's what Wendell kept insisting.

For a moment, Alicia allowed herself to go back. Back to the beginning when she first realized the manipulative, controlling person Jack Renton really was.

She pictured him again. Blond and confident, intelligent and articulate. They'd met at a jewelry store of all places. Alicia was buying a battery for her watch and Jack was doing the same thing. She would never forget the way he looked at her that first day.

"Sorry if I'm staring." His eyes had sparkled. "You look like an African angel."

An African angel.

Something no one had ever called her. And like that she was hooked. From the beginning Jack made Alicia feel like a princess. He brought her a diamond bracelet on their third date. He left her notes on her windshield wishing her a happy Tuesday or telling her she was the most beautiful woman in the world.

Alicia didn't realize what she'd gotten herself into until one morning as she headed out the door for Hamilton High and there, sitting on the curb next to her car, was Jack.

That was the moment the fear took root. When Jack turned around and looked at her, his eyes were dark and lifeless.

"You never came home last night," he said. His words were laced with hatred. Then he stood and pressed in close to her. So close she could feel his breath hot against her face. "Where were you?" He narrowed his eyes. "Who were you with?"

Alicia felt like she'd fallen into some twisted nightmare. "With?" Her mouth went dry. "What . . . what are you talking about? I went to the mall after work."

He gritted his teeth, like a poisonous rage was consuming him. "I checked your odometer, Alicia. Tell . . . me . . . the truth."

Alicia had to unlock her car door and let Jack inside for a clearer look at her mileage before finally he sat back in her driver's seat and exhaled. "Okay, fine. It's possible."

Jack stared up at her, where she was still standing on the curb, shivering. "Do me a favor, Alicia. Don't go to the mall without telling me. Never again."

He stood and shut the car door behind him, his eyes never leaving hers. Then he pulled her close and kissed her. Rougher than usual. "See you tonight, baby."

Then he walked to his own car, climbed in and drove off. Alicia could still remember the adrenaline coursing through her body, the way she felt sick to her stomach. For several reasons, of course. But the one that stood out the most was this:

Jack was checking her mileage.

He'd known it before that morning. Otherwise he wouldn't have been able to calculate how far she'd gone after work. A sickening chill ran down her arms, and all that day she had tried not to think about it.

After that things got worse, and finally one day Jack took Alicia's cell phone and slashed her tires.

While she was at work.

It was Wendell who had rescued her that day and it was Wendell who had been rescuing her ever since, standing up for her, defending her. Leading her toward the light. But tomorrow when she told him her decision, Wendell would go his own way. She would leave him no choice. And she would be alone.

Just her and the ever-haunting presence of Jack Renton.

5

One Year Later

Every fall on the first Saturday in October, the Baxters and their kids met at Hanson's pumpkin patch. The big day seemed to come earlier this year. But Luke Baxter didn't mind. He could hardly wait. His family looked forward to this almost as much as they looked forward to Christmas.

Luke drove their black SUV into the parking lot, and his wife, Reagan, pointed to a van in the row of cars closest to the cornfield. "Ashley and Landon are here."

"Good." He sighed. "I really need this." Luke had been so busy at the office, so caught up in a number of high-profile cases, that he hadn't been back to Bloomington since the Fourth of July.

"Makes me think of last time we were here." Luke reached for Reagan's hand as he looked for a parking spot. In the back seat the kids were laughing and talking about seeing their cousins. So for now in the front seat he and Reagan had this moment to themselves. He smiled at her. "Remember the Fourth of July?"

"Mmmm. One of the best moments this year. Or maybe ever." Reagan turned to him. "You know what I thought that day?"

"What?" The lot was crowded, but right now Luke didn't care. He loved this time, talking with Reagan.

"I sat there beside you on that bench at the park, my head on your shoulder while those fireworks lit up the sky, and I couldn't get past it."

"That was a beautiful night." Luke glanced at her. "But not as beautiful as you."

"Thanks." She smiled. "But that wasn't what I was thinking." She leaned closer and kissed his cheek. "I was thinking the Fourth of July is a celebration of freedom. And there I was sitting beside one of the most well-known freedom fighters of our time. Centuries after we won our independence, my husband was working to keep this country free. Like the celebration was as much for you as it was for our nation's birthday." She paused. "I'm so proud of you, Luke."

He felt her words to the center of his

heart. He saw a car pull out ahead of them, so he stopped and faced Reagan. "You thought that."

"I did." She smiled. "I still think it. But that night, that moment. The fireworks, you beside me. That park bench." Her eyes held his. "I'll remember it forever."

"I'm glad you told me." Luke had never loved Reagan more. "What did I do to deserve you?"

"Well." She sat back in her seat. "You're taking us to the corn maze, for one thing." Her laughter was soft. Just for him. "I do love a good corn maze. As you know."

Luke laughed. "That's all it took, huh?"

"A corn maze and you, Luke." She gave his hand a quick squeeze as he pulled into the space and killed the engine. "God has given me all I could ever want or need."

Their eyes held for a moment as Tommy popped his head up between them. "So we are doing the corn maze today, Dad?" At fourteen, Tommy was nearly six inches taller than he'd been last year. And his voice was deeper. He sat between his sister, Malin, who was nine, and brother, Johnny, who was already five.

Luke smiled at the kids. "Are you kidding? I wouldn't miss it."

"Just don't get lost like last year." Reagan

grinned at him and then at the kids. "Remember? We had to make a search party to find your father?"

"Yeah, Dad." Tommy laughed. "For someone so smart, you might want to use a compass app."

"Very funny." Luke chuckled as he climbed out of the SUV and grabbed the picnic basket from the back of the car. He shaded his eyes and scanned the nearby field. Twenty yards away he spotted Ashley and Landon and their four kids, along with Brooke and Peter and Kari and Ryan and their families. Their father and Elaine were also among the group.

Dayne and Katy would join them a little later. They were flying in today from Los Angeles.

Luke felt the joy of this together time all the way to the center of his soul. After weeks of courtroom battles and fighting for the chance to even mention God's name in public, today would be a very great respite.

"I love our family." Luke put his arm around Reagan's shoulders. "I need time like this. Especially when life gets crazy."

Reagan looked at him, a bit of concern in her eyes. "You've been doing it again."

He didn't have to ask what she meant. "I'll cut back. I'm sorry."

"Some cases need more time at the office." She kissed his cheek. "I know that. But just . . . be careful, Luke. Please." She looked at the kids and back to him. "This matters."

"Absolutely, it does." He held her close. She was right. He was staying late at the office a couple days a week. It was important work, but if he wasn't careful things would get as unbalanced as they'd been a year ago.

It was Ashley who spotted Luke first. She left the group and hurried to meet him. In a blur of motion, she threw her arms around his neck and then did the same to Reagan. "It's been way too long." She grinned at them both. "This day is going to be perfect! I love fall!"

The group snagged four picnic tables and set their things out.

"Dad says we're doing the corn maze first!" Tommy put his fist in the air. "This year the boy cousins are going to get through it first."

Luke laughed. "Yeah, we better do the corn maze first. While I still have energy to get through the thing."

Cole hopped up onto one of the picnic tables and grinned. "Didn't you get lost last year, Uncle Luke?"

"Yes . . ." Luke laughed. He crossed his

arms and nodded. "Yes, I believe I did."

Everyone was gathered close now. Landon sat on the picnic table across from Luke. "I remember thinking I should call in one of our fire crews to find you."

"Right." Luke laughed harder. "Thankfully I had my cell phone. Tommy talked me through it."

Tommy took a bow for the rest of the group. "I told him to use his compass app. Same thing he should do this year." He grinned at Luke. "Like you always say, Dad. Boy Scouts will come in handy at some point."

Reagan slipped her hand into Luke's and smiled at him. "We just didn't know it would be for getting through a corn maze at Hanson's."

"Okay, okay." Luke waved them off. "I get it. I'm directionally challenged."

His dad and Elaine had gone back to the car to get their picnic basket. When they returned, his dad looked at Luke. "You giving the corn maze another try this year, Son?"

Luke shook his head. "I'll never live it down."

A few minutes later the group set their sights on the entrance. Dayne and Katy and their kids arrived in time to join in, and after

101

a few minutes of excited conversation everyone was ready to begin. Luke's dad and
Elaine were the only ones to sit it out.

And like that the day was just as Luke
hoped it would be. A reunion of all the adult
Baxter kids and their families. Even getting
lost amid the corn couldn't ruin a day like
this.

Reagan linked arms with him as they
entered the maze. "How about I stay with
you? Just in case." She grinned at him. "You
know us girls. At least we ask for directions."

"True." Luke leaned in and kissed her.
"Let's win this thing!"

An hour later they were all gathered again
at the picnic tables. The boy cousins were
back first, just like Tommy and Cole had
promised from the beginning. Next were
the girl cousins. Amy giggled and said, "All
we had to do was follow the boys. They were
the loudest group in there!"

And last came the Baxter siblings and
their spouses. "We were chatting," Luke an-
nounced as the group arrived at the table
area last. "Not lost. Not this year."

Ashley took pictures of the different teams
and texted the photos to everyone in the
family. Then they settled in for a picnic
lunch. Like they'd done the last several
years, everyone brought a dish to share.

Luke and Reagan's chicken salad and fresh-made salsa, Elaine's homemade bread and pumpkin pies, Ashley's cold butternut squash soup, and half a dozen other dishes.

Only a few clouds dotted the Bloomington sky overhead, and the breeze was mild. The crowd at Hanson's was light that day. The afternoon couldn't have been more perfect. Before they ate, they formed a circle and held hands, the way the Baxter family always did when they came together. Their dad led the prayer.

"Lord, You are good. Thank You for fall, for the season of harvest. Thank You for bearing Your fruits and vegetables for Your people and for providing in so many other ways." Luke's dad paused as a gentle breeze drifted over the group. "We are grateful for Your love and mercy and for our redemption in Jesus Christ. And we are thankful for each other on this beautiful autumn day. In Jesus' name, amen."

Moments like this, Luke wondered how heaven could be better. And today, as they began to eat, he wondered something else. Whether anyone other than him understood how privileged they were to hold hands and pray in Jesus' name here in public.

Later, after the meal was finished and the entire group had taken a hayride to the back part of the farm to pick out pumpkins, the kids took another run through the corn maze. The adults were gathered around a few of the picnic tables when Luke's dad brought up the subject.

"You've been busy, Son. Religious freedom cases are popping up all over the place."

"They are." Luke's heart sank a little. He, better than any of them, knew the rate at which religious liberties were vanishing across the country. "It isn't just the lawsuits, it's the way people are thinking."

Ryan had his arm around Kari. He sat up a little straighter. "Some of the kids at Clear Creek High wanted to start a Bible club. We're talking just kids, now. Not a single teacher or administrator." He looked around the group and settled on Luke. "The principal told them they couldn't meet on school grounds. That it was a violation of church and state."

Frustration stirred in Luke's gut. "Not true. Absolutely not." He kept his tone in check. His passion for the subject knew no bounds. "Those kids have the right to freedom of speech. Freedom of religion. No one can make a law that prohibits their exercise of faith or their right to assemble."

"That's what I told them." Ryan shrugged.

"I think it's a matter of perception. Today, most people think it's illegal to talk about God in public."

Ryan was right. Luke used to handle the isolated cases, where a group of football players were sued for praying before a game or an office worker was fired for keeping her Bible on her desk. Now these things were commonplace. So much so that lawyers like Luke couldn't keep up.

In addition to the lawsuits, people didn't need to be forced into silence. They were silencing themselves out of fear and a lack of knowledge of their rights.

"Sometimes I think it's going to take a big case" — Luke leaned forward and rested his forearms on his knees — "something that really captures the heart of the nation. I'm afraid only then will people grasp the freedoms they're so quick to let die."

Ashley talked about being at the coffee shop in downtown Bloomington with a friend last week. "She was telling me about her family, and the message at church on Sunday."

"Wait till you hear this." Landon linked hands with Ashley and waited for her to finish.

"I know. I couldn't believe it." Ashley was clearly troubled by the situation. "So there we were in the coffee shop, sipping our lattes, and my friend is telling me about the sermon."

"Just a normal conversation," Landon added.

Ashley nodded. "So all the sudden my friend looks over one shoulder and then the other. Like someone might be listening. Seriously. Then she leans real close and whispers God's name. 'God is really speaking to me,' she tells me." Ashley shook her head. "I asked her why she was whispering and she told me. Because she was worried about saying God's name. Like it would be against the law to say the name God in a coffee shop."

The sick feeling in Luke's gut grew. "Two problems with that. First, your friend doesn't know her rights. And second, it seems she's okay with her perceived loss of rights, the idea that she might have to whisper God's name in public."

"What case are you working on?" His dad put his arm around Elaine. "I haven't seen you much. What's the state of things out there?"

"It's wild." Luke took a slow breath and thought about his recent docket. "So many lawsuits. I'm definitely enjoying it more than entertainment law."

"What you're doing now matters at a completely different level." His dad shook his head. "It's a crazy world out there."

Luke appreciated his dad's support. It mattered, knowing that his family believed in what he was doing. It always would.

The kids came running back, all the cousins together, including the little ones. Cole led the charge. "Can we take one more turn in the corn maze? We're trying to break our record." He grinned at Blaise, who at three was the youngest in the group. "It's not easy with the little ones, but we're all helping each other."

A chorus of pleading from the older cousins, and Luke and the others easily agreed. Another run through the maze was a great idea. The conversation among the adults was just getting started. The kids ran off, and the others leaned in.

"Who exactly is doing the suing?" The question came from Peter, Brooke's husband. Both of them were doctors. "We're pretty removed from all that in our world."

"Not me. Not on the coaching field." Ryan narrowed his eyes. "A coach in our district is fighting for his job because he allows the players to pray. Our country is changing and we never got a vote in the matter."

Luke nodded. "Exactly." How many times had he heard that before? He looked at Dayne. "There have been a few movies on the subject. *God's Not Dead,* for instance."

"Right. Film is a powerful tool." Dayne looked at his wife, Katy, and then at the group. "I have an investor who approached me yesterday looking to put money into a film defending religious freedom. I'm searching for the right story."

Luke chuckled, but the sound was more sad than humorous. "We need to have lunch, Brother. I have far too many stories." He looked at Peter. "Back to your question. The people suing are often atheistic legal groups, brain trusts whose intent it is to wipe religion — and the Christian faith in particular — from the landscape of America. There's a dozen of these groups now, and more all the time."

Reagan sighed. "The suing isn't just being done by those groups now. That's where it gets crazy."

"She's right." Luke felt the gravity of the situation. "Now it's school districts suing teachers for mentioning God. Parents suing schools for allowing such a mention." He hesitated. "Like I said, it's out of control."

The conversation shifted to the U.S. Supreme Court and the seats that would no doubt be filled in the next few years. Luke and his legal team had talked about that at length lately. "For now, things are better with the Supreme Court. But honestly, there could come a time when churches will gradually be outlawed in the United States." He looked at his family. "And it could happen in our lifetime."

Brooke looked doubtful. "How could that happen? The Constitution guarantees freedom of religion."

"Simple." Luke gave her a sad look. "The courts have been interpreting that very clause to read freedom *from* religion. As if belief in God were a dangerous or bad thing for culture."

His dad shook his head. "Nothing could be further from the truth. Studies have shown that faith is what keeps a society like ours working. It's the difference between a productive people living in the providence of God Almighty and . . . well, anarchy."

Another breeze washed over them and Luke exhaled. He didn't want to keep talking about this. Today was a time to celebrate. Still, it was important everyone understood that their rights truly were in jeopardy. "Here's how close we are to losing our churches." Luke made eye contact with his siblings and their spouses and then his father and Elaine. "The government would simply analyze the beliefs of a given church. If those beliefs line up with the Bible, then they could very well be determined to be hate speech in today's climate. Churches would be considered hate groups in the eyes of the government. They'd lose their tax-exempt status first, and then they'd lose their ability to meet."

Reagan raised her eyebrows. "Isn't that crazy?"

"And those conversations in coffee shops where people are afraid to say the name of God out loud aren't helping." Ashley leaned forward. The issue clearly troubled her. "Once people stop believing in their rights, those rights are a whole lot easier to take away."

"That's exactly it." Luke nodded. "Anyway . . . there've been lots of cases, and all of them have dealt with situations that would've never made it in front of a jury even a few years ago." He paused. "That's how quickly this whole religious freedom thing is changing."

The kids came running back, all of them laughing and out of breath. Some of the older kids had the little ones by their hands. Tommy was out in front, holding up his phone. "We did it! We beat our record!"

Hayley raised her arms in the air, her face bright with childlike joy. "We asked God to show us the way, and that's just what He did."

Luke smiled to himself and let the scene wash over him. No one had ever told Hayley not to talk about God in public. In fact, no one had ever told any of the kids that.

Help me to be like them, Lord. The silent prayer came from Luke's heart. *Let me keep the faith of a child. And let me keep the prayer of a child.* Hayley's words echoed in Luke's soul. *We asked God to show us the way, and that's just what He did.*

As the group cleaned up their picnics and loaded the baskets and pumpkins they had picked into their cars, Luke couldn't help but think about his job. No matter how difficult the cases, Luke was grateful.

If things got bad enough, he would just remember Hayley's prayer. And Luke would ask God to show him the way. And that's what God would do. He had to believe for such a time as this, while he was blessed to be a religious freedom fighter.

While there were still religious freedoms left to fight for.

6

In her new life, the one without Wendell
Quinn, the same crazy thing happened to
Alicia Harris every morning. Today was no
different. Alicia opened her eyes and in the
bleary line between night and day she literally could see the man she still loved. As if
Wendell was standing before her. His kind
brown eyes would look into hers and she
would feel the way she did whenever she
was with him: Safe. Loved.

Whole.

And in the dream she was sure she was
talking to him in his office. Talking about
how they might have a future together
and . . .

And then the reality hit. The way it did
every morning.

She rolled onto her side and stared at the
alarm clock.

Her life no longer included Wendell. The
world of Hamilton High was behind her.

These days she worked at a different high school, across town, and she only kept up with Wendell through the Facebook pages of her former co-workers.

Since their breakup, Alicia had not once looked into Wendell's kind eyes. She hadn't once walked into his office and talked to him about her fears, hadn't felt his arms safe around her. Hadn't dreamed with him about a life together.

Other than when she slept, her days with Wendell were, and always would be, part of her past. A million miles from the here and now.

Alicia sat up in bed and took a slow breath. The panic attacks had been gone for months now. Nothing in her new life triggered the anxiety. Just two Xanax a day and her doctor was happy with her progress. "You seem to be doing fine," he'd told her at her last appointment.

But her aching soul was another story. *Why, God . . . why do You let these dreams happen? I've asked You, please . . . take him away from me. Won't You do that?* She squeezed her eyes shut for a moment. She hated that she was so weak, that she was prone to anxiety. Hated the disorder with everything in her. But she couldn't change it. Some days she wondered if her life would be better if she'd never met Wendell Quinn.

At least then she wouldn't have to suffer the heartache of losing him.

Alicia opened her eyes. The thing was, Wendell thought Alicia had broken up with him because of the Raise the Bar program. But that was only part of it. She leaned back against the headboard and remembered that awful day once more. The one when she came home from Hamilton High with a decision to make.

She remembered every detail. How she had warmed up a plate of food and checked messages. That's when she noticed she had a second message from Jack Renton. In the two minutes it took to listen to his voice, Alicia had yet another reason to walk away from Hamilton High and Wendell Quinn.

Alicia closed her eyes and Jack's words came back to her again. She didn't have them memorized. Over the past year, she had done her best to forget them. But his evil intent remained, ingrained on her heart, forever etched in her mind. Jack had told her he was tired of waiting, tired of playing nice. She would be his one day soon. Period. If that meant getting rid of people in the way, so be it.

Jack's final words had been chilling.

"I'll have you, Alicia, or no one will. I'd

rather spend the rest of my life locked up than see you with someone else."

The memory still made Alicia sick. She pictured Wendell and his four kids, how they'd looked that day at the pool, all of them laughing and playing. She could never put them in danger. Even if it meant being single and alone forever.

How could I believe I might marry a man like Wendell Quinn? That he and his beautiful kids might someday be my own? I could never be good enough for them.

She opened her eyes and after a minute, she climbed out of bed. Her heart would always ache for Wendell. She missed him with every breath. During the day she didn't give herself time to think about him, to miss him. But in the morning — after seeing him in her dreams — she allowed herself the pain of remembering just a little. Enough to keep the good times alive.

Deep breath, Alicia. Deep breath.

A few minutes of stretching would clear her head, get her ready for another day of teaching. She bent at the waist and hugged her knees to her chest. The tension that had built up in the past twenty-four hours eased from her legs and spine.

After Jack's ominous message, Alicia had known just one way to be certain nothing would happen to Wendell and his kids. She broke things off with Wendell the next day, and requested a change of schools. It was one thing to stop dating Wendell. But to walk by his office every day would be too much.

Wendell had been hurt, of course. They both had been. But he'd respected her wishes. Anything to help her find relief from the panic attacks. A few weeks into the fall semester, Alicia was moved fifteen miles away to Jackson High School.

At first her old boyfriend left messages for her every day and her anxiety grew. Panic attacks happened every day, because this time Wendell wasn't there to help her. The calls lasted all fall semester. The threats were always the same: She'd better not date. No sneaking around with another guy. He would kill anyone who got in the way.

Alicia saved the messages — in case they were ever needed in a trial. But she only rarely considered using them to press charges against Jack. What could the legal system do? Again she thought about filing a restraining order, but then what? They wouldn't arrest a millionaire do-gooder for a couple of threatening phone calls. He would find his way free of any charges and then he would kill her.

Just like he promised.

So she let the messages build up in her answering machine. Then around Christmastime the calls abruptly stopped. His silence didn't make sense until last spring, when Alicia saw an article on Facebook about Jack. He had married the daughter of a bank president.

WEALTHY INDY PHILANTHROPIST MARRIES, the headline read.

"She's the love of my life," Jack was quoted as saying. "I've never felt like this before."

Alicia read the article six times through before she could feel anything. And then she was overcome by a tsunami of emotions: disbelief and shock and even anger. How dare Jack Renton destroy her life and her relationship with Wendell and then just move on?

As if he'd never known her.

But the strongest emotion that day, and every day since, was relief. Yes, Alicia was alone. She still spent two days a month analyzing her bills and trying to figure out how to pay off as much of her debt as possible. But no longer did she look over her shoulder on her way into work. She didn't check her rearview mirror to see if Jack was following her home. She wasn't afraid to walk out to her car every morning.

Jack Renton was finally and fully out of her life.

She thought about contacting Wendell and letting him know things had changed. She wasn't worried anymore about Jack hurting them. But she always stopped herself. Wendell had single-handedly turned things around at Hamilton High. She knew because her teacher friends talked on Facebook about the changes at the school.

Wendell had followed his faith and his heart, and she had been too fearful to stand beside him. Too worried she'd lose her job. Too scared Jack might do something to harm Wendell and his family.

She couldn't interrupt Wendell's life now. He deserved someone stronger. And so Alicia carried on alone, teaching and paying her bills and spending her evenings by herself. Only in her dreams did her rebellious heart journey back to Wendell Quinn.

A sigh worked its way up from her soul and filled her quiet bedroom.

Alicia finished stretching and looked at the clock on her bedside table. She was getting up earlier these days, allowing time for a part of her routine she'd never had before. A time of talking to God and sorting through her life.

The years she had yet to live.

She walked to the mirror over her dresser. There were faint lines at the corners of her eyes now. Alicia turned her face one way and then the other. She was still pretty. But her eyes looked a hundred years old.

The price of her anxiety disorder. The cost of living a life in fear of the next panic attack.

Alicia walked to the chair in the corner of the room. The temperature outside was only in the forties. Too cold to open the window. She sat down and stared at the old oak tree that stood between her house and her neighbor's. It was glorious today, with leaves the most brilliant reds and oranges.

She reached for her Bible on the small table near her bed. Her fingers moved over the leather binding and her name, engraved in the lower right corner.

A new Bible was the single extra purchase she had allowed herself since breaking up with Wendell. If belief in God had motivated Wendell to risk everything, then she wanted a faith like that. One that didn't run.

And so with fresh hope she began to read. She'd started with Matthew — the first book in the New Testament — and she hadn't stopped since. Her lonely nights were less so because of Jesus. She didn't fully understand Him, especially after she'd let her beliefs grow cold over the last few years. Her soul had paid the price.

But maybe . . . if she turned to Him now, He would keep her company on mornings like this.

Alicia stared out the window again. *Lord, do You see me? Do You want me to reach out to Wendell? Is that why You fill my head with visions of the man every time I lay my head on my pillow?*

Outside, a few red and orange leaves fluttered to the ground. Autumn was giving way to winter. Now if only she could find a way to change the seasons in her own life, to find the courage to move ahead. Try something new. Maybe even contact Wendell.

Alicia spent the next hour reading Matthew and when she came to the end of chapter eleven, verses 28 through 30, she paused. Alicia read the words several times over and let them permeate her mind. *Come to me, all you who are weary and burdened, and I will give you rest. Take my yoke upon you and learn from me, for I am gentle and humble in heart, and you will find rest for your souls.*

Learn from me.

She barely whispered her thoughts. "What do You want me to learn, Father?" She read the scripture again. "You want me to set aside my weariness and burdens and come to You. . . . I get that. But are the dreams about Wendell meant to teach me something? Are they from You?"

My daughter, two are better than one, because they have a good return on their labor. Remember that. And know that I am with you always, wherever you go.

Alicia felt chills run down her arms and legs. *Two are better than one? Was that God speaking to her?* The words came from the message at church last week. They were in Ecclesiastes, Chapter Four.

Two or three times before Alicia had sensed this sort of a heavenly response, something deep that resonated in her being. Like a voice that could be felt and not heard.

But she had never experienced it this clearly.

The response stayed with her as she got ready and drove to Jackson High School. Today's commute was like any other. No sign that something had gone terribly wrong during the night.

Not until she walked through the front doors did Alicia learn something devastating had happened. Along the hallway students were huddled together. Some of them seemed to be praying. Others were crying, weeping even.

Alicia walked quickly to the principal's office and found a number of her co-workers there. The woman closest to her took her hand. "Two of our students . . . they're gone, Alicia."

The story spilled out in sad, desperate bits. Two of Jackson's most popular student athletes — a couple recently nominated for homecoming king and queen — had come to school last night, sat in the bleachers and taken a handful of synthetic pills. Something called Pinky.

Whatever was in the potent drug, it was deadly poisonous.

One of the football coaches had found their bodies this morning. Lying on the bleachers in the same spot where they'd taken the drug. Their bodies had only been removed from campus minutes earlier.

In that moment Alicia knew what she had to do. She was finished with fear. Now there was only one way for the staff at Jackson High to get through this awful situation.

She looked around the principal's office at the circle of teachers and she felt her heart beat fast against her chest. *I am with you always . . . I am with you . . .* Alicia cleared her throat. "If you don't mind, I'd like to pray."

And like that Alicia took a step into her future. A future of dependence on God and reliance on His strength. A belief that with Him she really could do anything. She kept that mind-set all day as she prayed with grieving teachers and crying students. And even as the parents of the two students came to the school and broke down in her arms.

God was with her everywhere she was needed, every hour of the day.

By the time she climbed into her car that evening she knew two things. First, she had never really lived until today. And second, if two were better than one, then there was someone she needed to see. Not just in her dreams. But in front of her, for the first time in a year.

Wendell Quinn.

7

The Raise the Bar program met Tuesday and Thursday that week, and even still Wendell couldn't believe how the group had grown. After that first meeting, Wendell had moved the meeting to the band room. Two weeks after that they had so many students, they had to come together in the auditorium.

At the six-week mark nearly one hundred students showed up to hear about Jesus and His teachings, His promises, His gift of eternal life. Every week Wendell expected the phone call. Police were on their way to the school to arrest him. He would be fired for saying unthinkable things.

But the call never came.

Even his staff stayed quiet. The early handful of protests from his teachers gave way to busy schedules and classroom demands. Or maybe apathy. Perhaps they didn't have the energy to put up a fight. Or maybe they saw the good the club was doing. Whatever it was, no one had formally complained.

And every week kids continued to show up. Wendell couldn't explain the growth. Yes, he had believed the program would work, and yes, he felt called by God to step out in faith and lead it.

But almost a hundred kids?

The list of miraculous moments from the past year was too long to remember.

The young people in the club prayed for each other. They looked out for each other. One girl asked God that her dog would be found and by the time she got home from school, the pup was waiting for her. Another prayed for his mother's cancer diagnosis. That it would be gone at her next appointment. At her next meeting with her doctor, the woman was given a clean bill of health. No more cancer.

Now it was the second week in October, and already new students were joining. Wendell walked into his office and found the report on his desk. The one he believed he would need one day. Yes, in the past year he could see the changes. They were obvious. There had been only one incident of gang violence. Arrests were down and so were teen pregnancies. Test scores were improving.

But Wendell couldn't be completely sure that the Raise the Bar club was actually the reason for the changes.

So he had contacted a researcher from the School of Humanities and Social Sciences at Indiana University East. The school put him in touch with a master's student who needed a significant social project in order to complete her degree. AnnaMae Williams was a brilliant girl with a bright future.

She was also an agnostic.

Wendell didn't care. As soon as he explained the project, he saw the girl's interest ignite. She was to take every statistic that made up Hamilton High and compare it, one year to the next. AnnaMae didn't know about the Raise the Bar program. As far as Wendell was concerned, the girl didn't need to know. At least not yet.

What she did need to know, she would learn through researching teachers' grade books and police records. She could talk to the teen pregnancy center on campus and interview the nurse in the mental health office.

AnnaMae had been given the assignment the first week of school. And now, nearly two months later, she had finished the report and left it on Wendell's desk. Wendell had been looking forward to this moment since the beginning of the semester.

He approached his desk and sat down. A yellow sticky note on the top in AnnaMae's handwriting read: *The results are amazing. Whatever you're doing, keep it up! Way to go, Principal Quinn!*

Wendell's heart thudded against his chest. The report was titled "Hamilton High — A Comparison of Years." Wendell stared at the words. A comparison, indeed. *Lord, show me the difference You've made. Not just in lives, but in numbers.*

In case anyone ever wanted to know.

He opened the front cover and pored over the table of contents. AnnaMae had done a thorough job. Her categories went beyond what Wendell had requested. She covered criminal activity, and broke the statistics into felonies and misdemeanors.

Next was the mental health part of the report. She researched everything from suicides to suicide attempts, drug abuse, reports of depression and even student absences. From there she included student scores on standardized tests and assignments, as well as papers, and tests in each subject.

The report couldn't have been more thorough.

Wendell could barely breathe as he made his way from one page to the next. Arrests for violent crimes were down by seventy-five percent and misdemeanors were cut in half. Wendell let his eyes settle on the numbers. Tears gathered. *God, You are so faithful. This is beyond what I had hoped.*

And suddenly a slight gust of wind came through the open window behind him. *My son, I am able to do more than you can ask or imagine. Trust Me.*

The words blew across the surface of his soul, and Wendell held his breath. He was on holy ground here. But of course, God could do more than they could ever ask or imagine. His word promised that in Ephesians 3:20. And the report was absolute proof.

Wendell turned the page. Category after category, the results were beyond dramatic. Not a single suicide. Attendance was up and reports of depression were down.

Looking at the results, it was clear only God could have done this for Hamilton High School. And to think the Raise the Bar program had been kept a secret from the media all this time.

"All You, Lord. . . . Only You." He whispered the words, his eyes still on the report.

But while things had turned around at

Hamilton High, Wendell's personal life was still only about his children. Some days he missed Alicia with every heartbeat.

The two of them had liked having dinner at quiet cafés and catching a movie every now and then. He missed the happy, light-hearted approach she had with his boys, and the kind way she related to his girls. Times when anxiety seemed the furthest thing from her. No question, Wendell's heart was still hooked.

But there was no point thinking about her. Alicia had moved on. He hadn't heard from her since last fall. Whatever her life these days, she clearly wasn't looking back.

And she apparently had no idea of how her absence had hurt him. How it had left a gaping hole in his life.

Wendell made it through AnnaMae's entire report, and then he saw the one beneath it. The one put together by senior Cami Nelson. Wendell smiled as he picked it up. Cami had been attending the Raise the Bar meetings since the first week. In that time she had come to believe in the Lord and love Him.

She was a changed person, and she was just one of so many. A few weeks ago it had occurred to Wendell that statistics were only part of the story.

The results — no matter how stunning — would never take the place of personal testimonies. Cami Nelson was a journalism student. She loved writing the way some people loved singing. The way his own son Jordy loved running the football into the end zone. Writing was something Cami Nelson was born to do.

So Wendell gave her an assignment.

Starting with herself, she was to capture the stories of students who regularly attended the Raise the Bar club. Ask them what life was like before, and how it was different now. Then write a one-page narrative on each of them. Place them together in a single folder and get them on his desk by this Monday morning.

Wendell would see that she got extra credit for her work.

And sure enough, there beneath Anna-Mae's report was Cami Nelson's. The presentation wasn't as professional, but Wendell was certain the information it contained would be powerful. Numbers and percentages were proof that Hamilton High was improving. But the students' stories were proof that lives were actually being changed. Not only changed, but saved. Wendell opened the cover of Cami's report and saw that the first story was her own.

Hers and every account that followed appeared to be written in first person.

As if Cami had merely let the students tell their stories, and she had done her best to capture them. The one after Cami's was titled: "Dwayne Brown, Hamilton High Junior."

Wendell was gripped from the opening sentence.

It wasn't whether I was going to kill myself before I started attending the Raise the Bar program. It was when and how. The story went on to tell about Dwayne's life of drug abuse and meaninglessness. *Football had become my whole life. Other than that, I had no hope, no future, no direction. No one who cared whether I lived or died. Then I learned about God through the Raise the Bar program and everything changed.*

More tears blurred Wendell's eyes. He brushed at them with the palms of his hands and kept reading. Over the next hour he read through every story. The Raise the Bar kids had a whole new perspective on life.

They lived the Gospel.

Students in the club had developed initiatives to do peer counseling and tutoring, and they were responsible for so many positive changes. They volunteered as study partners with the elementary kids down the block, and they picked up trash and painted over graffiti at Hamilton. The ripple effect was obvious. They had made Hamilton High a better community.

Both reports proved it.

By then he'd gone through several tissues. If he cared for his students before, Wendell loved them even more now.

"I guess this proves You right, Father. You told me to start this program, and I obeyed." Wendell spoke softly. "Now look at the results . . ."

The program had come with a cost — though not the great cost Wendell had pictured when they started meeting a year ago. The most difficult part for him was, of course, the loss of Alicia Harris. He couldn't change her fear. Only God could do that.

Enough about Alicia. Wendell drew a deep breath. Parents' Night was in a few hours, and Wendell had already decided to share the good news.

Like the Bible said, a person couldn't light a lamp and put it under a bowl. God had changed the students at Hamilton High. Now it was Wendell's job to tell the world. Whatever the cost. In doing so, maybe other kids would join in. Parents might get behind the program.

He would talk about the club in basic

terms, then Jordy and Cami would share their experience. It was important that the community of parents know the truth about how God was working, and how a voluntary program was doing so much to affect Hamilton High.

Wendell was ready for possible pushback. He would go into the meeting with more than AnnaMae's report. He had his own research from the summer a year ago. If anyone had any questions, they could pore over the material themselves. There was no denying the reality that helping students find faith in God had changed their lives.

Wendell took a deep breath and settled back into his chair. He was about to read through the statistics of AnnaMae's report once more when there was a knock at his door. And there, like a vision from an already perfect day, stood Alicia. She looked beautiful, but she'd been crying. And something else. Her eyes looked different. Despite her sadness, they seemed stronger.

He went to her and opened the door. Everything in him wanted to take her into his arms and tell her how much he'd missed her.

But he did none of that.

"Alicia . . ." He searched her eyes.

She didn't look down. Again he sensed a

new resolve in her, a determination that hadn't been there before. She held his gaze. "I need to talk to you. Please, Wendell."

When they had dated more than a year ago, they would sometimes talk at their favorite place on campus. The baseball bleachers. Off to the far side of the school, the baseball field was the perfect place to meet. A line of trees separated it from the rest of the campus, so the two of them could talk without being spotted.

And if they were, that was fine, too. They had nothing to hide. Now, with school out and football practice under way, Wendell figured their favorite spot was exactly where they would go. At the last minute, he grabbed AnnaMae's research report and the two of them walked to the baseball field.

They didn't talk until they were seated next to each other. Wendell turned and studied her. Sitting this close to her, he missed her more than he could say. They'd lost so much time together. "It's good . . . being with you here."

Alicia nodded. Her expression was heavy, more troubled than before. "My school . . . it's falling apart, Wendell. The kids are as bad off as they were here." She stared at her hands for a minute and then looked straight at him. "Two kids died in the football stadium last night. They took some kind of street drug. Pinky, it's called." She shook her head. "Whatever was in it, they both died." Her voice broke. "Two of them, Wendell. They took that poison together."

Wendell felt the gravity of the situation. Losing two students in one day would be a terrible blow for any campus. Wendell groaned and lifted his eyes to the cloudy sky. "God, help their families." He looked at her again. "I'm so sorry."

She stared at him, like she was trying to figure him out. "I've been reading my Bible." Her smile was sad, but deep at the same time. "All the time." She hugged one knee to her chest and looked straight ahead at the empty baseball diamond. "Today when I saw everyone crying in the hallway and in the principal's office, it's like . . . I don't know, like the Word of God came to life inside me."

"Hmmm." No wonder her eyes looked more resolute.

"I had this . . . boldness. I prayed with teachers and students and the parents of the kids who died." She paused. "When the day was over, I knew I had to find you."

His head was spinning, trying to take it all in. "I'm . . . glad you did."

"Me, too." She looked ahead again, like

she was seeing answers that had evaded her before. "I was wrong to walk away from you. Even with my panic attacks." Her eyes narrowed as she faced him. "But there was more to the story." She sighed. "The day before I broke up with you, Jack Renton threatened to kill me. You, too. Anyone who got in his way."

"What?" Understanding dawned in Wendell's heart. Another reason why she had requested a transfer. "Did you call the police?"

"No." Another sad smile tugged at the corners of her lips. "I talked myself out of it. What would they do to Jack Renton? I even considered a restraining order, but that would mean I'd have to see him in court." She paused. "Then the calls stopped." She seemed to think for a moment. "Jack's married now. He's out of my life for good."

Wendell had known nothing of this. "You wanna catch me up?"

She angled her pretty face. "If you wanna listen."

"Of course." He moved to take her hand, and then stopped himself. He had to be careful not to blur the lines. Never mind the ache inside him, or the way it hurt to sit this close and not reach out for her. He folded his hands and waited. If he'd known

136

about Jack's threats, he would've been there for Alicia in a heartbeat. They'd missed out on each other's lives, and Wendell regretted it.

He didn't blink, didn't look away. "I still care, Alicia."

He stopped short of telling her how much he had thought about her. Nothing good could come from that. Not now.

"I know." A quick half smile tugged at her lips. "Thanks, Wendell." She drew a deep breath and then she began to tell him all he'd missed. She filled in every detail. How back then she couldn't afford to lose her job because she had lived beyond her means for Jack. But no longer. She was paying off her debt, but there was one purchase she'd had to make.

A new Bible.

When she was finished, Wendell had just one question. "How are you? Really?"

Alicia nodded slowly, her eyes never leaving his. "Better. I'm still on the medication, but I'm coming off it. I just feel, I don't know . . . stronger."

Hope ignited in Wendell. His prayers for the past year had been answered. "So Jack . . . he's the reason you took so long to come see me?"

"Yes." She hesitated. "Wendell, I didn't

want to mess up your life again. I figured you deserved someone braver than me." She faced him. It seemed like she might have more to say, something deeper about her feelings for him. But instead she lifted her eyes to the horizon and then turned back to him. "What happened today . . . it changed everything." Her eyes held his for a long time. "It made me realize . . . we have no guarantee of tomorrow."

He imagined her telling him she still had feelings for him. How his heart would have loved that. Like it had been given a second chance at life.

Instead Alicia looked at him. "I talked to Jenny Anders."

Wendell nodded. Jenny was a history teacher at Hamilton High. She was a regular attender at the Raise the Bar meetings. "Jenny's been a big help."

Alicia squinted against the glare of the clouds. "She told me how the kids are improving here. In every possible way. How things have changed."

Was Alicia really just finding out now? He kept his tone gentle. "You could've asked me. Things started changing as soon as we began the program."

"It's God. It has to be." Alicia shook her head and her eyes filled with awe. "I can't believe no one's called the school district or the police."

"The police?" A breeze drifted off the baseball field and brushed against his face. Wendell made sure he had the right words before he continued. "It's not a crime to tell kids about God, not if they're interested. Not if they're coming of their own volition, Alicia. You know that, right?"

"It . . . it seems like a crime." Clouds gathered in the distance. "You're still risking your job, Wendell. The jobs of teachers like Jenny Anders."

He nodded slowly. "We understand that."

Alicia looked beyond him to the football team practicing in the adjacent field. "The changes here at Hamilton . . . Jenny tells me more students attend your club every week."

Wendell's heart swelled with the reality. He held up the report he'd brought from his office. "The numbers just came in. Every measurable area at Hamilton has improved." He kept his joy at bay, mindful of the heartache she was carrying from the losses that day at her own school. "You're right. It's all God. He's the difference."

"Yes." She made a sound that was more disbelief than anything. "No other explanation."

A deep joy took root in the soil of Wendell's heart. Alicia was growing in her faith. Not just in knowledge but in belief. He was glad for her, glad for his answered prayers.

He handed her the report, and waited while she looked through it. When she was finished she handed it back to him. "Every school in America should see these results." Her voice fell. "Including mine."

"They're about to . . ." Wendell could feel the thrill in his heart. "I'm sure of that."

The wind played in the trees overhead and Alicia stood. "I have to go. We're having a vigil at school tonight." The courage in her eyes was unmistakable. "I'm doing the opening prayer."

His heart was full as he stood and faced her. God had worked a miracle in her, too. "Proud of you, Alicia. Really."

She looked at him, deep into his eyes. "I've missed you, Wendell. I'm sorry for how I treated you. Sorry I wasn't brave like you."

Wendell let that sink in. He pulled her close and hugged her. Longer than he should have. The spark was there for both of them. Wendell spoke words he hoped she would take with her. "You are now."

She smiled and they walked back to the main part of campus. When they reached his office, Alicia looked at him one more time. "Thank you. For what you said about me being brave now." Her eyes were softer this time, less troubled. "God's doing that, too. I can tell."

Then, with only a single glance back, she walked down the hall and out of the building. When she was gone from sight, Wendell exhaled. After his wife died, she was gone for good. There were no second chances, no way to see her again or look into her eyes once more.

But with Alicia there had always been hope.

And maybe it was still that way. Wendell allowed the possibility to linger. No . . . he was wrong. Today wasn't a beginning, it was an ending. They'd lost their chance. But at least this was a better ending than the one they'd shared a year ago. He felt the ache of missing her again. With everything in him he wanted Alicia back in his life.

Wendell tried to focus again on the parent assembly tonight. In just a few hours he would reveal at least some of the incredible changes at Hamilton to the parents. Because God hadn't only asked Wendell to trust Him and to teach young people about His ways and His truth. God had also asked him to share the proof of His power at work.

Which was just what Wendell was about to do.

Only Cami and Jordy and a few other students from the Raise the Bar program would be there tonight. Otherwise, the gathering was for parents only.

If parents chose to be critical of the Bible study and prayer times the kids and Wendell were having twice a week, they'd have a hard time saying so in the face of the students' stories.

Wendell settled in at his desk again. Sometimes he felt like the apostle Paul, a man bound for chains and prison because of his public support of God Almighty.

But whatever the price, he would pay it — all in an effort to obey the Father.

Wendell sorted through a stack of papers and found the report that had started it all. The one he'd put together two summers ago.

The one titled "In This Moment."

His football from Les Green still sat on the top shelf of his bookcase, the words crying out to him every day, every time the Raise the Bar club met. *What good can I do in this moment?* Wendell smiled. Yes, he had answered the call, and his mission remained the same. To love the students at Hamilton High. And live up to the job duties he'd

142

agreed to when he was hired. To *establish a schoolwide vision of commitment to high standards and ensure the success of all students.*

A text message flashed across the screen of his cell phone. He glanced down and saw Alicia's name.

I'll be praying for you tonight. You're doing the right thing, telling those parents about the good news at Hamilton. So glad you're being bold for Jesus!

Wendell's heart skipped a beat. *Alicia . . . you still care. Thank You, God, for this.* Wendell texted his reply. Thank you. That means more than you know.

He pushed the happy thought from his mind. The approaching meeting needed all his attention.

Tonight he would tell the parents how Hamilton High had changed, and how students now had a vision of commitment to high standards. How so many more students were actually succeeding. How their lives had been changed. And he would tell them that he couldn't take credit for the dramatic changes at Hamilton. Not when it was the Lord alone who deserved the praise. He would tell all of this to the parents — some of whom were bound to be shocked or even angry.

And then Wendell would trust God for whatever happened next.

8

One of the best things Cami loved about her new life, since she'd given her heart to Jesus, was the way she walked through her days not in the presence of anger. But in the presence of God.

Last week their after-school club had talked about the fruits of the Spirit. As people developed a friendship with God, the fruit in their lives showed. Love and joy, peace and patience. Kindness. Gentleness. Self-control. They were an outgrowth of believing the Lord and obeying Him. The fruits were the most amazing thing Cami had heard in a long time because they were true.

Cami was already feeling all of them. More love toward her friends and her family, a joy that couldn't be described — even on days when all she could think about was how much she missed her mother. Cami felt peace over her father's drinking and her little sisters' constant questions about their mom. And patience was so much more a part of her routine.

Patience hadn't stood a chance before, when anger was her constant companion.

Cami could be kind and she could be good — even when her father was mean to her. She wasn't perfect, but she desired only to grow stronger in her faith. Self-control was another thing. Most of her senior classmates still didn't attend the Raise the Bar meetings, and often they asked Cami to join them at parties on the weekends.

But drinking with them was the last thing she felt like doing. When she finished her homework and studying each night, she only wanted to read over the Bible passages from the week.

School was out for the day, so Cami took her books and her backpack to the football stadium, where Jordy and the team were practicing. This afternoon she was especially glad for the peace that filled her heart.

Because truth be told, she should be a little more afraid.

Yes, her life was better than it had ever been. But her father had no idea who she was or what she had become. And he definitely didn't know that Cami liked a guy in the club. She settled on the top row of the bleachers and found Jordy. He was the quarterback. Number 7. Easy to find among the mix of players.

Never had she imagined a year ago when she attended the first Raise the Bar meeting that she and Jordy would ever like each other. No one at school seemed to mind that she was white and Jordy and his family were black.

What mattered was their hearts, the way God had brought them together. The closer Cami drew to God, the more aware she was of Jordy's incredible qualities. Next year, they both wanted to attend Liberty University.

Cami wanted to study professional writing, and Jordy wanted to play for Liberty's football team. Then he wanted to earn his master's degree in business administration.

They weren't dating yet. But their feelings grew stronger every day.

There was just one problem — Cami's father.

Her dad didn't know about the Raise the Bar club, and he didn't know about Cami's newfound faith. He certainly didn't know about her feelings for Jordy. Cami felt bad not talking to her dad about any of that, but what was the point. Her father's hatred toward all things Christian was steadily growing. He blamed the Lord for losing his wife to a church man, and he was becoming more outspoken about having God's name removed from public conversation.

A whistle blew on the field, and Cami watched Jordy take charge of the huddle. The players clapped and then lined up in front of the ball. Jordy yelled out a few commands, and the ball was snapped into his hands. He danced back four steps, and then unwound his six-foot-three frame in fluid motion. The ball soared across the field and into the hands of one of his teammates, who ran straight for the end zone.

"That's what I'm talking about, Jordy!" the head coach yelled as he ran onto the field. He smacked Jordy on the back. "Just like that."

Cami smiled.

Everything was going so well for both of them. A gust of concern made its way over the otherwise calm landscape of her soul. So long as her father didn't come to the parents' meeting tonight.

Practice ended and Cami left for the library. Principal Quinn had told all of them to be there a few minutes before Parents' Night began. Cami had homework first. Her heart pounded as she walked across campus. What if her dad *did* show up? She tried not to think about it.

The meeting, she told herself. *Think about that.* The last time they got together, Principal Quinn had explained that he was going to talk about the Raise the Bar program with the parents. He had been waiting for statistics on the improvements. But he already knew how dramatically the lives of Hamilton High students had changed for the better. That's when Principal Quinn had asked Cami to share how the club had helped her. She was happy to talk to the parents about the changes in her own life.

Unless her dad showed up.

Cami swallowed her fear. It wasn't likely. Her dad probably didn't even know about Parents' Night. Of course, other moms and dads would be there and any of them could have a problem with the club. Which was why every student in the program was praying for the coming hours.

Cami's dad wouldn't come, though. Of course not. For most of the last year, he had come home from work and downed a six-pack before thinking about dinner or whether the girls had homework. There was no reason to expect he'd remember a meeting tonight at Hamilton High. But if he did . . . if he heard what Principal Quinn was doing, if he heard what Cami was planning to share . . .

Cami didn't have to wonder what her father would do.

He'd be through the roof livid. As her dad liked to say, heads would roll. And the first head would be that of Principal Quinn.

Cami shuddered at the thought. *Please, God . . . keep him out of this school tonight. Let him go straight home.* But if not . . .

She found a table in the library and waited for Jordy. As soon as he arrived, Cami pulled her history book from her backpack. They were using a new text this year, a decision made by Principal Quinn and the History Department. Jordy had explained the situation to her at the beginning of the semester.

"Lots of schools teach what's called revisionist history." Jordy always had the inside scoop. Principal Quinn was his father, after all. "What that means is that some people have rewritten history to remove God from the text."

Now they were using a textbook that drew its information from original letters and documents written by the founding fathers.

"I found this quote." Cami opened her history book and lifted her eyes to Jordy. "It's one of my favorites." The quote was from Alexander Hamilton, the school's namesake. Hamilton said, *There is a certain enthusiasm in liberty, that makes human nature rise above itself, in acts of bravery and heroism.*

Cami smiled. "That's what your dad did for us." She looked at the quote in the history book again. "For the sake of liberty, your dad started the Raise the Bar program. So that we might know God."

"I never thought about it that way." Jordy's eyes softened. "Like what he did for us has been an act of bravery. Heroism, even."

"Exactly." Cami loved this, the way she felt being with Jordy. The way they had so much in common now.

One hour blended into another and the two of them finished their homework. The whole time Cami tried not to think about her dad. But occasionally her fear won out. What if he'd learned about Parents' Night? What if the school had emailed him and this time he read the letter?

"You're worried." Jordy looked at her.

"A little." She glanced at him. "Not about my talk. But whether my dad will show up."

"I knew you were thinking about that." He closed his book and stared deep into her eyes. "Whether he comes tonight or not, Cami, you'll give your talk, and you'll be

151

amazing."

She smiled again. "Thanks."

Finally, they made their way to the auditorium, where the meeting was about to start. They entered behind the stage and moved to the wings, where the other students were gathered — the ones from other groups who would speak tonight. Cami tried to scan the audience. Was he there? She couldn't see every seat, but he didn't seem to be in the room. She felt a fresh rush of peace. *Thank You, God. . . . Thanks for protecting this program.*

"He's not here," Jordy whispered. He gave her a side hug. "Everything's going to be okay."

Principal Quinn started the evening. He took the podium with a presence that was kind and confident. Cami watched and thought that this was how Jesus Himself might've talked to the crowd.

"Thank you for coming tonight." Principal Quinn smiled at the parents. "I have wonderful news to share with you. A reason to celebrate." He went on to explain the Raise the Bar club.

"Some have asked me," their principal paused, "why I would share openly about the benefits of an after-school Bible study program. As if it might be illegal to have such a club." He looked around. "The reason is very simple: It's not illegal. And what God is doing at Hamilton High is too great to hide."

So true. Cami felt chills run down her arms. She scanned the audience again. The place was full, the parents definitely listening. Some looked puzzled, others nodded. A few even smiled. The main thing was that Cami's dad wasn't there. *Good.* She felt herself relax. Everything was going to be okay.

She turned her attention to the front of the room again. Principal Quinn was sharing about the tremendous changes that had happened in the past year. The statistics and personal stories. The more he talked, the better Cami felt. She was so thankful for the club. And because of her new faith, she wasn't angry anymore. Principal Quinn was the best.

No one cared for Hamilton High's students more than he did.

When the time came for the students to share, Cami followed Jordy. As she took the stage and approached the mic, she checked once more. Still no signs of her father. *Help me, Lord.*

Don't be afraid, My daughter. I am with you. The words whispered across the surface of her heart and worked their way deep into her soul. God was with her. She could feel Him here. She took a quick breath. "Good evening. My name is Cami Nelson, and I am one of the original members of the Raise the Bar club." Her notes trembled in her hands. "Principal Quinn asked if I'd share my experience. But the truth is . . . I want to share."

Cami looked at her principal, standing a few feet away. His expression was pure encouragement. She looked at the parents again. "Before attending Raise the Bar, I was angry. Not a little angry, but really mad. All the time." She was settling in, finding her passion. "I felt trapped by darkness. Like the days didn't matter . . . and neither did I."

She explained how she attended the first Raise the Bar meeting almost in protest. "I was going to report them to the police because I thought it was illegal. Reading the Bible on school grounds." Peace filled her heart. "But what happened next, I never could've imagined." She saw movement near the back of the room. A man standing and moving closer. "God took hold of my heart and —"

Cami stopped cold. She could see the man's face now. Coming closer, taking one of the seats up front. A parent with the meanest eyes ever.

Her father.

What? The room started to spin. This couldn't be happening. Maybe she should leave. Run out of the building and never look back. Cami clenched her jaw. No. She couldn't do that. Jesus had gone to the cross for her. She could go to bat for Him.

Even if her dad glared at her through every word.

Cami looked at her notes. Where was she? Her heart pounded so hard it was all she could hear. *Thud. Thud. Thud.* Cami blinked twice. *Help me, God, please.* Suddenly she remembered where she was in her speech. "God took hold of my heart and now life makes sense." She felt her courage double. "I have dreams about my future. I want to help people. And I have faith that I'll be in heaven one day."

As she spoke, never once did she look at her dad.

Not until the very end.

"The Raise the Bar club is the best thing that ever happened to me." This time she looked straight at her father. "I hope you think so, too. Thank you."

At that exact moment, Cami's father got up and stormed out of the building. He didn't need to stand up and yell his disapproval. Not at her or the program or Principal Quinn. His actions told Cami all she needed to know.

Later, the Quinns dropped her off at home, and her principal tried to encourage her. "It'll be okay, Cami. Just talk to him." Cami wanted to believe that. She thanked him and said goodbye to Jordy.

But as she walked into her house her heart raced. She had a feeling something terrible was about to happen. Good thing her twin sisters were staying with friends tonight. Her father was by himself when he met her at the door.

Rage burned in his eyes. "Cami Ann Nelson." He spat her name through clenched teeth. "Get yourself into the kitchen and sit down."

"Yes, sir." She dropped her backpack just inside the door and followed her father. He was bursting with hatred. More than Cami had ever seen.

In the kitchen, she saw at least six empty beers. *Great,* she thought. *He's drunk* and *furious.* She took the far seat, her back against the window. Her dad followed her to the table. Then he took slow steps in her direction. "Don't . . . you . . . move."

What was happening? Why was he talking

156

to her this way? Cami's heart raced so fast she could barely breathe. "Wh . . . what's wrong, Daddy?"

His words came like so many bullets, in a fit of anger greater than anything Cami had ever known. "I was at the parent meeting tonight. I heard your little speech." He slammed his hand down on the table and a cracking sound came from under it. "You're reading the *Bible*? Is that what you're doing? At a public school? Behind my *back*?"

Cami had always known this day could come. Many times she'd thought about telling her dad she was in the Raise the Bar club. Better to break the news before he found out about it. But there never seemed to be a right time. She swallowed hard. Her legs and arms shook with fear. *What's he going to do to me?*

"It's an important club, Daddy. All the students . . . everyone is happier now." Tears filled her eyes. Her father seriously looked like he might kill her. "Did . . . did you hear all the good things I said about it?"

"Oh, yes. I heard." The words came out like a hiss. Her dad turned and walked to the fridge. He took out another beer and downed it. Then he crushed the can and sneered at Cami. "Imagine my shock when I hear my daughter talking about her changed life." He slammed the can in the trash and turned to face her. "Star student in the club. Little Miss Give-your-life-to-Jesus."

He crashed his hand on the kitchen counter. "Well, I can tell you this much, missy. It's all over. You following some fairy-tale faith, and . . . and this club meeting on campus." He came closer to her, his breath hot against her face. Again his words were seething with hate. "I could overlook a few kids reading the Bible together after school. But when my own daughter is being *brainwashed* . . . something has to be done." His final words boomed. And then, suddenly, his voice fell to a whisper. "And as for that principal of yours, he can finish up his time behind bars. Then he can rot in hell."

Cami wondered if she'd throw up right here on the kitchen table. She couldn't breathe, couldn't speak. Her heart was beating so wildly, she thought it might stop altogether.

Her dad said his final words with a loud burst, every one like an arrow aimed straight for her heart. "Get. To. Your. Room!"

There was nothing Cami wanted more. She ran to the front of the house, grabbed her backpack, and sprinted down the hallway. But instead of shutting her bedroom door behind her, she left it open just a crack. She wanted a warning, wanted to know what her dad was going to do next.

As it turned out, she didn't have to wonder. Her dad was calling someone on the phone. He was too drunk to talk quietly or in any sort of professional manner. He must've dialed the local newspaper. Because from where she sat, on the edge of her bed, she could very clearly hear his side of the conversation.

"Yes, this is Andy Nelson from Haughville." His words were slurred — as much from his anger as the alcohol. "I need to talk to the main editor." He paused. "Hurry up. It's an emergency."

Cami felt the floor beneath her turn liquid. Suddenly she wasn't listening from her bedroom down the hall. She was in a ship, tossed by the worst waves any storm could ever stir up. *No, God . . . please, no.* This was going to ruin everything. She squeezed her eyes shut and waited.

"Hello, this is Andy Nelson." Now he sounded almost sober. He explained that his daughter was a senior at Hamilton High, and that the principal — Wendell Quinn — was leading Bible study and prayer meetings twice a week. "He's converting students to Christianity, and I want action immediately."

The blood rushing through Cami's head made it impossible to hear every word. But she caught much of it. Her dad said he was going to hire a lawyer and sue Principal Quinn and Hamilton High and the school district. Maybe the entire state of Indiana.

Whatever it took to shut down the program and see the people behind these acts punished.

The reporter must've promised to show up on campus the next day, because Cami heard her father repeat the name of the school. "You can see for yourself. We just had a parent meeting, and this . . . principal was actually proud of what he'd done."

Her dad was still talking, but Cami didn't hear another word. She ran to the bathroom and threw up. Not once but three times. Because after today, every good thing that had happened to her and to Jordy, every beautiful change that had taken place in the lives of the students at Hamilton High would all be brought to a sudden and dramatic end.

Cami couldn't imagine the trouble they were about to be in. They would probably all be arrested for talking about Jesus on a public school campus. Their Bibles would be confiscated and maybe burned. Something awful like that. And Principal Quinn could be locked up for life. Cami began to shiver. The students and administration at Hamilton would need a miracle to survive whatever was coming next. Her father would see that people were punished to the letter of the law. She knew that much about him.

As Cami crept into bed and turned off the light, as she lay in the dark shaking with fear, she couldn't feel even one fruit of the Spirit. Not love or joy or peace or patience. Not kindness or goodness or faithfulness or gentleness. Certainly not self-control.

But she knew this much. Even now she was not alone.

She drew a deep breath. *Calm, Cami . . . you can do this. Stay with me, Jesus. Please stay.* Gradually she felt control restored to her soul. Because there were two things no lawsuit or reporter or human being could ever change. First, God was with her. And second, He loved her.

Even if she was about to lose everything else that mattered.

9

Reagan couldn't sleep. Luke had come home late again, caught up in another important case. She climbed out of bed and walked without a sound into the living room. Anxiety ran like ice through her veins.

He'd been late three times this week. Reagan didn't want to admit it, but the problem was coming back. Luke was working too many hours, ignoring the kids and her. She dropped to the leather sofa and covered her face with her hands. *Please, God . . . not again.*

If she talked to him about it, he would do his best to change. But she didn't want to always be the nagging wife. Luke needed to see this on his own. He should want to be home more than he wanted to be at the office.

What am I supposed to do, God? She leaned back and looked around the dark room. *Will You please get Luke's attention?*

Let him realize what he's doing by being gone so much?

No answer came, but gradually a sense began to dawn on her. *Love Luke.* At first the idea grated on her. Love him? That wasn't the problem here. It was Luke who needed to love *her.* Luke was the one working too late.

But the idea wouldn't let her go. *Love Luke, My daughter. That's what I'm asking of you.* If the voice that echoed in her heart was God's, then Reagan had better listen. She sat up a little straighter.

Love Luke? Was that what God was asking of her?

It took another thirty minutes before she was sure. God wanted her to love her husband — no matter what. Her Bible study had been talking about this very thing. How to be the wife of a happy husband. The idea had seemed a little outdated at first, but every week the truth from Scripture and the stories of the women in her group were undeniable.

Bottom line, marriage took work.

It wasn't a fifty-fifty venture. It was each person giving a hundred percent, all of the time. Because that's what God asked of her. Not because Luke always deserved that. Some days, sure. But other times marriage simply meant Reagan needed to love Luke because that's what God called her to do.

Period.

Reagan let the message wash over her. *Love Luke.* The words filled her heart and soul. Rather than hold on to her frustration she needed to turn her efforts toward serving him. Loving him. Find some way to shift her mind from his late hours to something kind she could do for him.

As a way of honoring God . . . and her husband.

Reagan thought for a minute and then it hit her.

Luke's birthday was coming up just after Thanksgiving. All his life the family had celebrated it on or near Thanksgiving. Just last week Luke had joked about it with Tommy. He'd said something about how he never really had a birthday growing up. He had an extra-special Thanksgiving.

A smile lifted the corners of her mouth. A surprise party! That's what she could do. She would contact everyone in the Baxter family and get them on board early on. So they were all available. They'd let Thanksgiving come and go and that Sunday she would throw Luke his best birthday party ever. She would plan for the celebration and pray for her husband.

And maybe in the process she wouldn't notice how much he was gone.

The sun hadn't yet risen over downtown Indianapolis and already Wendell Quinn had a bad feeling. There was no reason, really. His meeting had gone without any of the complaining or arguing he'd expected. Not that everyone there agreed with Wendell or the Raise the Bar program.

But it was hard to argue with the results.

Maybe that, or maybe the fact that Hamilton High parents were too busy trying to make a living to complain. Because some of the parents definitely didn't like the idea of their kids learning about the Bible or praying together. Wendell had overheard some of them leaving the meeting.

"It's illegal, what that man's doing with our kids." The statement had come from a father who had been talking to a couple of women as they headed for the door. The man shrugged. "But hey, if it's keeping my boy off drugs, I say more power to him."

"Gotta hand it to the guy," one of the women said. "I wouldn't risk jail time for something like this."

"Me, neither." The second woman laughed. "I wouldn't risk missing dinner for it."

Wendell had watched them leave. *She wouldn't risk missing dinner?* What was that supposed to mean? He'd felt a sense of outrage then and he felt it now. They needed more parents who cared about the fate of the teens at Hamilton. More people willing to risk everything to see the kids grow up law-abiding, productive, successful citizens.

Now, first thing this morning, Wendell tiptoed to the kitchen and opened his briefcase. Inside was a sign-up sheet. Four parents had written their names on the piece of paper. Four out of all the parents who had attended. These four had agreed to bring snacks to the meetings. Snacks and dinners. Chick-fil-A was still providing a meal once a week, but the other meetings typically took place without food.

Wendell looked at the names of the volunteers. *Bless those parents, Lord. Bless the ones who care and bring more like them. We need all the help we can get.* Wendell studied the list once more and then shut his briefcase and headed for the shower.

This was his usual morning routine. He would get ready while his kids slept, and then around six-thirty, Jordy would get up and wake the other three. Leah scrambled eggs for her siblings and made sure they wore clothes that at least matched. Jordy

166

would feed Luvie.

Then an hour later, Jordy would drive everyone to school and they'd be one day closer to Christmas break. Most days, Wendell enjoyed the quiet of the morning. He tried to enjoy it today. In the shower he hummed "Amazing Grace," and while he got dressed, he prayed. For his kids and his home, for the students at Hamilton High and for protection of the Raise the Bar program.

Normally he was so happy by the time he headed off to school, it almost didn't matter what the day brought. Wendell would be ready to face it. But today was different. The bad feeling had been there since he opened his eyes, and it was worse as he walked to his small office at the front of the house and took a seat in the chair near the window.

Wendell tried to spend at least half an hour here every morning. This time was for him and God. The first appointment of the day. Get this one right, and the rest of the day would fall in place. Wendell grabbed his Bible from the small end table next to him.

He stared out the window and watched the sunrise begin to break across the horizon. *Nothing like the mornings, Lord.* He breathed in deep. There was something about seeing darkness flee, watching it dissolve in the power of the sunshine. It reminded him of one of his favorite Bible verses. Lamentations 3:22–23. *Because of the Lord's great love we are not consumed, for His compassions never fail. They are new every morning; great is your faithfulness.*

The words were true. They had always been true.

Wendell let the weight of the Bible settle on his lap. Maybe the concerned feeling was simply his heart, missing Joanna and the way life used to be. When everything was simpler. Wendell turned his eyes to his desk and the photo that had sat there for five years. A photo that would stay as long as Wendell was given another day.

The picture was taken many summers ago, when their youngest, Darrell, was only six years old. Wendell smiled at the image. He could still hear the kids laughing as the photographer tried to get them situated around the bench in her studio.

"I need the oldest kids in the back." The woman had been beside herself. "Please, could you all stop tickling each other? This is serious business."

Serious business? A family photo? Wendell chuckled in the morning glow just now hitting his window. The kids had all been laughing, talking about something Jordy had said or a song Leah had been singing. Alexandria had been just eight that summer, and the four kids got along like few siblings ever had.

Wendell credited Joanna with that. His wife had always wanted to be a mother. His eyes settled on Joanna, the first woman he had ever loved. "Dear God, I know she's happy in heaven. But could You please tell her . . . how very much we miss her down here?"

The pit in Wendell's stomach grew. Much the way it had felt the day of Joanna's accident. Wendell turned to the window again and lifted his eyes to the pink streaks making their way across the morning sky. And suddenly, like it did every now and then, the past came to life and Wendell was a middle-school boy, first day of seventh grade.

And Joanna was the prettiest girl he'd ever seen.

She was from California, more talkative than most of the girls. Her eyes were wide, her hair pulled into a ponytail and gathered in a bright pink bow. Wendell thought she looked like a model, and when the teacher assigned him a seat in English class far away from Joanna, Wendell did something he had never done before.

He disobeyed the teacher.

There had been an open chair right behind the new girl, so Wendell took that. And when the teacher called roll and looked for Wendell in the seat across the room, Wendell simply raised his hand. "I'm over here." He smiled at the man. "I'm sitting over here."

The teacher didn't really know how to respond. He looked down at the seating chart and up at Wendell. Finally he gave a shake of his head. "Okay. You're sitting there."

As the teacher moved on to the next students, Joanna turned and giggled in his direction. "You're funny."

Wendell smiled and felt his breath catch in his throat. "You're pretty."

He didn't kiss her until their wedding day, but after that middle-school English class, they were never apart again. Wendell blinked and took a long breath. The morning sky was lighter now, a few streaks of pale blue and orange giving way to a clear autumn sky.

He looked at the photo once more. He could still hear Joanna's voice when they'd reviewed the proofs from that shoot. Some of the pictures were perfect, in the most professional way possible. The kids all looking at the camera, everyone's clothes neat, their smiles on point.

Those weren't the photographs Joanna wanted.

No, she wanted the one that sat framed on his desk. The picture where the photographer had caught them all mid-laugh. Jordy was looking at Leah, and Alexandria was trying not to let go of Darrell. Wendell's arm was around Joanna's shoulders and her head was tipped back.

Laughing the hardest of them all.

Wendell let his eyes settle on her, on the way he would always see her. The way he would remember her.

Three weeks later Joanna was coming home from the grocery store. A trip she'd made a thousand times. Same car. Same street. Same groceries packed in bags in the back of their family van. Only this time a reckless teen rounded the corner on the wrong side of the two-lane highway.

The police said Joanna never knew what hit her. "Life to life." That's what Wendell had said about his beloved at her memorial a week later. Joanna Quinn had gone from life to life.

Jordy had said it another way. "My mom had three miscarriages between having us kids. She always talked about her babies in heaven. Three babies there. Four babies here." He had paused to dry his eyes. "She spent all these years here with us. It only makes sense that God would let her spend the rest of her time with her other babies. The ones in heaven."

Wendell let the memory fade. He swiped his finger beneath one eye and then the other. He had this morning time with God in part because of Joanna. Because years ago she had once told him: Mornings were the best time to hear God. The best time to talk to Him.

Yes, he and the kids missed her. They still talked about her and laughed at things she used to say. But they weren't without hope. One day they would all be together again, as a family.

Of course, the logistics of being a single dad to young children hadn't been easy. God had been good to provide a constant help in Joanna's mother. She had sold her house and moved in with them — taking the role of Joanna in raising the kids and tending to their daily needs.

Wendell had thrown himself into an even stronger faith — making sure he had his daily morning talks with the Lord, and doing everything in his power to live out his faith in the hallways of Hamilton High.

It was there that he first met Alicia Harris.

In the early years after Joanna's accident, Alicia became his friend. She would stop by his office and talk to him about the happenings of the high school. They would walk to the baseball field and sit in the bleachers, and eventually the conversations grew deeper. Especially after Joanna's mother died of cancer, leaving Wendell once again on his own with the children.

In their conversations, Wendell told Alicia about Joanna, how the two of them had fallen in love and about Joanna's strong belief in God. Alicia would listen, and once in a while she would admit something Wendell only suspected. "I wish I believed the way Joanna did."

Alicia was eight years younger than Wendell. She had spent her early teaching career helping her sick parents, and along the way she had missed out on the dating years. She had once dreamed of having children, but not anymore.

As Alicia and Wendell grew closer, Alicia admitted something to Wendell during one of their talks. Something she had never said before.

"You know what makes me most afraid?" It was a winter day, snow piled a foot high across the baseball field.

"What's that?" Wendell angled his body so he could see her eyes. He could feel himself being drawn to her, pulled in by her kind heart and deep beauty. Her skin was a light brown, her complexion smooth as silk. The smell of her perfume filled his senses.

Alicia hesitated, as if by saying the words the reality might somehow be worse. "I'm afraid of being alone." Her expression grew sad, sadder than Wendell had ever seen before. "My parents are gone. I have no family." She shrugged. "Sometimes I ask God . . . is this all there is for me?"

And in that moment Wendell felt his feelings for Alicia deepen. Before he could stop himself, he had reached for her hand. "You won't be alone." He looked intently into her eyes. "You have me. You always will."

But in the end that hadn't been true. His decision to lead the Raise the Bar club had driven her away.

He looked at the clock on his desk and stood. It was time to head to school, time to face another day without Alicia. Maybe that was all this was, the bad feeling stirring in his soul. Maybe he was just feeling afraid, the way Alicia had felt back then. Not because someone might fire him or throw him in jail for talking about Jesus on a public school campus.

But because — once his children were grown — he might spend the rest of his days alone.

10

Cami was terrified to go to school, but she had no choice. Her sisters had gone to stay with an aunt across town. Until the trial was over, their father had said. So the twins wouldn't be a part of the media circus that was bound to come. Already Cami had seen more people than usual driving by their house. A few of them definitely had cameras.

So her sisters were safe. But Cami still had to go to Hamilton High. She couldn't stay away forever. She thought for a minute. Maybe no one at school knew yet. Could it be she'd only imagined her father's phone call? Maybe he hadn't called the press. He could've been talking to one of his friends from the airport.

But as Cami stepped off the bus and headed through the front doors of Hamilton High that morning, she was sure she was only kidding herself. Of course her father had made the call. He had contacted the newspaper, and sometime today everything about her life was going to fall apart.

And not just her life, the life of Principal Quinn.

Before she got halfway down the hall to her locker, Cami saw Jordy round the corner with a group of football players. She stopped and waited until he saw her. At the same time, the guys gave Jordy a slight shove, the group of them laughing.

"Don't talk too long," one of them said. "Can't miss history class. Coach'll bench you for sure."

"I'll be there." Jordy grinned and gave the guys an elbow in return. These were his teammates and friends. Close friends. Some of the players who had been attending the Raise the Bar meetings for most of the past year.

Normally Cami would've stepped into the conversation and asked them how practice was going. She would've said something about the Friday night football game. But this morning she was too afraid to do anything but stand there. Silent. Waiting.

Jordy walked up to her and searched her expression. "Cami?" His smile faded. "What's wrong?"

She wanted to tell him, wanted to share every horrible thing about her father and last night. But class was about to start and besides . . . what if nothing came of it? Maybe this morning the reporter would forget he or she had ever talked to Cami's father. "Nothing." She tried to smile, but it felt flat.

"That's not true." He squinted at her, angling his head like he was trying to see past her words. "You look scared to death."

"No." A single laugh escaped her lips. But it sounded forced. "We have that history test." She nodded to the classroom down the hall. "Remember?"

"You've aced every history test you've ever taken." He lowered his brow, still clearly confused. "Something's wrong, Cami."

"No. Everything's fine." *For now,* she told herself. *It was fine for now.* Her blond hair was pulled back in a single long braid, the way she liked it these days. She smoothed out the ends and suddenly she did something she hadn't planned on doing. She reached for his hand. Everything was going to change after this. Jordy would hate her for what was about to happen. For her father's decision. She took a step away from him. "Come on. We can't be late."

The feeling between them was electric. This was the first time their hands had touched this way.

Their fingers locked together as they hurried down the hall toward history class. And Cami had a very distinct, very sickening thought. If the reporter acted on what her father had said, if Principal Quinn was arrested later today, then this might be the last time she and Jordy would ever be so close.

In fact it might be the last time they ever spoke. Because after today Jordy wouldn't merely be finished being her friend.

He would hate her.

The bad feeling stayed with Wendell as he arrived at his office and long after the first bell rang. He couldn't figure out just what was causing it, but the uneasiness was there.

Wendell spent the first hour walking the halls of Hamilton High, checking into each classroom. All seemed well. As was the trend recently, most desks were filled with students. The teachers seemed happy, and in each room a productive lesson was under way.

So what was the problem?

He returned to his office, sat at his desk and tried to grab a full breath. But his chest muscles felt too tight. *God, give me peace today. Something isn't right. Go before me, please.*

179

It occurred to him then, that he hadn't had time to read his Bible this morning. He had spent the time remembering Joanna. And thinking about Alicia. Yes, he'd talked to God. That was a constant every day for Wendell. But he hadn't opened the Bible. That had to be it. The bad feeling was simply him missing the Word of God today.

Wendell kept a Bible on his desk and he opened it up to 2 Chronicles. It was a chapter he'd read and loved before. Much of it was highlighted and underlined.

He felt himself drawn into the text. Chapter twenty was about a battle the Israelites were in, but it was the last part that captured Wendell's attention. He read verse 17 twice over. *You will not have to fight this battle. Take up your positions; stand firm and see the deliverance the LORD will give you. . . . Do not be afraid; do not be discouraged. Go out to face them tomorrow, and the LORD will be with you.*

The deliverance of the Lord.

A truth Wendell always tried to remember. He had scribbled something in the margin next to the text. A date — first day of school a year ago. Back then the words had meant something very clear to Wendell. His students had been under siege from the culture. Gang killings, crime, suicide, depression. A lack of achievement and desire to excel. God's Word had literally provided the answer then. The students were winning now, Wendell, too.

So what was this feeling inside him? And how come the message in 2 Chronicles seemed almost cryptic? Like he ought to again pay particular attention to the words? Wendell closed his Bible just as the phone in his office buzzed. He answered it on the second ring. "Principal Quinn. How can I help you?"

There was the slightest hesitation on the other end. "Is this Wendell Quinn?" The voice belonged to a woman. Her words came in a sharp staccato. She sounded fierce.

"Yes." Wendell leaned forward in his chair. "This is he." The three presentation folders were on his desk. He glanced at his Bible.

The woman drew a sharp breath. "I'm a reporter from *The Indianapolis Star.* Last night we received a call from the parent of one of your students, telling us about a Bible club that meets at your school two days a week." She barely paused. "Is this true?"

Wendell stood and paced to his office door and back. His mind raced. "The club is voluntary. The students choose whether to attend or not."

She seemed to ignore that. "Our understanding is that you run the club, is that right, Mr. Quinn?"

"I run it, yes." His heart beat hard against his chest. He was ready for this. But that didn't make the moment any easier. "Again, it's voluntary."

"How many students would you say attend the club, Mr. Quinn?" She barely gave him time to finish his sentence before firing the next question.

"It varies." He returned to his desk and pulled out his presentation folder. His hands shook as he looked at it. *In This Moment.* His coach's words came back to him. *What good can you do in this moment?* He tried to grab a full breath.

"Mr. Quinn?" She sounded beyond impatient.

"Hold on." He thumbed through the folder.

He needed to share some of the quotes he'd gathered, quotes from the founding fathers. Or let her have a copy of the independent report, the one done by Anna-Mae Williams. "Our school is a better place since we started the club. I could give you —"

"Mr. Quinn, the *Star* will run a story on

182

this matter in the next few hours. Do you have anything you'd like to say, anything we should include?"

Wendell felt like he was slipping through a dark hole. "You can't run this story now. It'll ruin everything."

"Is that your final statement?" She sounded angry and impatient. Like she didn't have time for his thoughts.

"No." Panic slapped him in the face. "First of all, which parent called you?"

"I'm not at liberty to say." Her answer sounded rehearsed. "I need to know if that's your final statement, Mr. Quinn."

"No." His frustration grew. "That's not my statement. What I'm saying is, I have a lot to add to the story. You need to come to my office and I'll explain why we started the program. I can show you what's happened since."

"There's no time for that, Mr. Quinn." She huffed, as if she was completely put out at how Wendell was wasting her minutes.

"This is my statement, then." Wendell was pacing, again. How could he quickly sum up what had happened at his school? "Since our Bible program began, since our students have been praying, we've seen miraculous results at Hamilton High. God has heard our prayers and met us where we are. We are a different student body because of Him."

As soon as the call ended, Wendell tried to remember exactly what he'd said to the reporter. He called his secretary, Ellen Boggs, into his office. "We may . . . be getting other calls from reporters today. I'd like you to put them all straight through to me."

Ellen nodded, her eyes the slightest bit fearful. "Is everything okay?"

"Yes." Wendell nodded. "Yes, it is. There's just . . . there's some interest in our Raise the Bar program. That's all."

It didn't take long for Wendell to realize how wrong he was. Saying the media had some interest in Hamilton High's Bible study program was like saying North Korea had some interest in taking over the world.

The Indianapolis Star's article ran online exactly two hours after the reporter's call to Wendell. And immediately Wendell's office phone began to ring. Ellen put the calls through and Wendell said the same thing to every one of them. Yes, the program had been meeting for a year. Of course attendance was voluntary. Yes, he'd been running the program. And sure, he definitely believed God was working a miracle in their midst.

Over and over and over again.

He took calls from the *Dispatch* in Ohio and the *Free Press* in Michigan. Reporters from Illinois and Kentucky and Oklahoma called, and nightly news programs contacted Wendell from stations throughout the Midwest.

By two o'clock, something else began to happen.

Local ABC, CBS, NBC, and Fox News vans pulled up in front of the school. Reporters attempted to come onto campus, but Wendell met them at the entrance. "This is a closed campus," he told them. "You do not have permission to be here, and you may not talk to our students."

By the time Wendell returned to his office, Jordy was waiting for him. He looked like he was about to pass out. "Dad . . . what's happening? Hamilton High is trending on Twitter."

Wendell wasn't sure what that meant, but it couldn't be good. "Some parent called *The Indianapolis Star* about our Bible study program."

"Why?" Jordy's anger was instant. "They don't want us to raise the bar? They want us shooting each other and doing drugs and failing out of school?" He dropped his backpack on the floor of Wendell's office and pulled his phone from his pocket. "Listen to this." He held up the phone. *"Principal Quinn said that God has heard the prayers of the school. We are a different student body because of Him."*

Jordy stared at Wendell. "As if that's a bad thing?" He huffed. "What are we going to do?"

Wendell had no idea. Outside his window another news van pulled up. The media that had arrived earlier were setting up cameras and reporters just off school property. When the final bell rang, in less than an hour, the press would be ready. Wendell turned to his son and held out his hand.

Whatever fear and frustration was coursing through Jordy, making him angry and coloring the tone of his voice, it faded in that moment. Wendell came close and took his hand.

"Let's ask God what we're supposed to do." Wendell felt an otherworldly calm come over him. "I don't see any other way through this."

Jordy nodded. The hint of a smile eased his expression. "I knew you'd say that."

"Yes." Wendell looked at his son for a few seconds. "We'll get through this, Jordy. We will." He prayed then, that God would protect the students at Hamilton, and the program he'd started. "Lord, don't let one student be dissuaded from attending the Raise the Bar club, but bring others into our midst because of whatever happens here today. And we ask for Your protection through it all. In Jesus' name, amen."

"Amen." Jordy hugged him, the way he used to when he was a little boy. When he pulled back, the concern was still strong in his eyes. "It's trending on Facebook, too."

"That's what you said about Twitter. Trending?" Wendell shook his head. "When we get home, maybe you can show me what that means."

That night Jordy tried to explain it. By then the story was on the home page of Fox News. Wendell couldn't possibly read all the comments under the hashtag #Hamilton-High, but the ones he did read were dramatically mixed.

Some people applauded him, but most wanted his head on a platter. They called him a right-wing racist, forcing his religious babble on the hearts and minds of innocent kids. Wendell wondered if they knew he was black. Could a black man be considered racist for believing in God? He wasn't sure, but anything seemed possible in today's culture.

One thing was certain. Based on their

posts, the majority of people shouting at him on social media seemed to hate God even more than they hated Wendell Quinn. Eventually Wendell had to walk away from the computer and fix dinner for the kids. Spaghetti and acorn squash. Leah's favorite.

When they were all around the table, Wendell looked at the kids, one at a time. "You've heard what's happening in the media. With Hamilton High?"

"Yes." Darrell, the youngest, had looked frightened ever since he got home from school. "Everyone's mad at you. Right, Daddy?" Tears welled in his eyes. "That's what my teacher said."

Was it possible that they were talking about the news even at Darrell's junior high? Wendell made a note to call the school's principal the next day. Neighboring teachers didn't need to stir the concerns of the students. The news was definitely doing that for them. Wendell set down his fork. "They aren't mad at me, Darrell. They're mad at God."

"What did God do to them?" Alexandria was clearly trying to be brave. But now that they were finally talking about it as a family, tears fell onto her cheeks, too.

"Well." Wendell drew a deep breath. "God doesn't care if those people are angry with

Him. But He wants them to bring their anger to Him. Pray about it or talk about it. Not spread rumors on social media."

Leah took a bite of her squash and stayed quiet.

"Hamilton is still trending on Facebook and Twitter." Jordy held up his phone. "You should hear this one, Dad."

"No, Son." Wendell raised his brow. "Put your phone away. Not during dinner."

Jordy looked surprised, but he slipped his phone back in the pocket of his jeans.

"Daddy . . ." Only then did Leah look at him. "Rachel said the police are going to put you in jail. Is that true?"

There were so many false rumors flying around. So many false beliefs. Wendell sighed. "No, it's not true. A person can't go to jail for talking about Jesus." He thought about Alicia's fears. "Lots of people think that's true in America today. But it's not." Wendell worked to keep his tone in check. "The Constitution guarantees us freedom of religion, Leah. Which means the kids at Hamilton High have a choice to pursue the Christian faith . . . or not." He hesitated. "It's their choice. And no one is going to jail."

Relief filled her eyes. "Are you sure?"

"Completely." Wendell smiled at her. He

looked at his plate; he'd barely touched his food. No matter how calm he tried to appear to the children, the pit in his stomach was worse than ever. "Everything will be okay."

Wendell told himself that throughout dinner and while they cleared the dishes. He did so again later as they prayed together and as all of them said goodnight. Everything was going to be okay. No one was going to jail. Really.

His reassuring thoughts lasted until the next morning.

The reporters were camped off school property but just a few yards from Wendell's marked parking spot. As he walked past them he learned several things — things the media had apparently found out before he did. Their questions came at him rapid-fire, even when he didn't stop to answer them.

"Mr. Quinn, have you had any personal issues with parent Andy Nelson before this?"

Another woman pushed her way closer. "What is your statement about the lawsuit filed this morning on behalf of Mr. Nelson?"

The reality hit Wendell so hard he nearly stopped walking. Andy Nelson? Cami's father? Wendell felt sick to his stomach, but he kept on. The questions did, too. "How do you plan to handle the mandate from the school board, that you cease all further meetings with your after-school Bible study program?"

Wendell's head was spinning. Could all of that possibly be true? He ignored the reporters and headed into his office. Once inside, he closed the door. His hands shook, and the noise from outside echoed in his mind. A quick look out the window told him what he had hoped wasn't true.

The reporters were talking to students. Whatever students were willing to stop before they reached campus. Wendell's mind raced and his head began to spin. His school district had issued a mandate, ordering the club to stop meeting? Andy Nelson had filed a lawsuit against him?

Wendell turned on his computer and checked his email. His heart pounded as he spotted a message from an attorney for the school district. Yes, indeed, he was being sued. The charges against him had been filed by Andy Nelson, father of senior Cami Nelson. The letter was replete with legal jargon, but the bottom line was this:

He was being summoned to court. The date seemed to consume the computer screen. Everything the reporters had said was true.

In the most terrifying slow motion, Wendell felt the walls around him begin to crumble and fall in on top of him. The roof crashed onto his shoulders and the ground wouldn't stop shaking. As if the world's worst earth-quake had started to destroy him, only this one showed no signs of stopping.

Wendell held on to his desk and closed his eyes. *How am I going to survive this, Lord? Make the room stop spinning, please. I have to lead this school, I have to take charge. And right now I don't know how.*

Then, the way God always did, He whispered the faintest words to Wendell Quinn. The words Wendell had read yesterday morning in this very office. The ones from 2 Chronicles. *You will not have to fight this battle. Take up your positions; stand firm and see the deliverance the LORD will give you . . .*

Wendell repeated the words to himself. *You will not have to fight this battle. The Lord will deliver you.* Which meant one thing. If Wendell was going to stop the spinning and find some sort of steady ground, he couldn't just sit here.

He lowered himself to the floor. Slowly, and with the greatest certainty, he took his position, preparing himself for the battle ahead. And he did so from the only place he knew how to fight.

On his knees.

And there Wendell remembered the name of the person he had determined to contact if he ever wound up in this situation, his back against the wall: Luke Baxter. As soon as he finished praying, Wendell sat back at his desk and made the call to a man he'd never met before. And then he said one more prayer.

That Luke would know what to do next.

11

Luke Baxter jumped as high as he could and snagged the Frisbee from the air — just before his brother-in-law Ryan had a chance to grab it. "Mine!" Luke laughed as he ran with the Frisbee. "Who's on my team?"

A handful of voices called out from the other side of the yard. Luke spotted his son Tommy, also on his team, and wound up for the throw. But instead of making it to Tommy, the Frisbee soared up and off the field — like it had a mind of its own.

"Out of bounds!" Dayne ran to get the Frisbee while everyone laughed and caught their breath.

Luke loved days like this. He had never been busier at work, and he knew the reason why. He was one of a few dozen attorneys battling for religious freedom in the United States, and very clearly the battle was getting worse.

But no matter how busy things got, no

matter how many cases came his way, Luke had always been determined to have one thing on the weekends: time with his family. Recently, though, his resolve had given way to the pressure of the cases he was handling, the importance of the religious freedoms at stake.

It had been far too long since he'd made the trip to Bloomington. But this week God had seemed to make it very clear. He needed family time. Now. And so Luke and Reagan had driven their kids an hour west to Bloomington to hang out with their cousins at Ashley and Landon's house.

The Baxter house — the place where Luke and his siblings had been raised. Ashley and Landon owned the place now, and they hosted get-togethers here as often as they could. The kids loved playing kickball out front or running through the backyard and splashing in the creek and pond that made up part of the ten-acre property.

Today it was a game of Ultimate Frisbee, and Luke was right in the thick of the action. Only Ashley, Kari and the youngest kids weren't playing. Otherwise everyone was caught up in the game. His dad and Elaine were sipping iced tea from the porch, watching the action. Taking in every moment.

The next hour flew by as each team won a game, and in the final minutes, Dayne's group took the last match. Exhausted, both teams dragged themselves to the front porch for water bottles. When he could breathe normally again, Luke raised his water to the sky. "I call rematch. Next time we're together."

Ryan laughed. He had been on Dayne's team today. "You're on."

Everyone headed inside, where John and Elaine had joined Ashley and Kari in making dinner. The whole house smelled like pulled pork and baked sweet potatoes. Luke approached his dad and put his arm around his shoulders. "I'm telling you, Dad. You and Elaine could open your own restaurant."

"From doctor to manager of a restaurant." His dad chuckled. "I think I'll stick to days like this."

"Good idea." Ashley grinned at Luke. She was working on a salad across the counter. "Otherwise they'd be too busy to cook for us."

Elaine held up a plate of fresh sliced red peppers. "The secret is the local vegetables. Anyone can make a good dinner with the food we get at the farmers' market."

Half an hour later everyone was seated

around two large tables in the dining room. Ashley and Landon used the old wooden table the Baxters had eaten at when they were growing up, and on days when the extended family was together, they brought in a second one.

So they could all be together. The way they loved best.

Luke's dad led the prayer, and once the meal was under way, they went around the room and talked about what was new, how God had been working in their lives or how they needed prayer. Dayne and Katy and their kids were well. "We still haven't found the story we want to develop for our investor. But we're thinking it'll be about religious freedom."

Luke used his napkin and set it back on his lap. "I have a dozen cases I could tell you about." He hesitated, thinking about his workload. "Nothing really sensational, though. I'll let you know if anything comes up."

"Thanks." Dayne looked pensive. "It's so troubling. How commonplace attacks on religious freedom have become."

Luke remembered the case that had dominated the media the past few days. "You heard about the principal in Indianapolis? The one being sued because of his after-school program?" He shook his head. "Poor guy doesn't stand a chance, from what I can tell. He'll lose his job and the program . . . and unless I'm missing something, he'll lose the lawsuit." Luke looked around. "That's just the way things are now."

Everyone agreed.

Next Brooke and Peter talked about a new program they were developing at their medical clinic. "It'll be in conjunction with the initiative put out by the city of Bloomington earlier this year. Training people about the connection between physical fitness and mental health." Brooke looked excited about the new opportunity. "It's always something."

Peter nodded, and Dayne looked around the table. "I forgot to ask . . . while we look for the right movie, if you all could pray about the one we're working on. It's a love story."

"Yes, it's beautiful." Katy nodded. "Centered around the Oklahoma City bombing." She looked around. "Remember that? Like twenty-some years ago?"

The others nodded. Luke was young, but he remembered the tragedy. "A hundred people were killed, right?"

"Actually 168 people." Dayne paused to

let that sink in. "It's called *To the Moon and Back.*"

"*To the Moon and Back?*" Kari took a sip of water and turned to Katy. "Like the bedtime story?"

"Yes." Katy's eyes filled with emotion. "The main couple . . . both their mothers used to say that to them. But now it's more like the story of their lives. They've been to the moon and back and still not found peace."

"Wow." Luke caught the vision for the film. "Sounds amazing."

"It'll be powerful." Dayne took a deep breath. "Difficult, but powerful. A story of true healing and redemption."

The conversation shifted to Ryan and Kari and the football season under way at Clear Creek High. "Those Flanigan boys score half the touchdowns." Ryan laughed. "No one can keep up with them."

During a lull, Luke looked at his niece Maddie. "Speaking of the Flanigans, how are things with Connor?" The oldest Flanigan boy was a sophomore at Liberty University this year.

Maddie's cheeks turned pink. She looked down at her plate and then up at the others. "We're struggling a little. Still friends, though." She smiled at Brooke. "Mom and

I were talking about him on our way here."
Maddie looked at Luke again. "He wants to
talk to you about the cases you've been taking. He's really thinking about going into
film. But he's not sure. Sometimes he thinks
he might be a lawyer."

Hayley, Maddie's younger sister, motioned
with her fork toward the others. "And yes, if
you want to know, they are no longer of-
ficially boyfriend and girlfriend." She raised
her eyebrows. "But if you ask me, they'll get
married one day."

No one was more loving and kind than
Hayley, even when it came to a teasing moment like this.

"Thank you, Hayley . . ." Maddie's smile
didn't reach her eyes. "You never know.
We'll see."

The meal was nearly over when Luke felt
his cell phone buzz in his pocket. He took it
out and read the message. It was his answering service. Apparently an urgent call had
come in the day before. For some reason,
the message was only getting to him now.
Luke excused himself and headed out the
front door onto the porch to listen.

"Mr. Baxter, you don't know me. My
name's Wendell Quinn. I'm the principal at
Hamilton High School on the west side of
Indianapolis." The man paused. "Mr. Bax-

ter, I'm in a great deal of trouble. I run a voluntary Bible study here at the school, and now I'm being sued."

Luke felt his heart sink. There was nothing he could do for the man. He had read enough about the case to know that.

"The truth is . . ." The man sounded desperate. "I need your help, and I wondered if you'd give me a call. I was on my knees earlier and God reminded me of your name. I'm not saying that to coerce you, but . . . there's no one I'd rather have on my side than you."

Wendell rattled off his phone number twice — just so Luke wouldn't miss it. "I'll be praying for your call. I'm not afraid, Mr. Baxter. But I definitely need some help here. Please call me back at your soonest convenience."

For a long moment after the message ended, Luke stared out at the front yard where he'd grown up. Who would have ever imagined such a thing? A principal helps bring a school back from the brink of destruction, and now he's sued? All because the solution involved God?

Luke went back inside the house and found the adults around one of the tables, drinking coffee and still talking. Luke tried to smile. "Where'd the kids go?"

Reagan laughed. "Every direction." She explained that the younger boys had gone out back to explore the pond, while the older kids had gone upstairs to watch the last half of the Indiana versus Michigan football game. The little girls were coloring in the craft room.

The heaviness in Luke's heart made its way to the surface. "I just got a message from the principal we were talking about, the one being sued for holding the after-school Bible club."

His siblings and their spouses were instantly in tune. Dad and Elaine, too. "What did he say?" Luke's father leaned back in his seat. "You look upset."

"I don't know what to do." Luke sighed. "He wants me to represent him." Luke crossed his arms. "Only the case is a no-win. There's literally nothing I can do for the man. Much as I'd like to."

"I read about the case." Ryan leaned his forearms on the table and shook his head. "The program was voluntary. Seems like he should have a chance."

"Precedent isn't on his side." Luke had gone over this more times than he could count in recent years. Always when a case involved prayer or Bible reading, courts would look back to the original cases that had changed things in the United States. "It all started in 1962 with *Engel v. Vitale.* It happened in New York."

Luke explained that back then the children in the New Hyde Park school district recited the same prayer each morning. "I happen to think the prayer is beautiful." Luke looked at the faces around him. "The kids would say, 'Almighty God, we acknowledge our dependence upon Thee, and beg Thy blessings upon us, our parents, and our country. Amen.' "

Ashley looked as shocked as the others. "Kids in a public school used to start their day like that?"

"They did." Their dad nodded. "I remember praying something similar to that when I was in school."

Elaine nodded. "Me, too."

"It was commonplace." Luke hesitated. "Anyway, that year some of the parents formed a group and sued the school district, claiming that the prayer violated the Constitution's establishment clause — which basically says, 'Congress shall make no law respecting an establishment of religion, or prohibiting the free exercise thereof.' "

The case quickly gained national interest, with most Americans standing by the school district. People believed that such a prayer was certainly not establishing a religion, as it was vague enough to serve the interests of nearly all religions.

"But not vague enough for the Supreme Court." Luke took a quick breath. "That case rewrote the way prayer was handled in public schools."

"I remember studying that in school." Brooke took a sip of her coffee and looked at Peter. "People look back on that as the year God was kicked out of the public schools."

"Me, too." Peter put his arm around his wife. "Brooke was just helping Hayley with a history test on that the other day."

"And it didn't end there." Luke went on to explain that next came a case brought by the founder of American Atheists, Madalyn Murray O'Hair. The famous 1963 lawsuit became known as *Murray v. Curlett,* and it led to a landmark Supreme Court ruling that ended Bible reading in American public schools.

"The next year, I believe, *Life* magazine referred to Murray O'Hair as the most hated woman in America." John looked troubled by the matter. "Our schools have gotten further and further away from God and prayer every year since."

"Exactly." Luke sighed. "With this principal — Wendell Quinn — any lawyer for the plaintiff would call on precedent set back in the sixties, or a number of rulings since then, and Quinn would lose before the case ever got to jury."

Ryan seemed especially intrigued by the situation. "What about whether the kids *wanted* to read the Bible and pray? There has to be a way the principal can be vindicated."

"There really isn't." Luke didn't want to talk about the case all night. He wanted to hear more about how his nieces and nephews were doing, which of them were playing sports or dancing or acting in one of the upcoming Christian Kids Theater plays. He would have to call the principal sometime tomorrow after church and tell him the reality.

He'd love to help, but the man faced a no-win legal battle.

Later that night, Luke's father pulled him aside. "You have a minute?"

"Of course." They walked to the living room. John sat on the sofa and Luke took the seat opposite his father. "What's up?"

His dad crossed one leg over the other, quiet for a moment, as if he were ordering his thoughts. "I've been thinking about that principal. Son, I think you should help him."

Luke took his time responding. Of course he wanted to help. But there wasn't anything he could do. "I'd love to, Dad. You know me." He clenched his jaw. "I fight these cases for a living, and I love it. Anything I can do to help preserve the dwindling religious rights of the people of this nation, I'm ready to take it on."

His dad nodded slowly. "You just don't see winning this one. That's what you said."

"Right." Luke didn't want to get too detailed, but since his dad had asked, he would do his best to explain the problem. "There was a case back in 1971 that created a sort of test, a way for the courts to determine if a situation of prayer or Bible study was legal in any given situation."

John Baxter was a very intelligent man. That much was evident as he narrowed his eyes, following everything Luke was saying. "Okay. What's the test?"

Luke explained that it was three parts. First, the religious activity must have a secular purpose. Second, it must neither advance nor inhibit religion, and third, it must not result in excessive entanglement between government and religion. Luke leaned on his knees, his eyes locked on his father's. "From what I see, Principal Quinn's case violates all three of those."

His father nodded, disappointed. "I understand. I just . . . I can't get the case out of my mind. I really believe you could help him, Luke."

Reagan came and sat down, and now Luke's dad talked to both of them. As he did he tried one more time. "Do you know what happened to Madalyn Murray O'Hair's son William? The one whose class read the Bible together?"

Reagan thought for a few seconds. "Well, he's the child Madalyn sued about. So her son wouldn't have to read the Bible at school."

"Yes." John looked at them, taking his time. "But do you know what happened to William in his later years?"

Luke knew the answer. "William became a Christian."

"Much to his mother's fury." Luke's father let that sit for a moment. "But if there's one thing that story proves, it's this: The Word of God does not return empty."

"Yes." Reagan looked at Luke, her eyes soft. "And the fact that nothing is impossible with God."

As the night continued, the idea of Madalyn Murray O'Hair's son becoming a Christian stayed with him. He hadn't thought about William Murray's story in a very long time. His father was right. Reagan, too.

God's Word was indeed powerful — beyond explanation. And with God all things truly were possible. Luke wrestled with the reality the rest of the night. It wasn't until an hour later, that he knew there was one case he had to take. One thing he absolutely must do. Whether it made sense or not.

He needed to call Wendell Quinn.

Before everyone left Landon and Ashley's house that evening, Reagan made her way to the kitchen. Luke and the other men and most of the kids were playing some last-minute Frisbee out front, so Reagan went to the kitchen and found the others.

"Hey, I want to tell you about my plan." She kept her voice low.

Elaine, Katy, Brooke, Kari and Ashley all stopped what they were doing and circled around.

Ashley dried her hands and set the towel down. "It sounds important."

"It is." Reagan's heart had felt heavy since her husband took the business call in the middle of dinner. "Luke's doing it again. Giving all his time to the office."

More than anyone else, Ashley understood the situation. "I can feel it. He's distracted."

"Exactly." Reagan looked over her shoulder. She needed to get to the point before Luke came back in looking for her. "I know God's over this. He's speaking to Luke, otherwise we wouldn't be here today."

Elaine put her hand on Reagan's shoulder. "I was going to say . . . that's a positive sign. That he made time for this."

"It is. But still." Reagan tried to condense the story. "I was praying about it the other night and God gave me an idea. Rather than feel bad and complain about what's happening, I could find a way to show Luke how much I love him."

Kari smiled. "I like that."

The others agreed.

"So." Reagan dropped her voice to a whisper. "I need your help in throwing a surprise party for Luke's birthday. The Sunday after Thanksgiving." She looked at Ashley. "I'd love to have it here."

"Absolutely." Ashley didn't hesitate. "I'll talk to Landon, but I'm sure it's okay." She stifled a laugh. "I love it! Surprise parties are the best."

"I'll help with the cooking." Elaine's eyes lit up. "And whatever else you want."

Brooke and Ashley said the same thing, and like that Reagan had a plan. She felt a thrill run through her. "Tell the guys later, but not the kids. Not yet."

"Reagan?" It was Luke. He had leaned into the house, breathless from his time outside. "Are we leaving?"

"Coming!" Reagan said it loud enough for him to hear. "Just helping with the dishes." Reagan covered her mouth to keep from laughing out loud. "One minute. Really."

The others laughed, too, but they were careful to keep quiet.

Reagan felt the thrill again. "This will be the best party ever." She was whispering again. "Love you all! Thank you!"

She turned and hurried out of the kitchen. Luke was back outside, and as she left the house he took her hand. The kids were already buckled in as Luke and Reagan walked across the grass. He leaned his face close to hers as they approached the car. "I have the nicest wife in the world."

Her heart skipped a beat, and she felt a rush of panic. "Me?"

"Yes." He kissed her forehead. "You helped with the dishes. I love that about you."

Luke opened Reagan's car door and then walked around to the driver's side. Reagan sank into her seat, relieved. She thought for sure he knew about the party. But he'd only been talking about the dishes. A smile started at the center of her heart and worked its way to her cheeks. The weeks to come would be full of planning. Which was a good thing. Not only so Luke would know he was loved.

But so Reagan wouldn't miss him so much when he was gone.

12

By Tuesday, everyone at school knew two things: First, Principal Quinn was being sued, and second, the lawsuit was being brought by Cami's dad — Andy Nelson. Ever since the news broke, Cami had wanted to stay home, but her dad wouldn't hear of it. She should be proud to take part in liberating the school from religious oppression.

That was literally what he had told her. More than once.

Cami waited outside the school until a few minutes before the first bell. That way she wouldn't have to linger in the hallways, where people would see her and start talking. Since Monday it seemed that's all everyone did.

As soon as they saw her coming, they would form little groups and whisper. Cami heard it all. The quiet snickers and rude words. All aimed straight at her. From students angry with her, confused by her father's actions, and wondering if somehow she was behind them.

Those weren't the only comments she'd gotten. Several kids had approached her with compliments. "Way to go, Cami! You finally saw the light." Or "We knew you wouldn't stick with that Jesus stuff forever."

A few times, Cami had tried to explain that she wasn't behind the actions of her father. She still supported the club. She was happy to support it. But her peers didn't want a conversation.

They wanted the chance at a jab.

Before she left school yesterday, she'd wanted to stand on the tallest building with a megaphone and tell everyone in earshot to back off. This wasn't her fault. Kids wanted either to applaud her or silence her. They all had something to say. But she had only one thing she wanted them to know: She loved the Bible study club. Being part of the group had changed her life in every possible way.

But there was no megaphone and no tall building. So Cami simply went home, avoided her father — who had been drinking more than usual — and climbed into bed early. At least she could talk to God and ask Him how this had all happened.

And why it was happening to her.

Cami was still outside. She kept her head down, hiding behind a wall, waiting for the moment when she could hurry through the doors. She had one goal today.

Avoid as many students as possible. Especially Jordy.

But even as the thought filled her mind, she spotted Jordy walking with two of the football players. That was another thing. He hadn't returned her texts or looked for her after school the way he usually did. Yesterday he wasn't in the only class they shared.

So was he avoiding her now? Did he and Principal Quinn really think she could've had something to do with all this?

The possibility made Cami sick to her stomach. *Help me, God . . . help me get the word out. This isn't my fault. Please, help me, God.* She leaned against the building and took a few quick breaths.

My peace I leave you, My daughter . . . My peace I give to you. Do not be discouraged and do not be afraid.

The Scripture verse settled in around the scared edges of her soul and whispered truth. Truth Cami desperately needed. She could walk in the peace of God, even if everything around her was falling apart. And she did not need to be discouraged or

214

afraid. God was with her.

Literally with her. Right here at Hamilton High.

Cami took a slower breath this time. The thing was, she didn't believe her dad on this whole thing. He was angry at Cami's mother, yes. He thought any Christian man who would have an affair with a married woman must be a hypocrite and a fraud. Okay, Cami could see that.

Cami figured this was the only thing her dad could think to do about it, and now the whole matter had spiraled out of control. So crazy out of control that it didn't seem like there was any way to undo it.

Because there was no way her dad could've really wanted national attention on this thing. People around the country were calling him an atheist and an antireligious zealot. Some supported him, of course. They publicly applauded his efforts. But lots of people were angry, wondering how Andy Nelson could stop such a good thing at a messed-up school like Hamilton.

Whatever was going to happen now, it was too late to stop it.

Except for explaining how she didn't have a part in it all. She could do something about that, she could speak her mind and tell the kids at Hamilton how this wasn't her doing. Today at the Raise the Bar meeting, Cami intended to do just that. God would be with her, she knew that for sure. Because she had already asked Him.

The club still met in the school auditorium. Principal Quinn would give a message from the Bible and talk about it. Then the students would break into smaller groups and share what the message meant to them.

Then they'd pray.

Cami guessed that none of the club expected she'd be there today. They probably figured she'd be sitting with her dad in some lawyer's office dreaming up a way to destroy Hamilton High. As if she'd been a fraud the entire time.

The bell rang. Cami had no choice but to make her move.

She raised her chin and clutched her backpack a little tighter. *God, be with me. Please. I can't do this alone. Give me the chance to make things right.* She pushed on the double doors and walked through the school entrance. Most kids were in class by now, but even then she caught a couple of them staring at her. Two boys pointed in her direction as she hurried to her English class.

One hour blended into the next, and Cami

struggled to focus on her schoolwork. One thing kept filling her mind when she was supposed to be listening to a lecture in chemistry or geometry. All this time she had taken the school's Bible study group for granted. As if this were the sort of thing that happened at most schools.

After all, so much good had come from it.

Students reading Scripture, talking about God, praying for themselves and their school . . . all of it had made a difference.

But since the story broke about her dad suing Principal Quinn, Cami had realized something. Most people really were against God. Or at least the loudest people were. They were all over Twitter and Facebook. Even Instagram. They made memes mocking Principal Quinn and Hamilton High and they were angry with the teachers for not blowing the whistle sooner.

Like they really didn't care about all the good that had happened.

When school was over, Cami took her time getting to the club. She wanted to slip in once everyone else was seated, take a spot in the back row, where it was dark. So no one could see her or shoot angry looks in her direction.

Principal Quinn was already up front as Cami sat down.

"Today we are talking about forgiveness and grace." He pulled his Bible from the podium and sat on a stool. "How many of you have your Bibles today?"

Half the kids raised their phones in the air. The other half held up an actual Bible. Cami raised her eyebrows in the dark of her seat. A year ago she would've been surprised if a single Hamilton student had a Bible.

Principal Quinn asked them to find Matthew 18. "This is a story about forgiveness. About how many times God asks us to forgive the people who hurt us."

The way my dad has hurt me, Cami thought. She pulled her Bible from her backpack and opened to Matthew. Principal Quinn went on to talk about the conversation the disciples had with Jesus. " 'How many times should I forgive? Seven?' "

Seemed like a big number to Cami. If her dad mocked her and yelled at her and made her the pariah of her school, forgiving him seven times would be a lot. But that wasn't where the story ended. Principal Quinn kept reading. " 'Jesus tells the man not seven times. But seventy times seven times.' " He looked around the room.

Cami felt like Principal Quinn was looking straight at her.

"Jesus wants us to have a heart of forgiveness all the time. No matter how often someone hurts us or offends us." He paused. "Some of you have been seriously hurt in the past. You've been the victim of a crime or someone you love has been killed or hurt. You've had parents who have mistreated you or neglected you. Maybe they're angry at you, and you can't understand why. Don't know what you ever did to deserve the way you're being treated."

Cami might as well have been the only one in the room. She felt herself begin to shiver.

"God does not say you have to like the people who do you harm. But He does say to forgive." Principal Quinn held up his Bible again. "Now turn to James 2:13. The last part of the verse." He waited while the kids did as he asked. "Let's read it together."

Together they read the words of the verse out loud. "Mercy triumphs over judgment." Next they looked up another Bible verse. One that talked about grace. "The message is clear. Grace is always better."

Principal Quinn went on to explain that grace was a replacement for punishment and revenge. "Grace means you are willing to give people another chance. The way God is giving you another chance. The way He always will." Again he looked around the room. "I want you to think about the ways you've been hurt, and how you can forgive those people."

He talked of Matthew West's song, the one about forgiving people. "A line in the song sums it up." He hesitated. "The prisoner that it really frees is you."

It was true. Being angry at someone — even her dad — was a prison. It was all Cami had been thinking about. She could tell Principal Quinn was about to turn on the lights and ask the students to get in small groups. She needed to make her move — now or never.

As if she were being driven by a force not her own, Cami suddenly stood. "Principal Quinn. May I say something? Please?" She walked slowly up the center aisle until she was sure he could see her. "I need to talk to you and the group. If that's okay."

Principal Quinn smiled at her, and in that single moment Cami knew she was going to be okay. Because the way he looked at her should've been with anger or frustration. Sadness, at least. Instead he looked at her the way she imagined God might look at her. With fondness and joy.

"Come on up here, Cami." He held out one arm, welcoming her.

She climbed the six stairs to the stage and

took the spot beside Principal Quinn. He put his arm around her shoulders, the way a dad might do. Her heart felt warm and safe. "Thank you," she whispered to him. Hope filled her soul. Principal Quinn would never know what this meant to her. This public show of the very forgiveness and grace he'd been talking about for thirty minutes.

Cami drew a deep breath. "In the last few days, most of you have been wondering about me. By now you know about the lawsuit." She looked down at her feet. How could her dad do this to her?

"It's okay." Principal Quinn spoke quietly, just for her. "They're listening."

They were. He was right. She nodded and lifted her eyes to her peers once more. "Some of you might think this is my fault. Like I went home and told my dad about the club so the whole thing would fall apart."

One of the students had turned on the audience lights, and Cami could see the looks on their faces now. They were hurt, angry. Clearly. She glanced down again, just for a moment. *Don't be mad at them. Forgive the way you want to be forgiven.* Cami exhaled, releasing every angry feeling. "I want to tell you this is not my doing. My dad came to the parent meeting. He heard about our Bible study club there, and he blew up. At Principal Quinn, and all of you. But mostly he blew up at me."

She looked at Principal Quinn beside her. "I don't know what's going to happen, and I'm so sorry my dad is doing all this." She turned to her classmates again. "But I'm with all of you. I love this club." Her voice began to shake, and tears blurred her eyes. "Ever since we've been meeting and reading the Bible. Ever since we've been praying, I feel different. I *am* different." She caught the first few tears with her knuckle. "I never even wanted to come here. I hated my family and I hated my life. I had no dreams. I didn't care about school or my family or anyone but myself."

The reality of Cami's changes rocked her to the core. "I'm a different person now. I believe Jeremiah 29:11 that God has good plans for me. I talk to Him all the time, and I have hope. Real hope." She looked around the room. "I'm one of you. And on behalf of my dad, I ask your forgiveness."

Principal Quinn smiled at her and then he began to clap. Slowly at first, and then louder and with more enthusiasm, Cami's classmates began to applaud, too. She looked over the kids in their seats, and her breath caught in her throat at what happened next.

Like the others, Jordy was still clapping when he stood. Then the kids around him did the same until finally everyone was standing and cheering for her.

Cami couldn't stop her tears. They ran down her face and reminded her that the Bible was right about forgiveness and grace. They were proof of faith. Proof of God. Cami knew firsthand now.

It was grace.

Grace personified.

Cami was still riding the high of being loved by the other kids when she got home later than usual. The small groups had met and then her peers had prayed for her specifically and for the club. None of them knew how great the trouble was that lay ahead.

Turned out that was especially true for Cami.

When she walked through the door her dad was waiting for her. A half-empty bottle of some kind of liquor was on the end table beside him. Before she could say a word he stood. "Do not tell me . . ." He charged toward her, his feet unsteady, eyes blazing. "Do not tell me, young lady, that you were at that . . . that Bible club today!"

His words slurred, and for the first time in Cami's life she was sure her dad was going to hit her. She clung to her backpack and with her other hand reached for the doorknob. If she had to escape, at least she could.

"Don't run away. You will not make a mockery out of me. You unnerstand?"

"Daddy . . . w-w-what's wrong with you?" Her words were a shriek.

Her father rushed at her once more and this time he swung at her. Right at her face. Cami moved just in time and her dad's fist went through the wall near the front door.

That was all she could take. Cami hurried back outside and began to run. Tears streamed down her face, but she kept running. As fast as she could. Away from her dad, away from his anger. His toxic view of life.

When she was three blocks from her house, when her sides were shaking and her lungs were gasping for air, Cami used her phone to call Jordy. "Please! I need your help."

Jordy was there in minutes and he drove her back to his house. Together with his dad, they came up with a plan. Because she was eighteen, there was no need to call Child Protective Services.

Cami didn't want to press charges against him, but still, the main concern was her immediate safety. One of the teachers, Michelle Smith, lived a few blocks away with her husband and two kids. They had a guest room and at times they took in Hamilton students who needed a place to stay.

Of course, if Cami had told any of them that her dad had nearly hit her, they would have gotten her help right away. But Cami didn't want to make that part public. Not yet. For now, it was enough just to be away from her dad.

Cami was still crying when Mrs. Smith pulled up to take her home. Jordy hugged her. "Remember our talk . . ." He searched her eyes. "Before all this happened? Remember?"

It took Cami a moment, but then it clicked. The conversation they'd had more than once about college and staying close. "Y-y-yes." Her teeth chattered. "You're not . . . m-m-mad at me?"

"Mad?" Jordy pulled her close again and held her for a long time. When he leaned back, he looked deep into her eyes. "How could I be mad at you? None of this is your fault."

Cami nodded. Gratitude filled her heart. Jordy was still on her side. Even still . . .

"I'm so scared. My dad . . . he's going to kill me. N-n-now that I left him."

"No." Jordy put his hands gently on her shoulders. His dad and Mrs. Smith were talking in the kitchen, so for this moment they were alone. "He's not going to kill you. We are going to ask God for a miracle, and we are going to believe that will happen."

A miracle. Yes, that was what she needed to pray for. Gradually Cami felt herself begin to relax. Jordy pulled her into another hug and they stayed that way for a long time. In his arms she stopped shaking. Her fears faded and she felt safe. Protected. He made her feel like a princess, like the most important girl in the world.

They stayed in the embrace until Mrs. Smith and Principal Quinn returned to the front of the house. Cami pulled herself back a bit and let her eyes find Jordy's once more. "Thank you."

"It's going to be okay." He looked like he wanted to kiss her, but he couldn't. Not here, not now. "Believe, Cami."

She nodded. "Okay."

"Let's pray." He didn't blink, didn't look away.

The smell of him filled her senses, a mix of his cologne and his shampoo, maybe. Cami tried not to think about it. She looked at her principal and Michelle. "Is it okay if we pray first?"

"Of course." Principal Quinn smiled at Jordy. "God's still in this story. Jordy's right. We need to pray for a miracle."

That's just what they did. But as Cami rode with Mrs. Smith to her house, doubts pounded her. Cami remembered a terrible storm last spring where she'd been caught walking to the bus stop. Lightning and thunder had ripped through the sky and then it had begun to hail. Ice chunks the size of golf balls rained down on Indianapolis, and Cami could only hold her backpack over her head and pray she wouldn't be killed by them.

When the bus finally arrived a few minutes later, Cami had welts on her arms and shoulders from the pounding hail.

That was how she felt now. Only instead of hail, she was being beaten down by doubts. What if her father found her? What if he didn't let her get her clothes from her house? What if he came to Mrs. Smith's house and killed them all? What if Principal Quinn went to jail for reading the Bible with them? And what if they stopped allowing the kids to pray?

By the time Cami entered her new bedroom and shut the door behind her, she could barely breathe for the doubts assailing her. That's when she remembered her Bible. She took it from her backpack and found the marker in the middle. She had placed it in a section that had given her hope when she first read it.

Cami reviewed it again now. It was from Isaiah 41. *So do not fear, for I am with you; do not be dismayed, for I am your God. I will strengthen you and help you; I will uphold you with my righteous right hand.*

The words brought physical comfort. *Do not be afraid. Do not be afraid, do not be afraid.* Saying them was like a mighty shelter, protecting Cami from the doubts that flew at her from every side. *Do not be afraid . . . do not be afraid.*

And as Cami fell asleep she thought about Jordy, how wonderful she had felt in his arms. How deeply he cared for her. Then her mind drifted and she had the strangest feeling. A feeling that told her God was in control and she could fall asleep in His arms. Whatever might happen in the days ahead, He would go before her. He would protect her. She knew this for sure.

Because the feeling was complete and absolute peace.

13

Reagan felt the weariness in her shoulders. Luke had come home late again last night. Two nights this week already and it was only Thursday. The kids were at school and she had set aside the next hour to work on Luke's party. Ashley had already confirmed that Landon was fine with hosting the party at their house.

But all Reagan wanted to do was drive down to Luke's office and tell him the truth: Things were getting out of hand again. Luke meant nothing by it. He loved the kids and her. The problem wasn't the job. It was his way of thinking.

Like he'd lose the important cases unless he worked around the clock.

She felt sure God wouldn't want Luke to strive like that. If Luke would put his family first, God would make up the lost hours on his cases. Reagan sighed. Yes, a trip to the office wouldn't be a bad idea.

Yet even as she toyed with the possibility, a different thought hit her.

The photo booth.

Brooke had brought the idea up a few days ago when Elaine, Brooke, Kari and Ashley got on the phone with her and dreamed a little. "What if we get one of those photo booths for the party? They send someone to run the machine and handle the photo strips. They bring silly hats and props."

All of them had loved the idea, so Reagan had made a few phone calls.

Now it was settled. The photo booth could be delivered to Landon and Ashley's house Sunday after church and they would position it just off the entryway. Reagan could hardly wait to share the news with the others. She got everyone onto a group call, and the conversation quickly shifted to the possibility of an ice cream sundae bar and what type of dinner food they should have.

At the end of the hour, when Reagan hung up, she felt happier than she had in days. And suddenly it hit her. The sad feeling about Luke's excessive work was gone. And of course! This was just what she was supposed to do. Believe that changes in Luke would come from God, and stick to doing what she could do.

Love Luke with all her heart.

Wendell had never disobeyed authority in all his life.

Until now.

He took the call from the president of the Indianapolis Public Schools board on Monday — days after the story about Wendell and Hamilton High had sufficiently blown up. Thanks to the media, Wendell already knew this call was coming.

James Black, president of the school board, had always been a friend, someone Wendell had shared a meal with on a number of occasions. When things were falling apart at Hamilton, Mr. Black had assured Wendell that the trouble wasn't his fault.

"Kids these days have a mind of their own. Too many video games, too many absent parents." The words Mr. Black had spoken to Wendell at the end of their worst school year stayed with Wendell still. "You have to figure some kids are going to fail. Period. That's just the way it is." The man had shrugged. "No one expected you to turn your school around. If you can, well then, I applaud you."

The cheering indeed came when James Black and the others at the school district saw the changes at Hamilton High.

"Whatever you're doing, keep it up." Mr. Black phoned him halfway through the last school year. He had chuckled. "You're making us all look good."

Wendell had wondered then why Mr. Black never asked exactly what Wendell was doing to make such amazing improvements. He knew the statistics, but not the details about why things were changing for the better. Maybe he hadn't wanted to know. Whatever the reason, the applause had ended as soon as the school board realized what had caused the improvements.

"You should've known better, Wendell." Mr. Black sounded beyond disappointed. "Talk of God does not belong in a public school. Period." Then the man went on to tell Wendell he needed to disband the Bible study club immediately. "If I hear wind of you attending those meetings . . . in fact, if the meetings are allowed to continue, you will be fired." He paused, condemnation heavy in his voice. "You've been warned, Wendell."

So this was the mandate the reporters had asked about. Wendell wasn't surprised, really. He'd figured it was coming sooner or later.

Wendell ached for someone to share this with. He would talk to God. He prayed without ceasing these days. But if he wanted to talk to someone who could look into his eyes and take hold of his hand, there was only one person outside of his family who would meet that need.

Alicia Harris.

He and Alicia had connected recently, but not nearly often enough. She probably understood the depth of his situation, the gravity of all that was at stake. Wendell prayed that his troubles hadn't rekindled her panic attacks.

He missed Alicia like never before.

Not only that, but he was out of answers when it came to the Raise the Bar club. Good thing he had Luke Baxter. The lawyer would know what to do. Their first meeting was set for one o'clock that afternoon.

The morning flew by and at just before one, Wendell took a spot in the lobby of Luke's office. The building was on the right side of Indianapolis, five stories high, ornate brick and beautiful white pillars and molding. Wendell hadn't seen something this nice since the time he took a group of teens to Washington, D.C.

"Wendell Quinn? Luke Baxter." The man smiled at him. A smile that did nothing to hide the seriousness of the matter at hand.

Wendell stood and shook Luke's hand. "A

hundred lawyers must work here."

"Feels that way after work when we're all trying to get out of the parking garage."

Luke led the way and Wendell followed, his briefcase clutched tight in his hand. "Thank you for seeing me."

"Of course." Luke sat in the chair behind his desk and motioned for Wendell to take the seat across from him. "Thank you for coming in."

So far, Luke Baxter had not agreed to take the case. But at least he wanted to talk to Wendell. That was a starting point. The first miracle would be for Luke to agree to represent him.

They would need many more for Wendell to win.

Once he was seated, Wendell put his briefcase on his lap. "I have a few folders full of information I'd like to share with you." He had been looking forward to this ever since the news broke.

Luke Baxter's desk was much cleaner than Wendell's. The area contained a large calendar, a ceramic pencil jar that looked like it was made by a child, and a photo of what appeared to be Luke's family. Wendell took the first folder out and set it on the desk in front of him.

"This is something I put together before I

started the —"

"Mr. Quinn . . ." Luke's face was filled with kindness. "Let's talk about the case first. I need you to understand what we're up against."

We're up against. Not *you're* up against. Wendell took that as a sign that Luke had already fully committed to the case. He slid the presentation folder back in to his brief-case and set it on the floor beside him. "I'm sorry. I'm just . . . I'm anxious to show you why I think we have a chance."

"I understand that." Luke leaned forward and set his forearms on the desk. "You need to know, Mr. Quinn, that I'd love nothing more than to help you. But here's what we're up against."

Wendell was listening. For the next half hour the lawyer explained the history of prayer and Bible reading in public schools. Every case he brought up was more discouraging than the one before it. "A test is used for a club like Raise the Bar." Luke Baxter pulled a sheet of paper from the top drawer of his desk and handed it to Wendell. "A three-part test."

Luke gave Wendell a brief overview of each part of the test. Then the lawyer sighed. "In your case, though what you're doing is working effectively, none of the three criteria are being met."

Wendell looked again at the sheet of paper. *Have a secular purpose. Neither advance nor inhibit religion. Must not result in excessive entanglement between government and religion.* "No offense, Mr. Baxter. But I think you've got this all wrong."

"Call me Luke." He smiled, patient.

"And you can call me Wendell."

Luke nodded. "Okay, how do you figure?"

"Well, let's take that first one." Wendell lifted his briefcase again. "Can I use my folders for this?"

"Of course." Luke leaned back in his chair and folded his arms. "If you think there's something I'm missing, I want to know."

Wendell pulled his folder from the briefcase. The one titled "In This Moment." He opened to the first page — where the definition of his job description was written. "When I was hired to serve as principal at Hamilton High, I was asked to do the following." Wendell read from the page in front of him. *Establish a schoolwide vision of commitment to high standards and ensure the success of all students.* He looked right at Luke. *Let him hear me, God. Please, let him hear me.* "That's what they asked me to do. That was my secular duty. My secular purpose, if you will."

Very slowly, Luke leaned forward again. "Go on."

A surge of possibility raced through Wendell. "The second point is neutral. More of a nonfactor." He looked from the paper Luke had given him back to his folder. "Our group merely presents Bible verses and allows students to discuss them. No one is suggesting they should become Christians. When that has happened, it happens on its own. The kids lead that sort of discussion because, frankly, they are hungry for a reason to believe in something more than what they've seen. They want a purpose in life."

Luke winced. "I'm afraid a judge and jury will hear that as advancement of religion. Even just announcing the club during school hours could be seen as promoting religion."

Wendell felt his heart sink. "What? I thought . . . I was just telling them about an opportunity."

"But it's a religious opportunity." Luke's tone remained kind. But he didn't waver on the problem at hand. "A club you, yourself, are leading. That could easily be a violation of church and state."

"I can't believe this." Wendell was ready to stand and pace the room. His heart felt like it had fallen to the floor. "I thought . . . if I didn't tell them it would be the opposite. A prohibition of religion." Wendell forced himself to remain in his seat. "The kids want this. If we deny it — if I deny it — isn't that prohibition?"

A sigh came from Luke, but he didn't say anything.

"The third point doesn't seem to apply at all. Entanglement between government and religion? I'm a principal, Mr. Bax— Luke. Not a governor or senator. I don't write laws. I'm not shaping public policy or opinion. I'm simply facilitating students who voluntarily choose to be part of an after-school Bible study. No entanglements. I have plenty of students who are not attending."

"I understand." Luke tapped his fingers on his desk. The man was listening, Wendell could tell.

Wendell's own argument made complete sense to him. In fact, he would've liked a chance to tell the judge and jury some of this. "Those students who don't show up Tuesday and Thursday afternoons are not penalized. There's no different treatment, no push for them to come to the club meeting."

Luke stood and walked to his window. For

a long time he only looked out, as if he were silently calling on God for help, the way Wendell had done so many times in his own office. When Luke turned to face him again, Wendell could see the give in his expression.

So he took a quick breath and continued.

He pulled the other two folders from his briefcase. "This" — he held up the research report put together by AnnaMae Williams — "has a breakdown of every very real statistic that changed for the better after a year of the Raise the Bar program." He held up the document. "Page after page, Luke. It tells the story."

Wendell slid the report across the desk, and Luke walked over and picked it up. He glanced through it and set it down. "The third one?"

"These are the personal stories of a dozen students whose lives and educational experience have been changed because of our Bible study meeting." Wendell handed that folder to Luke. "It's all there. Enough to win this case. I really believe that."

Luke sat back down. For the next few minutes he went over the precedents one more time. "This country — our courts and legal system, and especially our government — has been for most of the past decade very opposed to the Christian faith." He hesitated. "You understand that, right?"

This wasn't going anywhere. Wendell didn't want to talk precedents. He thought about telling Luke how he'd studied the founding fathers and that he knew all too well how far the country had drifted from its faith roots. Instead he sat back in his chair and studied his lawyer. "Tell me about yourself, Luke. Your family. Your faith."

The question seemed to take Luke by surprise. "Sure . . . okay." He talked about being raised in a wonderful, godly family. "I was the golden boy, the youngest. The one who did everything right by God and my parents." That was, he went on to say, until he and his girlfriend allowed things to go too far. "It was the night before 9/11. Her dad worked in one of the towers and because of . . . because of me, she didn't take his final call. He tried to reach her that Monday night. September 10. And she was too busy with me to answer it. He died the next morning in the attacks."

Wendell felt his heart sink. Funny how you could sit across from a successful attorney like Luke Baxter and never know what he'd been through. What trials had shaped him. "What happened next?"

Luke nodded. "It was awful." He shook

his head. "I've never told this to a potential client before. But since you asked . . ."

He explained that his girlfriend, Reagan, broke up with him and went home to be with her grieving mother. While she was there she learned she was pregnant. Even then she wouldn't talk to Luke. "After that, I got caught up in a terrible relationship with a girl who didn't believe in God whatsoever. A complete rebellion on my part."

The story was more than Wendell could've imagined.

"Thankfully I had my parents. So when I was ready to turn back home, someone was waiting with open arms and the truth of the Gospel." Luke paused. "Eventually Reagan and I found each other again and I realized I was the father to a little boy named Tommy. Reagan's birth experience nearly killed her. She couldn't have more kids after that. We ended up marrying and now . . . well, now we have three kids. The last two were adopted."

Wendell listened to every word. His heart went out to Luke and all that he and his family had been through. But there was something Luke had said that stood out. "What was that part about your family? About them waiting with open arms?"

Luke seemed puzzled, like he wasn't sure where this was going. "Just that, my family was there for me. They forgave me and prayed with me and led me back to God. I don't know where I'd be without them."

"Okay." Wendell could feel the intensity in his eyes. "Now imagine you didn't have a family like that. Imagine the only way you'd ever find your way back is a group that meets after school twice a week to read the Bible. A group of students and volunteer teachers who pray with you and care for you and point you to Jesus every single time you ask."

Slowly, Luke began to nod. He clenched his jaw and stared at the material on his desk. "We'll have an uphill battle every step of the way."

"I realize that." Wendell resisted the urge to celebrate. Never mind that the attorney across from him had just bared his heart. This was still a professional meeting.

Luke stood and walked to the window. He turned and stared at Wendell. "We'll be headline news in every paper, every TV station. And nearly everyone in positions of power will be shouting for us to lose."

Wendell folded his hands on Luke's desk. "I know that, too."

For a long moment, Luke was quiet. Probably sorting through his options, his schedule. "I'll take the case, Wendell. Pro bono. My fees are covered by donors who believe in religious freedom."

The reality came over Wendell like sun on a rainy day. "That's incredible."

"It is. As bad as things are, there will be people out there on our side." Luke thought for a minute. "Usually I have a good feeling about the cases I take." His expression grew somber. "I don't have that feeling this time."

"I understand." Wendell gathered his presentation folders from Luke's desk. "I'll make you copies of these."

Luke ignored the offer — clearly he had his own way of doing things, and using someone else's presentation folder and materials was almost certainly not that way. Luke walked Wendell to the door. "Pray that I'll find a precedent case. Something like yours."

"I'll pray. So will my kids and my students." Wendell paused by Luke's office door. "Thanks for telling me your story."

Luke smiled. "Next time, you tell yours. We're going to need to be friends if God's going to use us to pull this off."

"Deal." The two shook hands and again Wendell contained himself. It wasn't until he was almost to his car that Wendell stopped and raised both fists in the warm autumn afternoon air. "Thank You, God!" Wendell felt his smile stretch across his face. "I knew You'd convince him!"

Just as he climbed behind the wheel, his phone rang. He didn't check to see who it was before answering. So when he heard the voice on the other end, his heart skipped a beat.

"Wendell." She sounded kind, strong. "I can't talk long, but this call is overdue."

"Alicia." Wendell's mind raced and he closed his eyes. "It's good to hear your voice." Clearly she was not too afraid to reach out to him. Even with the national negative attention he was receiving.

"How are you?" She cared. Her question was deeper than Lake Michigan.

"I'm okay. I really am." Wendell leaned back and opened his eyes. He stared out the window at the sky. "God is working. Even today."

"I'm sure." This was definitely a new Alicia. She drew a full breath. "You're in trouble, but you're going to get through this, Wendell. I've been praying." She paused. "So what happened today?"

Wendell hadn't thought the day could get better, but it just did. "Well . . . I now have the very best lawyer! Luke Baxter is going to work with me."

"Hmm." She paused for a second. "Luke Baxter. I haven't heard of him."

"He's the best religious freedom lawyer in the nation." Wendell couldn't stop smiling. "He's taking my case, Alicia."

"That's great!" She sounded truly happy for him. "God is already ahead of you. Working for you." Alicia hesitated for a longer beat. "I just . . . I wanted you to know I'm here for you. I miss you."

"I miss you, too." He had been willing to lose her if it took that to help the students. To help her. But right now . . . Wendell only wished he could drive his car straight to her house and see her.

She was the friend he needed.

"After this craziness . . . could I take you to dinner? Even as a friend?"

Her answer came soft and certain. "I'd love that."

Wendell could hardly believe her response. He put his hand on the wheel. "Until then . . . keep praying. And I'll keep praying for you."

"I will. Thanks." Her sureness was there again. "And hey, I've stopped my medication. My doctor is thrilled. No panic attacks. God is . . . He's healing me, Wendell. A little more every day."

"That's amazing." It was the best news of all. He remembered that she didn't have long to talk. They would catch up in detail later, over dinner. "So . . . thanks for calling. I'll keep you posted. About the lawsuit."

"Please." The love he'd felt from her before was there again. Not in words, and maybe only as a friend. But it was there. "Oh, and . . ." her smile was audible, "it's good to hear your voice, too."

He wanted so badly to see her, hold her hands. Take her in his arms. "Talk to you soon, Alicia. Goodbye."

"Goodbye."

Wendell spent much of the ride home thinking about her. She was right. He was going to get through this. He wasn't doomed, the way the media made it sound. And with Luke Baxter, his very talented attorney, Wendell could win this case. He believed it. Because in the most difficult moments ahead, people would pray. Even Alicia. And it wouldn't be only Luke acting as his advocate in that courtroom.

But God Himself.

14

Luke had a pit in the center of his stomach.

The hearing was in less than an hour at the Indianapolis Civil Court. Like he'd told Wendell last Monday, typically he didn't take a case unless he had a good feeling he could win it. The way he felt about his other current cases. Like the one that involved a teacher at Clear Creek High School who had blown the whistle on a group of students, including his niece Jessie.

Jessie was a sixteen-year-old sophomore at the school, and part of the cheerleading squad. Every week before the football game, she and the other cheerleaders created a paper banner to encourage the football team. The banner always included a Bible verse.

Now the teacher had contacted the school district, and the school district had ordered Jessie and the cheerleaders to stop making mention of the Bible verse on the signs.

Never do it again, they were told.

Well, that was a violation of their religious freedoms, and Luke didn't mind saying so. He had written a letter to the school district, and he fully expected the situation to settle out of court. The school district would not want a public battle, which they would certainly lose because it didn't line up with the three-part test.

But that was not the case with Wendell Quinn.

The good news — which he'd repeatedly assured Wendell about — was this: There would be no jail time for Wendell. "At least at this point, people don't get sent to jail for reading the Bible or praying in a public place," he had told Wendell when they met last week at Hamilton High. "But you could lose your job at any point."

Wendell understood that. He told Luke how James Black had promised to fire him if Wendell continued the club. But so far the district had kept him on.

Wendell had smiled. "The apostle Paul said to consider it pure joy whenever we face trials of many kinds."

If that was Wendell's role model, it was working. Luke couldn't believe how joyful the man was, how sure that somehow God was going to give them a miracle. Luke only wished he felt the same way. As a lawyer, he'd seen several cases go his way when they shouldn't have. But even then he had been mostly sure he would win.

This case was the opposite. He was almost certain they would lose. Something even Reagan and Luke's father had recently expressed concern about. But truly, if Luke lost this case, he'd be okay. The religious freedom incidents would keep coming, and he would keep getting better at defending them. Barring some landmark decision against religious freedom from the Supreme Court, Luke would have a job in this area.

But Wendell . . . Wendell could be out of work tomorrow. The situation was that serious.

Luke surveyed the courtroom. Like most it was plain, with yellowy wood-paneled walls and two rows of chairs, six to a row, for the times when a jury was needed. The spectator section held another forty seats or so, and the judge's desk sat at the center, on a platform high enough to preside over the room.

Wendell stepped into the space and approached Luke. A smile filled the man's face. "It starts today. We're going to win this thing." He looked around. "Where do I sit?"

"With me." Luke really liked the guy.

Already he'd been to the man's house and to his school. Wendell's faith and his love for his family and his students were as genuine as sunshine. He was a good guy, and it was an honor to represent him. No matter how the case turned out.

"We'll share this table." Luke took the inside seat and Wendell sat in the outer one. Luke pointed to the table on the other side of the courtroom. "That's where Andy Nelson and his attorney will sit."

Wendell seemed to survey the situation. He nodded to the judge's chair. "That's for the judge?"

"Yes."

"So the decision will come from there?" Wendell seemed to study the empty place. "Is that right?"

"I hope not." Luke chuckled. The hearing was slated for ten that morning. "The goal today is to convince the judge that we need a trial. That there's enough information on our behalf to at least let a jury decide."

Wendell nodded. "That's right." He narrowed his eyes. "The other option is the judge decides and we win or lose today?"

Luke hesitated. "Yes." If the judge decided without a jury, the case would most definitely go against them. He had been over that with Wendell. "That's right."

"Well, then, good thing I brought this." Wendell set his briefcase on the table and pulled out the three presentation folders. "I made you copies of everything I have." He handed the three folders to Luke. "Here you go."

There was no kind way to explain that Wendell's information couldn't possibly win this case. Luke set the folders to the side of the table and smiled. "Thanks, Wendell. If cases were won or lost based on enthusiasm, we'd have a slam-dunk win."

Next into the courtroom that morning were Jordy Quinn and Cami Nelson. Luke had met them at Hamilton High last week. The two were both in the Raise the Bar club, and if chemistry was any indication, the pair had a thing for each other.

Jordy walked to the edge of the spectator section and motioned for Luke to come closer. "Mr. Baxter, thank you for letting us be here today. All of our teachers signed off, so we could miss school."

"You're always welcome. It's an open courtroom." Luke admired the young man. Jordy was polite and well-spoken. It was obvious the boy had a strong faith, and the respect he showed his father was unusual for a high school senior.

Jordy looked at his father and then back

at Luke. "I'm nervous for my dad, sir. I'll do . . . whatever you need to help him out. I can testify or talk to the judge privately. Whatever would help."

Luke stifled a smile. The young man could make a fine attorney one day. "I'll keep that in mind. Thank you for the offer."

As it neared ten o'clock, Andy Nelson and his attorney entered and took their seats. Andy looked angry and shut off. He didn't make eye contact with Luke or Wendell, not even with his daughter — at least as far as Luke could tell. The two men whispered for a few minutes, and Andy nodded twice.

The bailiff stood at attention. "All rise . . ."

As soon as those in the courtroom were on their feet, the bailiff continued. "The Honorable Judge Catherine Wells."

From a door behind her grand chair, the judge entered the room. She took her seat and motioned to the small crowd. "You may be seated." She looked at her desk. "First on the docket is *Nelson versus Quinn.*" The judge was in her late fifties. Luke had represented religious freedom cases in her courtroom three times before.

All cases Luke had won.

But that didn't mean the woman was favorable to Christian beliefs or Luke Baxter. She always seemed put out about Luke's defense. Like it was a waste of her time to even talk about the rights of people to practice religion in a public space.

The right to worship in private churches and homes was one thing. A public display of faith was another. In schools most of all.

Okay, Lord . . . we're going to need You here. Please give me the words. When Wendell and Luke met together at the principal's house, the two of them had prayed about today's hearing. Luke wasn't sure if Wendell understood the gravity of today's proceeding.

But God did.

Since Andy Nelson was the plaintiff bringing the case, his attorney was permitted to go first. "The matter here is very simple, Your Honor." Andy was represented by Eli Landsford, one of the most experienced antireligion lawyers in the business, a manipulative, fast-talking man from Washington, D.C. Landsford flew around the country taking cases that were easy antireligion wins.

As soon as Luke had learned that Landsford was taking Andy's case, his hopes sank. This was one more reason to believe the obvious. The case ahead of him was a no-win situation.

Landsford was known for doing anything

to establish precedent and a general sense that indeed, a person might end up in jail if he or she so much as talked about God in public spaces. Something untrue, but that didn't matter. Perception was more than half the battle in the fight for religious freedom.

Landsford had said in interviews that if people thought they weren't allowed to talk about God, most of them would give up their rights without a fight. Wendell Quinn was not one of those. Like Luke, Landsford worked pro bono. Public support for this type of trial went both ways.

Luke felt his determination double.

"Explain the plaintiff's position." The judge sounded bored, as if she longed for something more interesting than a religious freedom case.

Eli Landsford was on his feet. The man's shoes cost more than Luke's car payment, if he had to guess. "As I said, Your Honor, we have a very cut-and-dried case here. The defendant, Hamilton High Principal Wendell Quinn, has been leading a voluntary student Bible study after school for the past year." He adjusted the cuff links on his shirtsleeves and smiled at Judge Wells. "As you know, precedent clearly dictates that Principal Quinn's actions are inappropriate and illegal. A complete violation of church and state."

With everything in him, Luke wanted to object. But this wasn't the time. Landsford had the right to establish his case before the judge. Also, he'd stolen Luke's assertion that the club was voluntary. Rightfully so. In recent years and cases, even voluntary participation in a Bible study or prayer group had been ruled unconstitutional.

Even sitting in a school-owned desk to discuss things of God constituted a violation of church and state according to some previous cases.

Landsford was wrapping up his presentation. "My client and I would like to ask Your Honor to rule in favor of the plaintiff, thereby ordering the defendant to cease and desist all further Bible study or prayer group meetings at Hamilton High. In addition, we would like it established that if Mr. Quinn does not comply with cease and desist orders, he will face court sanctions and possible jail time."

There it was. Luke couldn't believe it. He had heard a rumor that Landsford was threatening to invoke imprisonment for people who dared bring up God in a public space. It was another case of perception versus reality. Say it often enough and such a thing could become truth.

The possibility made Luke feel sick. He glanced at Wendell. The man looked more nervous than he had at the beginning of the hour. "It's okay. The guy's just posturing."

Wendell kept his eyes on Landsford. "Okay. I don't plan on going to jail."

Judge Wells looked at Luke. "The defendant will respond to the complaint."

Luke noticed that Andy Nelson didn't look up. He kept his gaze squarely on the table he shared with Landsford. Not sure if it made any difference, but Luke also thought the plaintiff looked sick to his stomach.

Luke was on his feet. He ignored the three folders Wendell had given him as he approached the bench. This was no time to take a chance. "Your Honor, this is a very high-profile case, as I'm sure you know."

"Go on, Mr. Baxter." She raised her brow, as if to say Luke had better not waste her time. "How would the defendant like to respond?"

"Not guilty, Your Honor." Luke took a quick breath. "I have students willing to testify in this case. Students who deeply wish to continue meeting on a voluntary basis to discuss matters pertaining to the Christian faith." He folded his arms and stood facing Judge Wells.

"Which is a violation of church and state." Judge Wells looked stern. If there had been any doubt that she was on Andy Nelson's side, there was none now.

"That is not our opinion." Luke needed to get to the point. "I can promise you this, Your Honor. If you rule in favor of the plaintiff today, without a jury trial, we will appeal." He let that sink in for a moment. "We will appeal all the way to the Supreme Court."

Of course, when Judge Antonin Scalia died, appealing all the way to the Supreme Court wasn't as hopeful as it once had been. Yes, the new administration had filled his seat with a conservative judge. Regardless, Luke's best chance was right here in this courtroom with a jury trial. Regular citizens.

Judge Wells looked down at her docket and then back at Luke. Her eyes grew beady and dark. Clearly, she didn't appreciate being challenged this way. "Do not threaten the court, Mr. Baxter." She raised her brow and stared at Luke. "Is that understood?"

"Yes, Your Honor." Luke kept a straight face. The admonition angered him, but he couldn't let that show. He had no choice here. He had to say and do whatever was legally allowable to win this case for Wendell Quinn.

For the United States and the future of the Constitution.

Finally, with an exaggerated breath, Judge Wells looked from Luke to Landsford and back again. "The court will hold this matter over for trial."

Good thing. Luke maintained his professional composure. Wendell deserved a jury trial. His entire educational career was at stake, not to mention the hearts of the student body at Hamilton High.

Across the aisle, Landsford huffed and slammed a document on the table. He shook his head, making a show of the fact that in his hardly humble opinion a jury trial was absolutely not necessary.

Judge Wells noticed Landsford, but she didn't call him out. Instead she checked her docket again. "Jury selection will take place next Wednesday morning at nine. I'd like to start the trial the following Wednesday. This case needs to be wrapped up well before Thanksgiving."

Luke responded. "Yes, Your Honor. Thank you. Those dates work for my client."

The plaintiff had the right to ask for more time to prepare. But this was where Landsford's arrogance worked against him. He

258

clearly saw this case as an easy win. Nothing worth preparing for. Precedent would be enough. "Yes, thank you, Your Honor." Landsford gave Luke a sarcastic sneer. "Those dates work for my client, as well."

Judge Wells banged her gavel on the bench. "Five-minute recess until the next hearing." She stood and disappeared through the door behind the bench.

Luke turned to Wendell and shook his hand. "Well, we got past the first hurdle."

"We got a jury trial." Wendell grinned. "That means the students can testify."

"Whoa." Luke chuckled. "Probably not. We can only respond to what's brought against us. We have a lot of work ahead."

Wendell rolled up his sleeves. "I'm ready."

Jordy and Cami came to the railing that separated the spectators from the courtroom participants. They congratulated Wendell and Luke. Jordy looked at Luke. "We needed a jury trial if we're going to win, right?"

"Well . . . yes. A jury trial means the case will be decided by someone other than the judge." Luke was thrilled with the win today. A quick smile broke through his professional demeanor. "Which is a whole lot better for your dad."

From the corner of his eye, Luke saw

something that dimmed his enthusiasm. While they were talking, Cami's father and the man's attorney slipped out the back door, caught up in what looked like a one-sided conversation. Landsford babbling about the easy win, no doubt.

But as he left the courtroom, Andy Nelson never even spoke to his daughter.

It wasn't until Luke was home that night, sitting at the dinner table with his family, that it occurred to him just how brave Wendell was. Tommy had been asking him about the case. "You got a jury trial, so that's great, right?"

"It is." Luke loved his oldest son's interest in law. He had a feeling when the time came, Tommy would be a very good attorney indeed. "We have a long road ahead, though."

"Tell me about this principal. Wendell Quinn." Reagan set her fork down and folded her napkin on top of her plate. "What's his motivation for all this?"

Luke thought about his clients. Most were just regular people who believed they were owed the chance to practice their religion. Since that was what the Constitution guaranteed. But some were more stubborn than faithful. They just wanted to make a name for themselves or take on the establishment.

"Wendell is one of the good guys." Luke smiled, thinking of the conversations he'd had with the man. "He stands to lose everything in all this. His job, his reputation. Even the woman he loves. She broke things off as soon as he started the club."

"Wow . . . I didn't know that." Reagan reached for Luke's hand. "That's awful."

Tommy leaned in, listening. "That's what I love about all this, Dad. The passions people have for what's right."

Luke looked at his son. "That's what I love about it, too."

Malin and Johnny excused themselves from the table to finish catching frogs in the backyard. Something Luke had grown up doing. "I'll be out there in a few minutes," he promised them.

"No one catches frogs like you, Daddy." Johnny grinned. He had the same blond hair Luke had when he was a boy. The family resemblance was a coincidence, since Johnny was adopted. But that didn't matter. All three of their kids were theirs. Period.

Luke turned back to Reagan and Tommy. "I guess I'm just now seeing how brave Wendell Quinn really is. I mean, this isn't just a case to him. This is his life at stake. The career he's spent all his years building. The relationships that matter most to him."

"What about his son? He's a football player, right?" Tommy squinted. "He's one of the best players in the state. Jordy Quinn."

"That's him." Luke thought of the similarities. "He's like you, Tommy. He backs his father, no matter what. He'd take the witness stand, fight the opposing attorney. Whatever he has to do."

"What a beautiful thing." Reagan stood and picked the plates up from the table. "I hope you can win."

"Dad will make it happen." Tommy grinned and stood to help his mother. Luke did the same. As they walked into the kitchen, Tommy fist-bumped Luke. "You always win these cases!"

You always win. It was a statement that stayed with Luke while they cleaned up the kitchen and as he hunted frogs with Malin and Johnny. It stayed with him as the kids went to bed and he and Reagan turned in for the night.

What if he didn't win this time?

You can do this, Lord. But precedent is completely against us. You know that. I don't want to let them down, but . . .

He was brushing his teeth when he felt the Lord respond.

One, My son. One.

The words seemed to appear on the surface of Luke's soul. Strong and clear. *One.* He finished brushing his teeth and stepped out onto the back deck, just off the master bedroom. Luke walked to the railing and stared into the night sky. "One, Lord?"

And then like the cool night breeze it hit him. *One.* Luke had told Wendell they'd need a host of miracles in order to win this case. Well, now they had one. Which was why Luke needed to trust in God, not just now, but through the entire upcoming trial. God was capable of one miracle. Which meant He was certainly capable of more.

As many as it took to vindicate a brave man like Wendell Quinn.

Andy Nelson was getting used to the feel of an empty house, but that didn't mean he liked it. Andy's twin girls, Ensley and Ellie, were staying with Andy's sister a few miles away. He had explained that Cami was gone, and with work and the trial, he wouldn't be able to care for the girls. They needed a more stable environment until things settled down. His sister had been happy to help.

On Twitter, Andy followed a host of news services. He sat on the sofa in the living room and pored through the feed. One after another, the story was still trending. *Sensational Religious Freedom Case Set for Trial . . . Angry Parent to See His Day in Court . . . Trial Set for Parent Offended by School Bible Study.*

Andy turned off his phone. Yes, the case was sensational. He had known it would be the day he called the newspaper. His attorney had told him they'd win the case. There was no doubt in the man's mind.

Good thing, Andy thought. He was just glad the guy was working for free. He certainly had no money to pay a lawyer. Andy stood and wandered to the front window. He should feel overjoyed about all of it. The slam-dunk case, the free lawyer.

A trial meant more eyes on the case. More people who would be served notice. Bible study and prayer were not allowed in public places — especially not schools. Period. The more people who knew, the more they would stay away from such things in the future.

All of which should make Andy thrilled. Ecstatic. The faith his ex-wife had tried to shove down their throats would eventually be extinct if this sort of case continued to gain public attention. Eventually people would be too afraid to even talk about Christianity.

Andy looked over his shoulder toward the kitchen. He needed another shot. Beer was a thing of the past. Too much time drinking for the same effect. Jack Daniel's was a whole lot quicker. He'd already had three shots since he got home from court.

His boss seemed to understand about the work Andy would need to miss. "No educator should be reading the Bible with his students," his boss had said. "Nothing could be more against our legal system."

The man had given Andy literally as much time off as it took to see the case through. Today Andy got home hours earlier than he would have if he'd been working at the airport. He took a nap, tried to eat a can of tuna and then found the bottle of Jack.

Weirdest thing was how Andy was feeling. He should be beyond happy. The best attorney in the nation represented him. Landsford was going to win and Andy was going to be vindicated, and together they were going to earn the respect of everyone from Andy's boss to high-profile politicians. Every media outlet would love Andy Nelson.

But Andy didn't feel a bit of that thrill.

He felt old and tired and sad.

The bottle stood like a beacon on the kitchen counter. Not a beacon of hope, exactly. More a symbol of darkness. The alcohol didn't make him feel better. It just made him not feel at all. He moved from the window to the kitchen counter. Another drink. That's what he needed. He poured the liquid and held it to his lips. A quick tilt of his head and another shot down.

Cami.

That's what was bothering him. Andy knew it, of course. Deep down he had known it every day since she left. He walked to the back bedroom, her bedroom — at least until the day he blew up at her.

He had been crazy that day. Crazy with anger and betrayal and frustration. He wanted her to know just how upset he was over the Bible study club. Andy sat on the edge of her bed and felt the beginning of tears.

He'd accomplished that, for sure. Cami was so aware of the way Andy felt, she couldn't get out of the house fast enough. He took a slow breath and stared at the photos on the corkboard that hung over Cami's bed. Cami and a group of friends at the prom last year. Cami and her sisters at the park.

Cami and Audrey, her unfaithful mother. Andy hated that picture. So what if the woman was Cami's mother. Audrey didn't deserve to have her photo on Cami's wall.

"I wasn't going to hurt you, Cami girl." His voice was soft. Like his heart was speaking all on its own. "My fist was always going for the wall. Not for you."

He lay down, his head on her pillow, and closed his eyes. *I'm sorry, Cami. I never meant to scare you. I'm so sorry.* The tears came harder, forcing their way out from between his eyelids. What sort of wretched man was he? And how come Cami would believe in a God that destroyed families?

Andy blinked his eyes open and rubbed his fists over his eyelids. Was that what had happened? God had destroyed his family? Andy sniffed and sat up again.

His wife had gotten the wild idea one day that she would start taking the family to church. When Andy refused, she took Cami and Ensley and Ellie. That went on for almost a year before Andy found out about the affair.

Even now the situation sickened Andy. An affair with a man from church? Audrey said the man left the congregation after that. He walked away from church and his family and his reputation. Ran off with Andy's wife.

Cami and her sisters had no mother because of what God had done. At least that's the way it seemed.

If God was real, then He wouldn't have wanted Andy's wife to have an affair. And He wouldn't have wanted a Christian man to leave his family and his church for another woman. Of course not. In fact, a God like that would probably be on Andy's side. Feeling sorry for Andy because of what had happened.

He sat up and reached out, touched another photo on the corkboard. Cami when she was just two years old. Bright smile, lopsided braids. A mouthful of baby teeth. Suddenly something occurred to Andy. After what he'd done to Cami a few weeks ago, she had every right to call the police on him.

She could've filed charges against him. Charges of child abuse or domestic violence. That would put a twist in the case everyone wanted to talk about. Suddenly Cami would be the victim and he'd be the tyrant. Refusing to let her read the Bible. Refusing to let her pray. Threatening her with violence for wanting a life different than his.

A chill started at his neck and ran down his back and arms. Why hadn't Cami said anything to the police? What in the world reason would there be for her to not say something? The club she loved so much was going to be shut down, and here she had information about her father that could throw the entire case into disarray.

Principal Quinn and the school district would win if people knew what Andy had done, how in his anger he'd almost hit Cami. Andy lay back on Cami's pillow again. He was so sorry. And again he was struck by a realization. There was only one reason Cami would spare him that sort of humiliation and punishment.

Cami didn't hate him. She truly believed in God. Faith in Him led Cami to take the higher road. The truth grew inside Andy. His daughter wasn't out to get him. She didn't want to see him suffer. He covered his face with his hand. Cami only wanted to learn how to live right. Learn a little more about God.

A sick feeling grabbed at Andy's stomach. What if Cami was right? What if there really was a God? If that were the case it wouldn't matter what happened with the trial. Andy would lose and he would lose big. Here and in the next world.

For all eternity.

Andy climbed out of bed and walked to the hallway mirror, the one Audrey had hung when the two of them were still married. Andy stared at himself. Before Audrey left, he had been the most clean-cut mechanic at the airport. A guy who cared about shaving and keeping his hair short and neat.

Now his stringy hair hung down to his collar and his beard looked scrappier all the time. On top of that, his arm was still throbbing. The spot on his bicep where he'd gotten a new tattoo this past Saturday.

Andy turned so he could see his arm better. He had asked the tattoo artist to use an angry font. Whatever that meant. Something full of rage. Andy surveyed the guy's work and couldn't help but approve. The tattoo was dark, solid, one-inch block letters, and the message was as bold as the text. A message that — if there was a God — would keep Andy Nelson out of heaven for sure. The message held two words, words that defined him now.

NO GOD.

15

Reagan was folding laundry on the couch when she heard Luke at the front door. It was just after ten o'clock. With everything in her she wanted to break down, tell him the late nights he was keeping were wrong.

But every time she prayed about his hours at the office, she felt the same response from God.

Love him. Just keep loving him.

Luke walked in and she turned to him. Their eyes met, and he set his briefcase down. "I'm sorry."

Love . . . just love. "It's okay." Reagan felt the tenderness in her smile. "You've got a lot of responsibility."

"I've got a family." He came to her and put his hands on her shoulders. "It's not right, what I've been doing." His voice was kind, grateful. "Staying late at the office. It's like it was last year all over again."

She didn't blink, didn't look away. "People

are counting on you."

"That's no excuse." He put his hands on either side of her face and kissed her. Longer than usual. With the passion they hadn't shared in too long. "I'm sorry, Reagan. I'll work on it. I promise."

Tears stung her eyes. God was so faithful. She had listened to Him, and now look. "Thank you."

"I love you." He kissed her again, his eyes locked on hers. "More than you'll ever know."

"I love you, too." Reagan had not expected this. A tear spilled onto her cheek and he caught it gently with his thumb. "Thank you."

"Let me finish the laundry." He stepped toward the pile of clothes. "You take a break. You deserve it." He kissed her once more. "And thank you, beautiful. For supporting me . . . even when I get it wrong."

Reagan wasn't sure what to say, what to do. A slight laugh slipped from her lips and she went to the kitchen. A cup of tea, maybe. Yes, that was it. Chamomile tea. While she made it she kept her eyes on Luke in the next room.

Folding clothes.

Reagan's heart soared. God had given her direction and she had taken it. And now, not only had Luke figured out that his late hours were a problem. But she was the heroine. The one who had supported Luke rather than nagging him. Everything was going to be okay now. She could feel it.

And bonus: Luke's surprise birthday party was going to be the best time ever.

The Raise the Bar club didn't meet as usual that Tuesday because it was Halloween. Instead Principal Quinn had opened the auditorium for not only the club but any student who wanted to join them. A Harvest Party, he called it. Cami was glad she'd stayed, glad that several teachers were there also. They hung around the front of the room, while the students talked in small groups and shared pizza and snacks — compliments, this time, of Hobby Lobby.

That was one thing Cami was thankful for. Though most of the world seemed to hate Principal Quinn, Christians everywhere had come out in support of Raise the Bar. Businesses and parent volunteers took turns providing food for the club whenever it met. Even in her own life, she felt supported. She was still living with her teacher's family. The woman had taken Cami by her house when her dad wasn't home so she could get what she needed. God had taken care of Cami and the Raise the Bar club. And He would do that again.

Even today.

She saw Jordy across the room. Her feelings for him had only grown over the past few days. She kept thinking about that night at his house. The way she felt in his arms. A feeling she would remember always.

Especially because it would probably never happen again. It was one thing for Principal Quinn to forgive Cami for what her father had done to him. But the man would never let Jordy date the enemy's daughter.

No, she and Jordy had no future. But that didn't stop her from thinking the world of him. She watched Jordy now. The way he talked to one of the kids and patted another one on the back. The way he listened. Jordy wasn't just strong and handsome. He was kind. Even now when his dad was under attack. Cami watched Jordy spot her and head over.

"Hey." Jordy led her to a quieter spot, away from the table of maple doughnuts and Oreo cookies. "I was looking for you." He seemed concerned. "Have you seen Dwayne?"

"Not since yesterday." Cami looked

around the room. "He was supposed to be here."

Frustration darkened Jordy's eyes. "A bunch of the guys on the team are planning something tonight. They say it's just a hang, but . . . I think it'll be a fight. You know, like every Halloween night."

A gang fight. Cami remembered. Two years ago a Hamilton High football player was killed. The murder was a terrible blow to their student body and the school.

"Oh, no." Cami felt a new kind of fear move through her veins. Dwayne Brown was a junior. One of the kids she'd featured in her Raise the Bar report. Cami brought her hand to her face and shook her head. "He can't go."

"I tried to stop him." Jordy's expression was a mix of anger and helpless frustration.

Cami took a few steps toward the exit and then turned around. "Is it too late? Can we go find him?"

"He left. Usually the guys eat somewhere first. Make a plan." Jordy sighed. "I just keep praying."

"What if something bad happens?" Cami felt sick. "Dwayne or . . . or any of them." She leaned against the wall. "Gangs are so stupid." She thought of something else. "Plus . . . if someone gets hurt it will ruin everything."

Jordy lowered his brow, as if he didn't understand what she meant. "Everything?"

Cami searched his eyes. "We're trying to convince people that our club matters. It's making a difference. Higher grades, less criminal activity. All the rest. The club's changing lives. That's the whole point." She crossed her arms. "If something happens tonight . . . no one will believe the Bible even matters. Everyone will know we're not perfect."

"What?" At first Jordy sounded annoyed. But then his expression softened. "No, Cami. That's not it. Only Jesus is perfect." He moved closer to her and put his hand on her arm for a few seconds. "You know that, right?"

No, she didn't know that. Cami looked at the floor of the auditorium. She tried to figure out what to say. Every week since the club had started meeting Cami had been there. Principal Quinn often talked about coming to Jesus broken, and letting Jesus do the fixing.

She looked into Jordy's brown eyes. "Your dad says Jesus can fix us." She tried to find the right words. Wasn't that how the faith thing was supposed to work? "Okay, so then after we become His people . . . once Jesus fixes us . . . then we should be different. Perfect. Because He's perfect. Because of God's power in us."

Jordy shook his head. "Cami, only God is perfect. Sure, the more time we spend with Him, the more we start acting like Him." His tone was gentle. "Jesus changes lives. But we'll never be perfect."

Chris Tomlin's "Good Good Father" played from the speakers. Cami looked around the room. Conversations seemed happy. These were kids who used to smoke pot and get so drunk they couldn't make it to school Monday morning. They were in gangs and they ditched school and slept with someone new every weekend.

Now they were different. They were changed. It felt pretty perfect to Cami.

She looked back at Jordy. "It still matters. What happens tonight."

"It does." His answer came quick. "Because kids' lives are on the line. Not because it might make us look bad."

"Okay. I get that." Cami felt tears in her eyes. The scared feeling inside her was like a rock, sitting in her stomach and making her feel sick. "But all these people who hate your dad, all the people who hate us . . . they won't understand. If something happens. They'll just think the club didn't matter."

Jordy didn't look discouraged. "It's possible."

"I'm just . . . I want everything to be perfect." She looked at her worn-out tennis shoes and then back at him. "So my dad and . . . and everyone else will just leave us alone."

The look in Jordy's eyes changed. "There's no other girl like you." His voice was softer than before.

Cami's cheeks felt hot. Once, a long time ago, before Cami's mother had left them, their family was watching a movie. A love story. The girl was named Katie — at least that's what she remembered. The guy's name seemed really different. Hubbell. That was it. Cami never forgot it.

Especially one of the early scenes. Katie crossed the street to sit with Hubbell and in an instant things between the two of them were different. Cami could see it in their eyes. Like something had changed in the way they saw each other.

Jordy was looking at her that way now. The way Cami always dreamed he might look at her. She was doing the same thing. She could feel it in her eyes. But just as quickly she stepped away. So there'd be

278

more space between them.

She couldn't do this, couldn't let herself fall for him.

Not when the two of them didn't have a chance.

Across the room she spotted the pizza. *Good. A distraction.* "Let's get food." She glanced toward the table stacked with Domino's boxes. Kids swarmed around it.

"I'm not really —"

"Wait." Cami started walking, she looked back over her shoulder at him. "I'll get you a piece."

Her steps were too fast and she didn't wait for Jordy to tell her what kind of pizza he might want. She couldn't wait. If she stood there another minute with him looking at her that way she'd start falling for him again. Dreaming about kissing him. Or about a time when their parents wouldn't think the worst possible thing was for Jordy and Cami to date. But that definitely wasn't going to happen.

Not now. Not ever.

Dwayne Brown gripped the steering wheel of his brother's car.

Okay, so he didn't ask to borrow it tonight. Who cared? His brother had taken a ride with friends and gone to Ohio. Some debate club meeting. Dwayne rolled his eyes. His brother was always trying to show him up. Prove he was the better of the two boys.

He didn't have to try hard.

Dwayne was a mess-up. He'd always been a mess-up.

This year was the worst — everywhere except the football field. Out there he was the best linebacker in the city. Gonna get a scholarship. That would show his momma and brother what for.

That's why he'd started going to the Bible meetings. Bunch of his friends had been going since last year, and truth was, the dudes were really changed. Sam didn't drink anymore. Like, not a drop. Allen was getting passing grades in all his classes.

Dwayne had asked Allen about it at the beginning of the school year when they were sitting at the cafeteria. "A Bible group is helping you in school?" Dwayne had laughed. Mostly because he was uncomfortable. "How's that even possible? Like, what do you do? Sit around asking Jesus to help you with math?" Another laugh. "Sounds like sissy stuff, man."

"Shut up!" Allen stood up and stared at him, real angry.

Allen's eyes got all squinty, and for half a second Dwayne thought the guy was going

280

to hit him. Allen was a lot taller. And bigger. An all-county lineman, so he could've, no problem. Would've knocked Dwayne out, first punch. But then Allen's face relaxed.

A lot.

Allen sat back down and took a bite of his burger. When he looked at Dwayne again, Allen had eyes like a kid. Like he didn't have a worry in the world. And right there he explained about faith and the Bible and math. "I'm a child of God." He raised his eyebrows. "You are, too."

Dwayne wanted to laugh. He was hardly a child of God. Allen mustn't know him that well. But Dwayne kept quiet.

"The Bible isn't just another textbook. It's a letter from Jesus to us. When I read it, it's like . . ." Allen smiled, and let out a quiet breath. "It's like God wrote it straight to me."

An uncomfortable feeling stirred in Dwayne's stomach. "How's that help you with math?"

"The words in the Bible . . . they're not just words. They're alive." Allen didn't look embarrassed. He seemed to really believe this stuff. Allen paused for a minute. "Like, there's this Scripture that says, 'I can do all this through Him who gives me strength.' "

Allen patted the backpack beside him.

"Even math. I remind myself of that every time I sit in Mrs. Barron's classroom. Next thing you know, I'm remembering the formulas and stuff." Allen took another bite. When he was finished with it he looked hard at Dwayne. "You only get one life, man. At least give it a try."

The memory stopped there. Dwayne turned left on Briar Street. His stomach felt tight and he could almost hear a voice in his head.

Turn back. Don't go this way, My son. Go home!

So strange, the voice. He had heard it before. Especially the third time he went to the Bible group. That day he sat with Jordy. Most of the time, Dwayne and Jordy didn't talk. Jordy was one of the good kids. Good grades. Good dad. Good looks. It was all a little too much.

But that day when Dwayne walked into the auditorium, Jordy looked right at him and smiled. Like they were the same kinda dudes. "Over here," Jordy called out.

Dwayne looked behind him, just in case Jordy was talking to someone else. But he wasn't. So Dwayne took the seat next to Jordy. "Can I tell you something?" Jordy looked at him. Right in his eyes.

"Sure." Dwayne squirmed a little. *Where's*

this going? he thought.

Jordy smiled. "I've been praying since last year that you'd come to this." He smiled and gave Dwayne a light smack on the back. "You're not a thug. I heard some of the guys on the team call you that." He paused. "It's not true." Jordy grew quiet. He clenched his jaw. "You want the truth? You belong to God. It's time you figured that out."

He wasn't a thug. Dwayne had liked that. And when Principal Quinn spoke that day, he talked about having a hero. "Everyone has a story. And every story needs a hero."

A hero? Dwayne remembered being confused by that. Like a superhero? What was the man talking about? He had focused, really tried to understand.

"We're all going to die. Every one of us." Principal Quinn had a booming voice. Not angry, the way Dwayne's mama got when he didn't come home till after midnight. Just powerful. Kind of like a coach. The man explained himself. "We only get so many pages, and the ending of the story will never go well unless you ask Jesus to be a part of it. He's the only One who can rescue any of us."

Dwayne let that thought stay with him. Only Jesus could rescue him. Sounded pretty good. Where Dwayne lived people got in trouble all the time. A definite rescue would be a good thing to have.

That's when Jordy leaned closer. "You listening?"

"Yeah." He felt awkward. Like when he asked Brianne Sanchez to prom last year. "I never thought of this stuff before."

"Maybe it's time." Jordy must've known how Dwayne was feeling.

Dwayne whispered, "How do you do it? How do you get Jesus?"

"I'll tell you after club." No hesitation from Jordy. Probably because he'd known about Jesus all his life.

Dwayne nodded. "Sure, man. Okay."

Principal Quinn wrapped things up then. "With Jesus, you never die. You just move your story from here to heaven, where there will be no more tears, no more dying. Where the story never ends." He smiled real big. "And when you learn to listen to Jesus, every page of your story is a whole lot better than it would've been without Him. He's the Hero."

Which explained Allen and the math.

After the meeting, Jordy talked to Dwayne and asked him if he wanted Jesus to be with him all the time. Inside his heart. If he wanted to turn away from all the wrong things he'd ever done.

Dwayne had felt unsure about that last part. "I don't think . . . I mean, I'm sorry . . . but I can't be perfect."

"You don't have to be." Jordy looked right at him.

Jordy opened his Bible and showed Dwayne some more verses.

When they were done reading, Jordy told Dwayne how to pray. For Jesus to come into his heart and for God to forgive Dwayne for all the things he'd done wrong. The drinking and lying. The cheating and the way he'd treated girls. And for the gang stuff, too.

None of that was what God wanted from His people. Dwayne understood now. He still had a lot to learn, of course. Even after the Saturday field trip when everyone went to John Oliver's house. John was a wide receiver for Hamilton High, and his family owned four gas stations. His pool was heated and that day five kids got baptized.

Dwayne was one of them.

He blinked a few times and turned right on Martin Luther King Boulevard. So why was he doing this? Why fight tonight? Just because a bunch of the guys on the team were going?

It was Billy Benson who'd convinced Dwayne. Billy and Dwayne used to be in the same gang. At least before Dwayne started believing in Jesus. Ever since Dwayne started going to the Bible club, Billy would laugh at him. Just shake his head and laugh. Yesterday after practice the kid found Dwayne at his locker. "You going to club today? That prayer stuff's made you soft." Billy gave Dwayne a shove in the shoulder. "You lost your edge, man."

Dwayne felt anger light up inside him. "Leave me alone, Benson." He clenched his fist. "I ain't soft."

"If you're still tough . . ." The kid snickered. "Prove it. Halloween's tomorrow."

Dwayne told himself he wouldn't do it. He didn't need to prove anything to Billy Benson. But at practice today, Billy had laughed at him again.

The Bible club was having a Halloween party. Dwayne tightened his grip on the steering wheel. A Halloween party? He narrowed his eyes. Halloween parties weren't for high school kids. They were for babies. If Billy thought he was soft before, he'd never let Dwayne live it down if he hung out at a Halloween party.

Up ahead was the alley where they were meeting this year. The two gangs always picked an alley. So they could hide in doorways and keep away from the cops.

Dwayne slowed his car. Gotta hide anything that might identify him. He leaned down and tucked his wallet beneath his seat. Then he slid his phone into his jeans pocket. Rules were simple on Halloween.

Each man for himself. No guns.

Usually his gang won. More guys, more of them on the football team. Fists would fly and threats would be made, but after ten minutes or so the other guys would back off. At least that's how it went last year.

Suddenly Dwayne remembered the year before last. When he was a freshman. Someone broke the rule and in the middle of the fight, at the worst of it, a gun went off.

And Jimmy Salvo lay in the alley bleeding. He died before he knew what hit him.

Dwayne parked his car and the voice came again. Like someone was sitting in the seat next to him talking to him.

Run! Don't do this! I have plans for you, My son.

What in the world? It was like the Bible verse from the other day had come to life here in his car. What was it again? Jeremiah something. All about God having good plans for him. Dwayne nodded to himself. He believed that. One day when he was grown up and out of Hamilton, one day when he moved far away from the gangs and the streets, good things were going to happen.

He believed God on that.

But for now . . . for now he had to take care of business. And if a few of his blows landed on Billy Benson, so be it. Anything could happen in a Halloween fight.

Dwayne waited till ten o'clock sharp. Then he slipped out of his brother's car. It was pitch-dark outside, cloudy. No moon or stars overhead. He raised the hood on his sweatshirt and shoved his hands deep in his pockets. All down the street he watched gang members do the same thing.

Soon as the police found out, they'd break things up. The fight wouldn't last long. He moved fast, his body smooth and athletic. A couple colleges were looking at him now. After today, after he proved he wasn't soft, Dwayne would get serious. The Bible club was good for him. Jesus was, too.

He met up with eight of his guys and together they turned the corner. That's when Dwayne saw them. Their rivals were coming, filling the alley. Walking closer. "This is it!" one of them shouted. "Halloween fight!"

"You oughta run while you can!" one of Dwayne's boys yelled back.

Dwayne's heart sped up. His blood rushed

through his body. No one was going to call him soft. He pushed his sweatshirt sleeves up, but before he could take a swing, before he could land his fist against the face of the guy rushing at him, there was a popping sound.

Just a single pop.

At first Dwayne wasn't sure what it was or where the sound came from, but then — in a single second — he felt it. Sharp pain in his chest and something hot. He looked down and saw the blood just as his knees buckled.

What had happened? Someone had shot at him and the fight hadn't even —

"No guns!" The voice was Billy Benson's. Dwayne could tell. "The rule is no guns, man! Someone call 9-1-1!"

Dwayne was on the ground now, sprawled out. He couldn't move his arms or his legs, but he could feel. The aching pain in his chest, the way his sweatshirt was wetter now. Soaking wet.

"Dwayne, buddy . . . talk to me." In all their high school days together, all their nights cruising with the gang, Dwayne had never dreamed he'd see this.

Billy Benson was scared.

His eyes were wide and his face was white as paper. He was saying something, screaming at the guys to call . . . call someone. Dwayne wasn't sure. Couldn't hear the noise anymore. Billy's voice, the other guys. People running out of the alley.

He couldn't hear any of it.

And suddenly a woman police officer knelt on his other side. "Dwayne, can you hear me?"

"Yes." Everything else was dim now. No sound at all. But he could hear the woman beside him. She didn't look like a normal person. Her eyes were too bright. Dwayne looked at her badge.

ASPYN.

Dwayne's eyes were heavy. The effort it took to play fourth-quarter football was nothing to what it took to keep them open now. He looked at the woman. "I'm . . . shot."

"You're going to be okay, Dwayne." She squeezed his hand. "God is with you."

God. Dwayne felt regret like a fire through his body. "I'm sorry, God. I'm so sorry. I didn't listen." The policewoman took his hand. Peace washed over him, peace like he'd never known before. Dwayne took a final look at Aspyn, and then he closed his eyes. "My friends . . . are wrong . . . about you police."

"It's okay, Dwayne." Aspyn's voice was

soothing in a way Dwayne had never heard before. She stayed there, very near his face. "Relax, child. God has you."

"You . . . you only . . . care. Right now." Dwayne's eyes were closed but he could see clearly now. Most police officers only wanted to help. The way God had tried to help him.

"God loves you, Dwayne." Aspyn was still holding his hand. With her other one, she touched her fingers to Dwayne's forehead. "You're going to be okay."

Dwayne wanted to say something. His body was letting go. He felt lighter than before. The pain fading. "God . . . God warned me . . . He told me to go home." The words in his head were slow now. He couldn't think right. And there, with the world fading around him, Dwayne remembered Principal Quinn's words. He could see the man. His smile and warm eyes. *With Jesus, you never die.*

But Dwayne was dying. He could feel the life leaving his body. He should've listened. Should've stayed at school. Dwayne's words were barely a whisper. "Is it true? With Jesus, you never die?" He had seconds left, no more.

"Yes, Dwayne." Aspyn's voice covered him in warmth and peace.

Dwayne tried to breathe, but he couldn't make his lungs work. What else was it? What had Principal Quinn said? Dwayne's mind was spinning now. Something about his story.

Yeah, that was it.

With Jesus as the Hero, your story just moves from here to heaven. No more tears, no more dying. Just like the Bible said.

Dwayne struggled to take another breath. Aspyn was right. Dwayne was going to be okay. God had not wanted things to end this way. Here in the alley.

He was just a high school junior.

No telling what his life might have been like here on earth. The plans God would've had for him. This wasn't even where he was supposed to be tonight. But as he drew his last breath, Dwayne smiled. Aspyn's words washed over him.

You're going to be okay, Dwayne. God is with you.

It was true because Jesus was the Hero of his story. And tonight, any second now, Jesus was going to rescue him and Dwayne would take his next breath in heaven. With Jesus. Light washed over him, and Dwayne let himself go toward it. God was calling him home now. Dwayne smiled. Home to heaven.

Where his story would never end.

16

It was just after two o'clock in the morning when Wendell Quinn got the call. At first he thought it might be James Black, calling to tell him he was fired. But that wasn't rational.

Not long after he'd threatened to fire Wendell, James Black had called again and promised Wendell could keep his job through the trial. The school district didn't want to draw attention to itself in the midst of the court proceedings. No, it wasn't James Black.

But as Wendell answered the phone, he couldn't make out what the man on the other end was saying. Something about a gang and wanting him to know before school in the morning. Only after a full minute did Wendell understand what had happened.

Dwayne Brown was dead.

The news knocked the wind from him.

Long after he hung up the phone, Wendell sat straight up in his bed. How could this happen? Dwayne was like one of his own kids. For two months he'd been attending Raise the Bar. He'd even been baptized. Wendell felt sick, his head spinning.

The young man had his whole life ahead of him.

Wendell leaned back against the headboard and stared out the window at the night sky. Dwayne was like a lot of Hamilton kids. Bad relationship with his family. No interest in the classroom. Dwayne had been a problem at the school since his freshman year.

Until this semester.

Tears filled Wendell's eyes and trickled down his cheeks. *Lord, I'm trying. I'd give up my own life for those kids.* He felt the heaviness of the situation to the center of his soul. Wasn't this the point of the Bible study meetings? To save kids like Dwayne Brown?

There was just one person he wanted to call, one who would understand the way his heart was breaking. Alicia Harris.

None of it made sense.

He grabbed his phone and was just about to hit her number when he realized it was the middle of the night. It would have to wait. Instead he opened his photo library.

There, in his album of favorites, was a picture of Alicia and him. A year ago summer. The two of them in a canoe paddling around Geist Reservoir near Admirals Bay. Someone hiking on the trail had stopped and taken their picture.

Alicia had come so far since her days of being paralyzed by anxiety. But she would be devastated when she heard about Dwayne. *Please, Father, help her through this. Keep her mind steadfast on You. Please.*

Wendell thought about Dwayne. In a few hours he'd have to tell the kids at Hamilton High what had happened. How Dwayne had died in a gang fight. Another senseless, tragic, heartbreaking loss.

"I'm gonna need Your help, Lord." Wendell looked out the window again. "I can't do this alone."

Not only that, but just before lunch he and Luke Baxter would attend the jury selection at Marion Circuit Court downtown. The place for more significant civil suits. And if the media attention had been any indication, the suit against him and Hamilton High qualified.

There was only one way to prepare for such a day. Wendell closed out the photo of Alicia and him and opened his Bible app. He turned to John 16:33 and let his eyes move over the words. *In this world you will have trouble. But take heart! I have overcome the world.*

Yes, that was his hope. Jesus had overcome the world.

Wendell had definitely had trouble. Not just at Hamilton High. Losing Joanna had been the toughest thing Wendell had ever been through. But God had seen him beyond that season. Then when Alicia left last year, again he didn't think he could survive the hurt. But once more the Lord had been faithful to carry him through. Faithful to heal Alicia.

Now it was this. The death of Dwayne Brown. Another time when Wendell was sure he couldn't get through it without divine help.

He dragged himself out of bed. Was this the cost of holding a Bible study at Hamilton High? The unseen enemy of his soul attacking all God had given Wendell? He breathed in deep and turned to another section of Scripture. Matthew 11:28–30. *Come to me, all you who are weary and burdened. . . . Take my yoke upon you and learn from me, for I am gentle and humble in heart, and you will find rest for your souls. For my yoke is easy and my burden is light.*

Alicia had mentioned reading those very

verses the day her school suffered such loss. Now they came to Wendell again.

Come to me, all you who are weary . . . He held on to that simple invitation. *That's me, Lord. I'm coming to you.* Today when he had to tell the students about Dwayne. And later when he had to appear in court to defend his right to lead kids in the ways of the Bible. Wendell would believe the impossible was possible. That he would not only find help in staying linked to God Almighty.

But he would find rest for his soul.

His ever-weary soul.

Wendell arrived at school earlier than usual, before sunup. He hadn't been able to go back to sleep, so he figured he might as well come here. The older kids would help the younger ones get off to school. This way Wendell could pray and prepare. It wasn't the first time he'd had to deliver bad news to his students.

But he could ask God that maybe — just maybe — it might be the last.

It was 6:15 when he parked his car and made his way inside. He went to the field house first and used his master key to open the locker room. Each locker was more of an open-air cubby. And each was identified with the name of a football player. Wendell walked down the row until he reached the one he was looking for.

Dwayne Brown.

The kid's helmet hung on the hook and his game uniform was clean and pressed, waiting for a contest that would never come. Wendell ran his finger slowly over the boy's name. *Why'd you do it? Why'd you go to the fight?*

He could picture Dwayne's smile. The one that lit up the kid's face so much more often lately. Dwayne was in heaven . . . Wendell knew that. He sat down on the bench and stared at the boy's locker. He had seen the changes in Dwayne. What being a believer in Christ had done for Dwayne. He had a new confidence. Improved grades.

Hope for the future.

So why did Dwayne go back to his old ways? And why was his body in a morgue this morning when he should've been getting ready for school? Between this and the trial, Wendell struggled to draw a breath. The weight of it all was so much.

He closed his eyes. *Come to me, all you who are weary and burdened, and I will give you rest . . .*

Wendell heard the sound of the door opening behind him. Probably one of the coaches. Before leaving this morning Wendell had sent an email to the faculty telling them the news. If one of the trainers had checked his messages, he might come down to the field house early, too. The loss was going to hit everyone hard.

Wendell turned to see who it was, but the person in front of him was not one of the staff. Wendell stood. The sight of her was like oxygen in the room. He could breathe again. "Alicia."

"Can I be in here?"

"Yes." He took a step toward her. "The boys aren't on campus yet."

Alicia nodded. Her eyes were red and swollen. Clearly she'd been crying. "I had to come." Before Wendell had time to believe she was even here, she was in his arms. "Dwayne. I . . . I can't believe it."

"I know." He ran his hand along the back of her head, over her hair and onto her shoulders. "It's awful."

"Jenny Anders forwarded me the email. She thought . . ." A quick few sobs interrupted her. She pulled back and looked at Wendell. "He was in my English class two years ago. There was something special about him." She dabbed at her eyes and seemed to try to collect herself. "Remember?"

Wendell thought back, and all the sudden

the memory was clear. Alicia had one student who had given her a hard time from the beginning. She had talked to Wendell about the boy, and he had given her a challenge.

Pray for him.

Not out loud or with everyone watching. Not in a way that the boy even had to know about. Just pray. "Devote yourself to this, Alicia," Wendell had told her. "Beg God day and night for a change in the kid and see what happens. God will answer. He's faithful that way."

Only now did Wendell understand. "The boy you prayed for . . ."

"It was Dwayne." Alicia laid her head on Wendell's chest again. "I believe . . . God is a God of miracles." She held him tighter. "But this is so hard to understand."

A thought hit Wendell. Alicia didn't know about Dwayne's faith. Of course she didn't.

He put his hands gently on her shoulders and took a step back. "Dwayne gave his life to the Lord, Alicia." Wendell searched her eyes. "He's been coming to our Raise the Bar club since school started." Tears blurred his own eyes. "I baptized him a few weeks ago in John Oliver's pool."

"What?" Now it was Alicia's turn to be shocked. She ran her fingers through her pretty dark hair and walked slowly to Dwayne's locker. "I had . . . no idea." She sat down and stared at the boy's name.

Wendell came and took the spot beside her on the bench. "God is faithful." His words were only a whisper. "Now you don't have to wonder."

She was quiet. Clearly processing. "Still . . . why would God . . . ?" Her voice trailed off. The new, more confident Alicia still had doubts. The way most people did in times like this.

An aching desperation came over Wendell. He wanted so badly to help her understand. Help them both. "God heard your prayer, Alicia. He heard mine." Wendell chose each word with care. "The Lord worked a miracle with Dwayne. He's in heaven. With Jesus now." The truth was hitting Wendell even as he spoke. "He found salvation at the Raise the Bar club. And now . . . now we will see him again."

The reality seemed to take a long while to fully sink in. Finally Alicia looked at him. "I like that."

He felt his shoulders relax some. "Me, too."

She looked at him, deep in his eyes. "I owe you an apology. I didn't say it the other day on the phone, but I wanted to."

Wendell waited, his eyes locked on hers.

"I never should've asked for a transfer. I could've worked through my anxiety in the background. And still been here to see . . ." She looked at Dwayne's locker, then back to Wendell. "Everything I missed. The victories. Like Dwayne."

"Alicia." Wendell reached for her hand. "What if God wanted you at Jackson High School? To pray with your students after those kids died?"

She hesitated, like she hadn't thought of that before. "Maybe." Two tears fell onto her face. "Still . . . I'm sorry. I'm so sorry, Wendell."

"It's okay." He allowed a quiet between them. It was still hard to believe she was here, beside him. "Those days . . . they're gone."

Another hesitation. "I'm so sad." She shook her head. "For Dwayne and his mama. For us. For what might've been if I'd stayed."

Wendell wanted to cry, too. A boy's life had been taken. The school would be in shock. He had to focus on caring for his student body. They had a memorial to plan. He looked out the locker room window. The sun was starting to break through the darkness. Pinks and blues streaked the sky. Like the night sky, they needed to find the light again after Dwayne's death.

They stayed that way for a minute or so. Then Alicia stood. "I have to go."

Wendell sighed. If only he could stop time. This was the first time they'd been together in nearly a year. And now she was leaving. He stood and closed the distance between them. Again he put his hands on her shoulders. "Thank you for coming."

There were so many things he wanted to say. "Remember how you prayed about Dwayne? That God would do something special in his life?"

"Yes." Alicia hadn't moved any closer to the door. She was so beautiful, but so hurt at the same time. "I'll always remember."

Wendell looked deep into her eyes. "Why don't you pray that way for us?" He gently took hold of her hands. "That God will do something special. A miracle like He did for Dwayne. So we'll know what's next for us. Friendship or . . . something more." He paused and his voice grew quieter. "Whatever it is, I don't want to lose you again, Alicia."

Uncertainty and love mixed in her expression. "I will. I'll pray." She stepped away and mouthed just one more word as she left. "Goodbye."

That was it. She reached the door and she was gone.

Wendell wanted to run after her, take her in his arms and ask her to never leave. He wanted to tell her that he felt dizzy and whole and wonderful just being around her. But all he could do was let her go and face the tragedy of Dwayne's death. That and do the same thing he'd told her to do.

Pray for God to give them a miracle.

The students took the news hard, the way Wendell had figured they would. He canceled classes and allowed them to gather in either the cafeteria or the auditorium. Wherever they felt most able to process. The school district sent in three grief counselors.

But most of all help came from the kids in the Raise the Bar program. Across campus they talked with their peers and prayed with them. They spoke words of peace and love and healing, and they assured the kids who were most afraid that Dwayne was okay.

He was in heaven now.

Still, Dwayne's death struck the students particularly hard. Several students from Raise the Bar came up to Wendell before he left for court. "Will the media talk about this?" a freshman girl asked. "Will people think things are the same around here? Like

305

nothing good really happened."

Much as they were devastated at the loss of their classmate, the students were nervous that this could mar the proof that the group was making a difference. Wendell wasn't worried about it. He ran into Jordy on the way to his car.

His son hugged him. Wendell studied the boy. "How you holding up?"

"I'm okay." The pain in Jordy's eyes made him look five years older than yesterday. "I keep thinking if I'd been a little more serious. If I'd forced him not to go. I could've convinced him to just stay with me and go to the Halloween party."

Wendell started to shake his head. "Son, you know that's not —"

"I know . . ." Jordy placed his hand on Wendell's shoulder. "I know it's not my fault. I just . . . I wish I could've kept him here. That's all."

"Me, too." Sometimes there were no answers.

"And you know what else?" Jordy's lips lifted in the slightest smile. "I keep thinking about something. With or without the club, sadly Dwayne would still be gone. But now I'm sure he's in heaven."

Wendell knew it was true. But hearing the words from Jordy now gave them new meaning. The Raise the Bar club really was a matter of life or death. He'd been dealing all morning with kids who thought the club should've made a difference for Dwayne. If he was getting closer to Jesus he shouldn't have gone to the gang fight.

But here . . . this was the truth. The club hadn't saved Dwayne from getting shot. But his faith in Christ, the faith he'd learned and accepted at the meetings, had saved him from hell. Which could still be true for many of the kids at Hamilton High. The Raise the Bar club was a matter of life or death.

If not in this world, for the next.

"Son." Wendell gave his boy another embrace. "You've given me something to take to my lawyer."

The two said goodbye and fifteen minutes later, Wendell met up with Luke Baxter in the foyer of the court building. Wendell looked around as he walked inside. The place was beautiful. Complete with ornate columns and beveled window trim and ceilings that seemed to stretch up forever.

Luke was there, sitting on a bench against the back wall. He gave a serious nod and stood to greet Wendell. The two shook hands, and Luke spoke first. "I heard about your student. Dwayne Brown." He hesitated. "So tough. I'm sorry."

"Yes. Long day." Wendell could still hear his son's words. He managed a slight smile, picturing Dwayne in heaven. "That boy found Jesus at our club. He's in heaven now."

"Well." Luke nodded. "If that's not something worth fighting for, I don't know what is."

Wendell patted him on the back as they headed for the courtroom. "That's what I like to hear."

Luke had already gone over the details. There would be no hearing today, just jury selection. Dozens of potential jurors would be gathered in the courtroom. Others would be on hand in case they were needed.

Wendell would simply watch while Luke did his work. If Luke were a very great artist, then this was the part of the process where he gathered his paints. He had told Wendell he already knew what types of jurors he wanted on the panel. Now it was a matter of finding them.

Luke had already submitted questions, as had Eli Landsford. Wendell had done his research. According to the Indiana Rules of Court, section 47-D, questions must be submitted ahead of time. Questions Judge

Wells would ask the entire panel of possible jurors.

The questions were pretty obvious. Landsford asked: Have you ever been a pastor or worked on the staff of a church? Or from Luke: Have you ever filed suit against a person or entity because of the First Amendment establishment clause?

General questions like that.

The more specific questions would come during the lawyer questioning, when each attorney would have three peremptory challenges — a chance to eliminate a juror for any reason whatsoever. Because it was a civil case they needed only six jurors and four alternates.

Once the judge finished, Wendell watched Luke ask the jury pool a number of questions, and Landsford did the same. Luke had said he was looking for average Americans with a sense of faith and family. Hardworking citizens who might be more likely to appreciate the benefit of the Raise the Bar club.

If Luke had his way, a majority of the jurors would be black — like Wendell. More sympathetic that way.

Landsford was clearly looking for a different type of juror. Single people living in the city, or married people with no children. At least it seemed that way based on the questions he was asking. He wanted people with liberal politics and an opposition to anything remotely Christian. People who didn't own Bibles or better yet, found them offensive.

Halfway through the process, Landsford was still pacing in front of the jury, eyeing them like a caged tiger hungry for dinner. As if the jurors were somehow on trial.

"What is your church experience, Mr. Janson?" Landsford asked a man who seemed to be in his late forties.

"Not much church experience. Except when I was young." The man looked uneasy in the hardback wooden chair provided for the occasion.

"What experience did you have when you were young?"

"My parents divorced. They said we kids didn't have to go to church if we didn't want to." He shrugged. "We didn't want to."

Landsford looked at the judge. "Acceptable juror, Your Honor."

Luke still had two peremptory challenges. He stood, confident. "The defense would like to challenge."

"Let the record show, the defense has just one remaining challenge." Judge Wells looked over her glasses at Luke. "Let's finish this up, Mr. Baxter. Jury selection shouldn't take all day."

Wendell wasn't a lawyer but he sensed the hostility Luke faced in this courtroom. The next six jurors seemed as opposed to Bible study and the Christian faith as Andy Nelson. Luke used his one remaining challenge, but after that there wasn't much he could do to stop three of them from being placed on the jury.

Thirty minutes later they had their jurors. Luke turned to Wendell. "It could be worse, but it's not what I hoped for. It'll be pretty split based on their answers today."

"I wondered." Wendell felt a ripple of concern. "We'll just have to pray. God's not surprised by anything that happened today."

"True." Luke smiled and shook Wendell's hand. "I'll be in touch tomorrow. We'll go over everything regarding the trial."

Wendell left the building with Luke. It wasn't until he reached his car that he noticed someone standing by the driver's side. His heart stopped when he saw her.

"Alicia." She had a way of showing up when he least expected her and most needed her. "Why . . . what are you doing here?"

She lifted her face, the strength back in her eyes. "I'm tired of walking away from you."

"Okay." Wendell didn't blink, didn't turn

away. He shoved his hands in the pockets of his jacket and waited.

"I don't like how things ended this morning." She took a step closer. "Today was jury selection. What sort of friend disappears when the stakes are this great?"

True, he wanted to say. But he remained silent.

"Forgive me, Wendell. I won't turn my back on you again." She reached for his hand. "Whatever happens after this trial, I'll be your friend, at least. I'm not going anywhere."

It was a start, a first step. Wendell wanted to say he still loved her. But for now this was enough. He pulled her slowly into his arms and held her. After a long moment, he stepped back and said the only thing he could think to say. "Thank you. For being here."

Her eyes held the hint of sparkle. "Let's get coffee. So you can tell me about jury selection."

Alicia followed him to the coffee shop a mile from the courthouse. He checked his rearview mirror six times — just to be sure she was really behind him. So he would know this wasn't something from a dream. An hour later, when they parted ways and he headed home to his kids, Wendell felt better about today's jury selection and the trial ahead.

Not because the process would be any easier. Luke Baxter assured him that the next week would be the most difficult of all.

But because he had a friend to see him through it.

17

Luke and his family filed into the CKT children's theater that Saturday night for the opening performance of *Seussical the Musical.* The play several of his nieces and nephews were in. He was keeping his word. Spending more time with his family and glad for it.

But today all Luke could think about was the case against Wendell Quinn.

"You look distracted." Reagan leaned close to him and searched his face. "You're thinking about the trial, aren't you?"

"Trying not to be." He kissed her cheek. "Sorry."

Tommy was sitting next to Reagan. He opened his program and turned to them. "Who's playing what parts again?"

Malin and Johnny listened, too, while Reagan explained it to them. "All of Aunt Kari and Uncle Ryan's kids are in it. Jessie's playing Horton — her biggest role ever." Rea-

314

gan looked at the program. "RJ and Annie are ensemble." She pointed to a column of names. "Aunt Ashley and Uncle Landon have three in the show, too. Amy is a Bird Girl, and Devin is the mayor. Janessa is one of the Who townspeople."

"I thought Maddie had a role." Luke was still struggling to stay focused. His family and the rest of the Baxters had been looking forward to this night for months. He needed to at least try. "Is she in it?"

"She's not in the cast." Reagan put her arm around his shoulders. "Maddie's an assistant director along with Bailey Flanigan."

Tommy nodded. "That's right. Maddie's dating Bailey's brother Connor."

"Not anymore." Reagan gave him a sad smile. "They're on a break. Maddie told us that last time we were all together."

"A break. Right." Luke looked into Reagan's eyes. "I remember how that felt." He kissed her again, this time on the lips.

"Not much fun."

"No." He loved Reagan with everything in him. Loved the way they'd overcome every kind of struggle to get where they were today. The theater was filling up. Ashley and Landon and Cole took the seats in front of them. Cole had a friend with him, a pretty blond girl who looked head over heels for him.

Luke raised his brow at the pair and then at Reagan. "Something new?"

"I'll have to ask Ashley." Reagan put her finger to her lips. "Later."

John and Elaine took the seats on the other side of Cole while Kari, Ryan, Brooke, Peter and Hayley filled out the row. After a few minutes, the theater went dark and the music began to play. Luke hadn't seen *Seussical* before, but he loved the Dr. Seuss stories. He had read them to his kids when they were little.

The Cat in the Hat entered the stage and the show began. Even so Luke struggled to keep his attention on the musical. He still had no idea how he was going to win the case against Wendell Quinn. No idea how he was supposed to find a precedent that might help them.

God, I need a miracle. Show me which way to turn. Please. He sighed and reached for Reagan's hand. His nieces and nephews did a wonderful job throughout the evening, but it wasn't until the second act that one of the verses hit Luke differently than the others.

The line was simply this: *Their whole world was saved by the smallest of all.*

Luke let the words play over again in his mind. *Lord, is there a message there for me? Could Wendell's whole world be saved by the smallest of all?*

Maybe the students would come through with something that might affect the jury. Luke wasn't sure but it felt significant. Like God wanted him to pay particular attention to this part.

Not until the show was over and they were home in Indianapolis did the line finally make sense.

Luke walked into Tommy's room to say goodnight, but the boy's bed was empty. Tommy was fourteen that fall, and it was after midnight. But with church in the morning, normally their oldest son would be in bed by now.

A quick check of the other bedrooms didn't turn up Tommy, either. Luke jogged down the stairs and found Reagan in the kitchen. "Where's Tommy?"

"In your office." She pointed to the glass doors on the small room just off the kitchen. "He's been in there since we got home."

Strange. Luke headed into the office, closed the door behind him and watched his oldest child. The boy was sitting at Luke's desk, Wendell's three presentation folders spread out before him.

Tommy looked up. "Hi, Dad." A serious look filled his face. "I can't stop thinking about your case. The one with the principal."

"Right." Luke moved slowly to the other chair, the one in the corner of the room. "I feel the same way." He waited a moment. "So what are you reading?"

"I mean" — Tommy looked at the documents and then back at Luke — "it's all super interesting. Having Bible study at the school has changed everything. Test scores, crime rates, all of it."

Tommy sounded like a seasoned lawyer. Luke stifled a smile to keep things serious. The paperwork was private between him and his client. But Tommy's interest was harmless. Besides, Luke loved that his son was intrigued by the case. "No question Principal Quinn's plan worked."

"Exactly." Tommy pointed to the first folder. The one that contained Wendell's research from two summers ago. "Wasn't he just doing his job, Dad? I mean . . . did you read this?"

Suddenly Luke felt embarrassed. He needed precedent, not statistics and historical quotes, not Bible verses and anecdotes. How many times had Wendell asked him the same thing? "No . . . I'm going to, but . . . not yet."

Tommy seemed unfazed. He opened the cover and read from one of the first few pages. "Listen to this. Here's the job description Principal Quinn agreed to carry out when he was hired." Tommy hesitated. "Establish a schoolwide vision of commitment to high standards and ensure the success of all students." Tommy looked at Luke. "Principal Quinn had tried everything else, right? Isn't that what he told you?"

Luke smiled. Tommy must've been paying attention when Luke and Reagan had talked about the case the other night at dinner. "Yes." Luke could see where Tommy was headed with this. "He'd tried everything else."

"So then — if he wanted to do his job — he had to think of something else, right?"

"Right." Luke's heart raced. Tommy was only a freshman in high school. His dream of being a lawyer felt pretty solid right about now.

"So he tried a voluntary Bible study, and it worked." Tommy picked up the second folder, the one with the research from the college student. "Which can only mean one thing."

Luke waited. Tommy deserved his shot at making the case here.

"Principal Quinn was just doing his job. He was establishing a schoolwide vision of commitment to high standards, and he was offering at least one way to ensure the success of his students."

Slowly Luke began to nod. "I really wanted precedent for this case. Something that would prove to the jury why this case might be an easy win for Mr. Quinn."

"But, Dad . . ." Tommy smiled and handed Luke the first folder. "Sometimes you have to *set* precedent. Right? I mean . . . someone has to blaze the trail for everyone else. Plus, you have God on your side."

Luke took Wendell's presentation folder, amazed at the astuteness of his oldest son. "Well . . . you have a point."

Tommy nodded. "I thought so." He yawned and stood, pushing the desk chair in before walking over to Luke. "I'm headed to bed. Goodnight, Dad. Love you."

"Goodnight." A sense of bewilderment came over Luke. "Love you, Tommy."

The boy seemed nonchalant as he made his way to the kitchen, kissed his mother and climbed the stairs. Like solving crazy difficult cases was a normal part of his Saturday night.

For a long time, Luke sat there in his office and stared at the folder in his hand.

The one Wendell had wanted him to read all those days ago. This was a different take, for sure. Landsford would never expect Luke to come at the case from this angle. But it just might work.

Like Tommy said, Principal Quinn was just doing his job.

And suddenly the scene from the musical came back to Luke, the one that had seemed so profound. The Whos had been in dire need, their town on the dust speck about to be boiled in oil. But in the end, little JoJo had made a single sound. And that one sound had saved the Whos.

Their whole world was saved by the smallest of all.

Dr. Seuss's message was clear. Every voice counted. Every life mattered. And in this case, no years of legal training and courtroom experience could match the simple understanding of a kid.

Someone like Tommy.

Luke wasn't sure if he had his answer. He had no idea if this was a trail he could follow to victory for Wendell Quinn. But he had something he didn't have this morning.

He had the hope of a child.

That night just after midnight, Cami agreed to meet Jordy at the park between his house and the Smiths', the place where she was still living. The trial was set to begin Monday morning.

The meeting was Jordy's idea. They needed a plan, he had told her. Some way that the kids in the Raise the Bar club could help his dad win the case against him. None of them could imagine what might happen if they were shut down. Cami loved the club. It had become her refuge. If Principal Quinn lost, the club would break up and she would lose the one thing she counted on.

It was cold and windy outside. Not quite winter, but close. Cami put on her down jacket and pulled a woolen beanie over her ears. Slipping out of the house without being noticed, she jogged the three blocks to the park. She spotted Jordy on the bench, right where he'd said he'd be. But he wasn't alone.

As Cami came closer she saw at least another twenty Hamilton High students gathered around Jordy. It took no time to figure out that everyone was there to help.

"This is our thing." One of the guys started the meeting. "The club is for us, so we're the ones who should testify."

"I agree." Cami pulled her coat tight around her waist. She shivered, not so much because of the cold but because of the matter at hand. "If we didn't want a Bible study we wouldn't go. But since we're all going, we should be the ones fighting for it."

Jordy was quiet during the meeting. It was his dad's career at stake. His father's reputation was his reputation, in some ways. It made sense that Jordy would let the others do the talking. He only spoke at the very end.

"What you're saying is true." He looked at Cami and then the others. "My dad only did this for you. For us. Because our school was falling apart."

"And now it's doing so much better." Another guy stepped up, his voice filled with passion. "Jordy, you find out which day we should be there. Then I say we skip class and show up. As many of us as they'll allow in the courtroom."

They agreed on the plan and the kids left for their own homes. Only Cami and Jordy remained. Jordy slid his hands into the pockets of his thick jacket. "Thanks. For being here tonight."

Only a few feet separated them. The nearby streetlight shone a splash of yellow over the spot where they stood. "Of course." She had done everything in her power to keep her distance from Jordy. What she felt for him still could go nowhere.

But Jordy was making it difficult.

Cami took a step closer so she could keep her voice quiet. "I still feel like this is my fault."

"It was never your fault." Their breath hung in the air between them. "When this is all over, I still want to go to Liberty with you next year."

"But my life's such a mess."

"It isn't." He closed the distance between them. "You have Jesus and you have me. You have everyone at the club." He put his warm hand against her cheek.

The feeling was wonderful. Could it be that maybe Jordy actually liked her? As more than a friend? She tried to focus. "God will get me through this. Just like your dad."

"Right." Jordy smiled at her.

He was closer now, their faces inches apart. Cami could practically hear his heartbeat in the silence of the night. All she wanted was for him to kiss her. But this was impossible. His dad would want someone better for Jordy. Someone more like him.

Her internal protest faded. None of that mattered now. It was just the two of them here under the night sky. So close she could hear him breathing. She studied him.

"Thanks, Jordy. For always believing in me."
She felt tears well up in her eyes. "You
believe in everyone like that. Dwayne. The
kids in the club. It's one of my favorite
things about you."

Then, what she didn't dare hope would
happen, did. Jordy still had his hand on her
face, and he brought his lips to hers. The
kiss didn't last long, but it warmed her
entire body. His eyes melted into hers. "You
don't know how long I've wanted to do
that."

She felt dizzy, like her feet were lifting off
the ground. The nightfall did a good job of
hiding the heat she could feel in her cheeks.
"You don't know how long I've wanted you
to."

He smiled and gave her a quick hug. "I
have to get home." For a long moment he
searched her face. "We're still going to be
here. Like this, Cami. When all this is
behind us."

She nodded. With everything in her she
wanted him to be right. He walked her to
the Smiths' house and this time he didn't
kiss her. Just hugged her and waited while
she walked up to the door. Cami turned and
waved goodbye as he took off running for
his home. As he disappeared around the
corner, she replayed the way his hand felt

on her face, the heat of his lips against hers.

The kiss had only lasted a few seconds, but it would stay with her forever.

And maybe — if God answered her prayers — Jordy would, too.

Wendell was waiting for Jordy when he got home that night. He pulled his bathrobe tight around his middle and sat in the living room chair closest to the front door. He heard Jordy turn the key and open the door. Once he was inside he seemed to take a moment for his eyes to adjust to the dark of the foyer.

Only then did Wendell stand up. "Where've you been, Son?"

Jordy jumped back. "Dad! You scared me."

"We have a rule in this house, young man. Let someone know where you're going. Not to mention it's past curfew."

"I'm sorry." Jordy was out of breath. "I didn't want to wake you."

"Next time, do. I can sleep later." This entire scene was completely out of character for Jordy. He had always been the best son, obedient, quick to help. Honest. Wendell had a feeling who was behind this. He worked to keep his tone even. "Were you with Cami Nelson?"

Jordy shifted his weight, and looked down

at the floor for a few seconds. "Yes." His eyes found Wendell's again. "But not just her. A bunch of kids from club were there, too. At the park a few blocks away."

Over the years Wendell had learned to take his time in moments of discipline. Let his kids be heard. Instruction and correction could come later. When all the facts were on the table. "A midnight meeting at the park. I see." Wendell paused. "Wanna tell me about it?"

"It was for you." Jordy was breathing more normally now. He locked the door behind him and motioned to the living room. "Can we sit down?"

"Sure. Of course." Wendell had all the time in the world. "How was this meeting for me?"

They both sat down.

Jordy shrugged. "All of us want to testify on your behalf. We think it's wrong that you're on trial when the club is for us. We're the ones who needed the bar to be raised." Jordy's tone was earnest. He was telling the truth, Wendell was sure.

He nodded. "I see. And since you have school, when exactly do the group of you plan to testify?"

"We need your help for that." Jordy's eyes shone with pure intentions. "Wednesday or

Thursday. Friday. Whatever day you want us there, we'll be there."

Wendell could hardly be frustrated with the boy. He felt his heart soften. "That's very kind, Jordy. Something your mother would've been a part of."

"Cami . . . she's . . . she's a lot like Mom that way." Jordy blinked, but he didn't look away. "She and I stayed and talked for a few minutes after everyone else left."

Wendell's heart beat a little faster. "You and Cami?"

"Yes." Jordy swallowed, clearly more nervous than a few minutes ago. "I like her, Dad. I know it's . . . it's awkward because of her father. But I can't help it. I like her a lot."

Wendell had seen this coming, and even still he could do nothing to stop it. "I was afraid we'd need to have this talk." His sigh filled the quiet living room. "You and Cami Nelson, Son. It could never work. Not in a million years."

Jordy rarely got angry, but here in the dark of night, with only the outside lamps lending light to the room, the boy's eyes flashed. "Dad . . . that's a terrible thing to say."

"It's true." Wendell didn't want to have to say this, but Jordy had left him no choice. "Black and white, no matter how far we've

328

come on race issues, things are worse than ever. Her dad's one of those closet racists. I could tell that the minute I saw him in court."

Jordy squinted his eyes. "What? Dad, are you serious?"

"Of course I'm serious. He glared at me as soon as our eyes met. Looked like he wanted to kill me. Like he'd never seen a black principal."

"Dad! Listen to you." Jordy stood and paced across the room and back. "He has something against Christians. Not *black* people. You have no proof of that whatsoever."

"Well, still . . . these days things are worse. People will hate you for dating a white girl. They'll hate Cami for dating a black guy." Wendell wished there was an easier way to spell out the facts. "Save yourselves a lifetime of heartache and find another girl, Jordy. Let this one go."

Jordy stopped and stared hard at Wendell. For a few seconds he worked the muscles in his jaw, as if he was so angry he couldn't think of exactly what to say. "So who's the racist, Dad?"

"Jordy."

"Please. Listen to me." Jordy seemed to force himself to lower his voice. "You're telling me her father looked like he wanted to kill you? Like he'd never seen a black principal? Why? Because he's a mechanic? Because he doesn't have his doctorate like you?"

Wendell had never seen such righteous anger from his son. He leaned forward in his chair and waited for Jordy to settle down. When the boy sat again, Wendell chose his words with care. "I'm sorry. You're right." Wendell could feel the Holy Spirit reminding him to be humble. He was wrong here, and he needed to say so. "There's no reason for me to assume the man's a racist."

"We can't buy the lie that all white people are racist, Dad." Jordy's expression became more hurt than angry. "Isn't that what you taught us kids?"

It was. Wendell felt awful. "I'm sorry. Forgive me." This was part of what made their family special. The ability to apologize freely. And freely forgive.

"Okay." Jordy settled back in his chair. For a minute he gripped the armrests and rocked. As if he were sorting through his feelings and trying to figure out which was the most important. "I know Cami's dad is a mean man." Jordy hesitated. "I know he doesn't like God or Christians." His eyes locked on to Wendell's. "But I like his daughter. That's all I know. Cami loves Jesus, Dad. She does. And what about Mom? She was half white, remember? You and Mom were the ones who taught us that skin color doesn't matter."

Wendell could think of a thousand times.

"You told us hurt people hurt people, and if anyone ever had a problem with us because of our skin color it wasn't our problem. It was theirs. You said some people got made fun of for being too tall or too short. Too heavy or too skinny. Too smart or too slow." Passion filled Jordy's voice. "You said none of that mattered, because in God's eyes we were all the same. We were all His children."

"True. I said that." Wendell was ashamed of himself for his words earlier. And grateful for his older son's ability to put the issue in perspective.

"So Cami and I, we're just a couple of children of God who happen to like each other." Jordy managed the slightest smile. "I don't know if I'll ask her out. I'm not sure if we'll be boyfriend and girlfriend or if we'll get married one day. But I like her. A lot." He paused. "I think Mom would like her, too."

"Yes." Wendell found his own smile as he

stood and helped Jordy to his feet. "I think Mom would like her, too." He put his hand on his son's shoulder and searched his eyes. "I guess I just want an easier road for you, Jordy. I don't want people taking out their hate on you. Not for any reason."

Jordy nodded, his eyes full of confidence and maturity. "I get that. But I can't live to please other people. Only God. Heartache and hate are a part of life. Our job is to love. Besides" — he grinned — "God created all the colors." He laughed. "Right?"

A chuckle came from Wendell. "When did you get to be so smart?"

The air between them was warm again, the tension gone. Jordy slipped his arm around his father's shoulders. "I had the best teacher."

"And I have the best son."

The conversation stayed with Wendell long after Jordy turned in, long after Wendell was under the covers, staring at the ceiling over his bed. If he could protect his kids from the sort of attack he himself was under, he would. He'd spare them every time.

But Jordy was right. Earth was full of heartache. Hurt people would always hurt people. Which was probably why Andy Nelson had filed suit against Wendell and Hamilton High in the first place. Someone had hurt him. And when the dust settled on this case, Wendell prayed he might find out more about the man. The one he had been quick to criticize.

In case there was some way Wendell might show the man love and mercy.

Instead of judgment.

18

Andy Nelson would've given anything to avoid waking up in the morning. The trial against Hamilton High's Wendell Quinn was set to begin in a few days, and there was nothing Andy could do to stop it.

He had dug this hole. Now it was no surprise he couldn't find his way out of it.

There were several options, of course. He could take a bottle of pills or load up the revolver he kept at his bedside. But any of those would mean destroying his girls' lives. And he couldn't do that. The lawsuit was bad enough.

If he killed himself now, the horrible news would be splashed across newspapers all over the country. The world, even. And his daughters would suffer more than they were already. And they were definitely suffering.

Cami most of all.

The house was dark, the lights out in every room including his own. His attempt at finding sleep. Because the only thing worse than waking up in the morning was staying awake all night to get there.

The blankets on his bed felt like they were strangling him. Which wouldn't have been so bad. At least his death would be by natural causes. But since the covers were making it hard for him to breathe, Andy flung them off his legs and sat up. He needed fresh air. Something to hurry the alcohol out of his system.

Andy had no idea how many shots of whiskey he'd had tonight. Not enough to kill him. But too much to pull a full breath into his lungs. He stumbled across his bedroom floor, down the hallway and out the front door. It was just after one in the morning, his neighbors would be asleep.

Since no one was watching, Andy didn't care that he was only wearing sweatpants and a white T-shirt. He tripped down the front steps and landed spread out on the grass. The ground smelled of wet dirt and fertilizer. He sucked in as much air as he could.

Ten minutes, fifteen. Andy had no idea how long he stayed that way, but eventually he blinked his eyes open and looked around. What was he doing out here on the front lawn? And why was he shivering? He pressed his face against the grass again. It was freezing. The yard was ice cold, that was why.

He struggled to his feet and dragged himself back in the house. His clothes were wet and covered in mud and grass stains. A wobbly walk to his bedroom and into the bathroom, where he flipped on the light and stared at himself in the mirror.

A lunatic, that's what he was. A raving, sick-in-the-head crazy person. What sort of man would turn on his own children? He felt a rush of nausea and he barely made it to the toilet in time. Another fifteen minutes. Thirty, maybe. However long it took for the alcohol to make its way out of his body.

Once more he got to his feet and looked around. He was more sober now, more aware of his surroundings. Why couldn't he just die? What on earth could God possibly still want with Andy Nelson? He shuffled to the sink and wiped off his face. Brushed off the grass and mud sticking to his T-shirt.

Then he made his way down the hall to Cami's bedroom.

Andy walked to the edge of his daughter's bed, to the collage of photos that hung on the corkboard. His head hurt and his stomach still felt queasy. But he could focus now. The streetlamp outside her window gave him just enough light to see. The pictures showed a life Cami no longer had. A life none of them had.

She was a beautiful girl. Just like her mother.

"That's why I'm so hard on you, baby." He reached out and touched one of the photos. "It's enough that you look like her. But when you started reading the Bible like she did . . ." He shook his head.

Tears filled Andy's eyes. Tears so foreign he almost didn't recognize the feeling. No, he couldn't stand to watch Cami go the way of her mother. Headed into some Christian lifestyle where she'd turn against Andy and everything she'd known before.

He wanted to save her from making the same mistakes her mother made. New anger washed over him. Of course he was justified in filing the lawsuit. Andy gripped the edge of the bed, unsteady on his feet again.

Something on her dresser caught his eye. A book or a journal. Whatever it was Cami had forgotten it when she left. When he terrified her that night. Andy used the wall to navigate his way to the object, and a few seconds later he had his answer. He was right. It was a journal.

A quick flip to the last entry and Andy squinted so he could make out the words in the dark. The date was September 6. The first week of school.

It's been a year since I started going to the Bible study club at Hamilton and my entire life is different. I'm happy and I have peace. All the anger I felt before about my mom . . . it's gone. I gave it to God and whenever I think about taking it back I just talk to Him. He's the best friend ever. Now if there was just some way to tell my dad . . .

Andy dropped slowly to the edge of her bed and read the entry again and then a third time. This was how Cami felt? Like God was her best friend? And her only problem was figuring out a way to tell him?

His body began to shake and bile rose up in his throat. Was this what he was afraid of? Cami's belief that God had become someone she could talk to? Someone who gave her joy and peace?

Fingers of regret wrapped themselves around his neck and choked the air from his throat. All of this was his fault. Why had he acted so quickly? He had no reason to call the reporter, no need to make such a mess of things. Now the whole world knew his name. Andy Nelson, the man who had sued to stop his own daughter from attending a voluntary Bible study. His actions sounded mean and controlling, even to him.

Why hadn't he seen that before?

Now he'd lost her forever.

She hadn't been in touch once since leaving, and how could he blame her? He closed her journal and set it back on her dresser.

Andy needed the bathroom again. He rushed out of Cami's room and barely made it to the toilet. He had nothing left to throw up but the hatred he'd allowed to fester. And that would never leave his system.

Not after what he'd done.

From his place hovering on the floor near the toilet, something else caught his attention. The tattoo on his bicep. *NO GOD.* As if he could just so boldly make the statement that God didn't exist. Like by permanently saying so, he could undo the hurt his wife had caused him.

Undo the hurt he'd caused Cami and Ensley and Ellie.

Maybe if he took a small handful of pills he could go to sleep and never wake up and the world wouldn't be the wiser. They would find him dead and assume he had died in his sleep. Natural causes. He could take the pills and then hide the bottle. Lie down on the bed and never get up again.

That way he'd never have to sit in a courtroom opposite his daughter. Never have to take the witness stand in opposition to Cami's best friend.

God Almighty.

He could skip the whole thing if he could just pull it off. Make it look like he'd suffered a heart attack before morning light. He struggled to his feet and slid himself to the sink. He opened the medicine cabinet. Inside were half a dozen bottles. Andy looked at them one at a time. Sleeping pills. Yes, that would do the trick.

Andy poured a pile into the palm of his hand and hesitated. If only he believed in God. If only the Creator of the Universe could help him the way He had apparently helped Cami. But there was a difference between him and his daughter.

Cami believed.

Do it. Get the pills down you.

He wasn't sure where the voice came from, but it was there and it meant business. *Take the pills.* The words practically shouted at him. Andy closed his eyes and smashed the handful of pills into his mouth. A swig of water from the faucet and the pills easily made their way down. There. Now he wouldn't have to face any of them.

Especially not Cami. His sweet daughter. The one he'd turned into a public enemy. Andy tried to keep his brain engaged. He didn't have long. *Focus,* he told himself.

Cover your tracks.

He returned the lid and placed the bottle of pills back in the cabinet. Then he shut the cabinet door and made his way back to bed. *Turn off the light. You have to turn off the light.* Already the room was starting to spin. It was all Andy could do to get to the light switch and hit it.

One last thing. He needed to find his way under the covers. So it would look like he'd simply fallen asleep. Like this was any other night. He stumbled as he made his way to the edge of his bed.

The place where he slept.

The place where he would die.

Somehow he made his way under the blankets and that was all. He couldn't move his hands or legs, couldn't turn his head. When they found him tomorrow or the next day, he could only hope he looked normal. So no one would know the truth: That Andy Nelson simply couldn't take another day. Couldn't come before the world as Cami's enemy.

His head was heavier now, his eyes, too. Andy wasn't sure when he took his last breath, but his lungs no longer worked and something was pulling at him. Sleep or maybe something else. It took Andy a few seconds to figure it out and when he did, he felt a rush of fear. Like maybe this wasn't what he wanted. Maybe he wanted to live.

He could've apologized to Cami. Called her up and offered to take her to lunch. Andy could've tried to make things right again. Why hadn't he thought of that before? Now he would never have the chance. Because the thing pulling at him wasn't sleep.

It was a terrible, all-consuming darkness.

19

Wendell wrapped up the Raise the Bar meeting that Tuesday and met with students for an hour afterward. Their questions were sad and chilling at the same time. Was this the last time they'd be allowed to meet? Wendell didn't know. Were the police going to show up and arrest people for reading the Bible? Most definitely not. Reading a Bible was a right afforded all Americans.

At least for now.

A few of the students told Wendell they weren't sure they could stay out of their gangs if the club stopped meeting. "This group of kids is my new gang. They're all I have," one junior told Wendell. "Please win this case. So we can try to make things right for ourselves. So we can keep learning about our real Father." The guy had tears in his eyes. "He's the only Father I've ever had."

The weight of it all pressed on Wendell's shoulders and made the drive home feel longer than usual. *I need to win this, Lord. Not just for me, but for the kids.* Sure, a few of them might find a way to keep meeting. But it wouldn't be the same. *They need a place to meet, a chance to learn about You. What else do they have?*

I am with you, My son. You will not have to fight this battle alone.

The response drifted across the barren surface of his soul like a warm breeze. There was no guarantee he would win. No promise any of them would win. But God would be with them. Somehow He would see them through. Even if telling students about God became a crime punishable by prison time, Wendell was up for the challenge.

I can do good here. In this moment. *Right, Lord?*

The trial was set to begin tomorrow morning.

Wendell's last conversation with Luke hadn't gone as well as either of them had hoped. Luke had read the presentation folders Wendell put together. He understood the historical foundation for a public expression of faith. He knew the quotes from the country's founding fathers, and he had memorized the improved statistics at Hamilton High.

The problem, Luke had reiterated, was

precedent. So far Luke hadn't found any for what Wendell was doing. And common sense wasn't an argument. Luke had mentioned to Wendell his son Tommy's insight after a musical he saw. Even though it was interesting and refreshing, Luke still wasn't sure he could use it as a defense.

The idea that Wendell was only doing what he'd been hired to do.

If they won the case, then sure — those things could become precedent for someone else. But typically religious freedom cases were won or lost based on cases that had come before. Luke even talked about Tommy's encouragement that *somebody* had set precedent on those previous cases.

Now it was Luke's turn to set it for someone else.

Luke had explained that believing it might happen was akin to believing in a miracle. Wendell had replayed Luke's words ten times today. *Don't get your hopes up, Wendell. I want you to be ready to lose this thing.*

Wendell was ready. But he wouldn't go down without a fight. If he could look in the eyes of those jurors and explain that he had no other option, no other way to reach the kids at Hamilton High, then surely they would listen.

God would see to that.

He exhaled long and slow as he pulled his car into the garage and cut the engine. The kids needed dinner. Usually it fell to Jordy to get the meal started. The boy loved cooking. He even talked about opening a restaurant one day. But tonight the job would be Wendell's. Jordy was headed out for a study group with Cami and a few other students.

As Wendell walked up the garage stairs he checked the time on his phone. Just after six-thirty. It would be three hours before he could think about the trial again. Dinner and dishes and homework would keep him busy until then.

And maybe that was a good thing.

He opened the door and suddenly he was looking into the face of Alicia Harris. "Hi, Wendell." She took his briefcase from him and stepped aside. "Dinner's ready."

Behind her the children all wore sneaky smiles. Even Jordy. "Surprise!" Their voices came together in the happiest sound Wendell had heard all day.

Spread out on the table in front of them was baked chicken, mashed potatoes, green beans and a salad. Cooling on the counter was what looked like a pan of brownies.

The worries of the day and the unknowns about tomorrow faded as the kids came to him. They surrounded him in a group hug.

"Do I have the best kids in the world, or what?" He winked at Alicia, who was standing back a bit, smiling bigger than all of them.

Leah was still in her band uniform. "We made this plan a week ago! Alicia called me and we put together a shopping list."

"Alicia bought the groceries on the way over." Jordy smiled at her and then back at Wendell. "It's like a pre-celebration. Because we trust God for a victory."

Wendell's heart melted. "Seriously?" He looked from Jordy to Leah as he kissed his older daughter's forehead.

"I made the green beans." Darrell grinned as he made his way closer to Wendell. "Alicia said they're the best ever."

Alexandria giggled. "She snuck a taste." She looked at Alicia. "Right?"

"I did." Alicia ran her hand along Alexandria's hair. Then she faced Wendell. "We've had the best time."

Wendell laughed. "Let's just say this is the highlight of my whole week."

"That's what we thought." Darrell pulled Wendell toward the food. "Now can we pray? I'm starving!"

Wendell put his arm around Alicia as they gathered in a circle near the table. Their eyes met and held. They would talk later.

But for now he didn't need words to tell her how grateful he was for her presence, that she was here tonight. Not just because of dinner. But because spending time with his kids meant they had something else to think about beside the trial.

They had a reason to smile and laugh and serve. All antidotes to fear and anxiety — not just for the kids, but for him.

Jordy reached out and took hold of his sisters' hands, one on each side of him. "Can I pray tonight?"

Again Wendell was beyond touched. How could he feel anything but hope and joy with a family like this? He thought again of the passionate way Jordy had defended his interest in Cami the other night. How God was so very real to the boy. Wendell smiled at him. "Yes, Son. Please."

Wendell took hold of Alicia's hand on one side and Darrell's on the other. When the circle was complete, Jordy began. "Father, You are always with us. Here and tomorrow and through whatever this week brings. We have already won because of You, and for that we thank You." He hesitated. "Thank You for this food, and thank You for the best dad any kids ever had. Thanks for Alicia, too." A smile filled his voice. "It's good to have her back. In Jesus' name, amen."

They sat at the table and the next hour was a celebration of laughter and conversation. Each of the kids shared something from their day. Jordy got an A on a big paper in English. Leah received a letter from her band instructor promising to recommend her for scholarships when the time came for college. Alexandria decided to audition for the lead in her club's upcoming performance of *Little Women,* and Darrell made the basketball team.

"What about you?" Alicia smiled at him from across the table. She sat between the girls, the way she had done before their breakup. Everything about the dinner felt like something from a dream.

"Me?" Wendell thought about his day, the somber warning from Luke Baxter, the way his students asked him nervous questions at their club meeting this afternoon. He took a deep breath, grinned at Alicia and then each of his children. "Today was the best day ever because the world's greatest kids made me dinner!"

Alexandria bounced in her seat. "Don't forget the world's greatest girlfriend!"

Wendell shared a quick glance with Alicia before he looked in Leah's direction. He smiled. "Yes, her, too." He nodded toward

Alicia. "Thank you for pulling it all together."

After dinner, Wendell worked with Darrell on his science homework and Alicia helped Leah memorize her history flash cards. Through the next few hours Wendell would catch himself watching Alicia, imagining that tonight wasn't merely her kindhearted way of helping a friend in need.

But that they might stay like this forever.

The kids felt the same way, Wendell could sense it. Each of them loved Alicia — the girls, especially. Being a single father was something Wendell worked his hardest at. But nothing could replace the role of a mother figure in the lives of his girls.

Tonight was proof.

When her homework was finished, Leah asked Alicia to come to the girls' room and check out a new lip gloss she'd gotten for her band performance. Not to be outdone, Alexandria clutched Alicia's hand as the three of them walked upstairs. "I have a new lip gloss too. It's clear, but it's really pretty. I'll show you."

Every moment, every bit of homework help and conversation filled Wendell's heart like nothing in months had. Not until the kids were upstairs getting ready for bed did Alicia join him in the living room. The two of them sat together on the sofa and Wendell played Matthew West's newest album in the background.

"What a night." Alicia's eyes sparkled. "Just like the kids and I planned."

Wendell searched her face. He wanted to remember everything about this night. "Thank you . . . it was amazing. I still can't believe it."

For a while they sat like that, a few feet between them, their eyes locked on each other. Alicia spoke first. "Do you feel it?"

"Chemistry?" Wendell's heart was pounding.

"Yes." Her eyes held the hint of a smile. "You need that."

"Definitely." Wendell didn't blink, didn't look away. He wanted to kiss her, but this wasn't the time. "You said you'd be my friend." His voice grew quieter. His heart to hers. "This . . . feels like more."

Alicia nodded, but she didn't look away. "There have been lots of reasons why you and I should only be friends, Wendell." She pressed her slim shoulder into the back of the sofa. "But now . . ."

The conversation was easy, like a slow dance. "But now . . . ?"

"I don't know if I can be 'just friends.'" Her expression was serious.

"What about your fear?" He didn't want to bring it up, but the last thing he needed was for Alicia to relapse. "Are you sure?"

"Ah, yes. My fear." Alicia stared at her hands. "I'll be honest. Some days it tries to come back." She lifted her eyes to his. Whatever she was about to tell him, she had clearly come prepared to say it. "At the courthouse that day, I was too afraid to go inside. That's why I met you at your car."

"Mmm." Again he wanted to take her in his arms, tell her she had nothing to be afraid of. Not now, not ever. Instead he stayed focused on her words. "I wondered." He smiled. "I mean, I was glad to see you. But the parking lot is a strange place to meet."

Sorrow filled her eyes. "I know. Ridiculous." She took a deep breath and sat a little straighter. "Anyway . . . I told you I've been reading the Bible." She uttered a slight laugh. "A lot, actually."

"Good." He chuckled.

The expression in her eyes grew deeper. "I may always battle anxiety, but with Jesus . . . and you, Wendell . . . I will battle it. And I will win." She shrugged, and as she did, she looked young and hopeful. The way she'd looked when Wendell first met her. Before Jack Renton. A smile lifted her lips. "What could possibly make me afraid?"

Wendell reached out and put his hand on her shoulder. "Alicia . . . I've prayed for this." He let himself get lost in her gaze. "If you only knew how often."

"I'm not afraid anymore, Wendell. Not at all." Tears shone in her eyes. "Whatever happens this week, I'm here." She paused. "If you'll still have me."

She wasn't saying she was ready for a relationship. But this was a step Wendell hadn't expected. "By my side, Alicia. That's where I want you. Please."

She checked the time on her phone. "I have to get home. The staff at Jackson has an early meeting in the morning. But even when I'm not at court tomorrow, I'll be here." She touched the spot over his heart. "Every step of the way this week."

Wendell stood and helped Alicia to her feet. As he did, he took her in his arms. The feeling of her body against his was as natural as his own heartbeat. "I'll picture you. Cheering me on."

Alicia stepped back and met his eyes. "Praying for you."

Wendell raised his brow.

"And for the kids at Hamilton."

"Them, too."

Alicia looked up the stairs. "And for those

precious babies of yours."

He had no words. Again he pulled her into his arms and held her until he had two choices. Kiss her or let her go. He stepped away. "I'll remember tonight forever." He smiled at her. "I mean it."

"Me, too." She leaned close and kissed his cheek. "Can I pray for you? Before I leave?"

Wendell's heart felt light as a feather. The pressure and anxiety from earlier, completely gone. "Yes. Please."

And so Alicia Harris — the woman who had been too afraid to stand by Wendell in any matter regarding faith — prayed for him. That God would go before him into the courtroom tomorrow and that the jury would hear Wendell's heart. That victory would happen for Wendell and Hamilton High and the students who desperately needed the Bible study club.

"And I thank You for a strong, godly man like Wendell Quinn." Alicia's voice broke. "A man who believes the words of Alexander Hamilton. That you have to stand for something, or you'll fall for anything." She hesitated. "Thank You, God, that I'm not falling anymore. Help us to stand together this week and trust You. For whatever's ahead. In Jesus' name, amen."

Wendell smiled. "Well," he stepped back

and looked deep into her eyes, "your Bible reading is paying off."

She gave him the sweetest look. "Isn't that what it says in Scripture? The Word of God is alive and active. It changes you."

He chuckled. "Indeed." They walked together through the front door and out to her car, where he hugged her goodbye. He wanted to hold on, wanted the moment to linger. But he drew back quickly, so he wouldn't kiss her. Tonight was about possibilities.

Possibilities that filled Wendell's heart with happiness. Nothing more. Not yet.

Alicia was part of his life again. She wasn't afraid. She believed in God with a faith that took his breath. Yes, tonight was about the best kind of possibilities.

And with God on his side, tomorrow would be, too.

Because with God, all things were possible.

Alicia didn't stop smiling the whole ride home. She couldn't guarantee things were headed toward a relationship with Wendell. But after tonight it sure felt that way. She replayed every moment, the way it felt to be surrounded by Wendell's children while they cooked him dinner, and how her heart leapt when they circled up and prayed before eating.

Chatting over dinner and doing dishes together, helping the kids with homework. All of it made Alicia feel like she'd come home. Like there with Wendell and his family was just where she belonged.

Her heart was so full from the joy of it all, Alicia didn't notice the car trailing her until she was almost to her condo. Years of dating Jack had taught her never to drive all the way home with a strange car behind her.

Tonight was no different.

She picked up her cell phone from the passenger seat and thought about calling Wendell. But first she needed to make sure she was actually being followed. Jack was out of her life now, so maybe she was only imagining it.

Alicia turned right at the next street and waited. The car behind her turned right, too. Her heart began to beat faster. Who would do this? How come she didn't notice sooner? Had the person been following her ever since Wendell's house? *God . . . help me here. What's happening?*

At the end of the street, Alicia made a left on a busier road. The main thoroughfare to the freeway. Sure enough, the car behind her did the same thing. She swallowed hard.

Should she call Wendell or 911? She was so busy glancing in her rearview mirror she almost rear-ended the car in front of her.

Don't be afraid, Alicia. Whoever it is, they can't hurt you. Then she remembered the plan she'd had before. When Jack would sometimes get out of hand. Drive to the nearest police station. Alicia made a right at the next intersection and watched her mirror. The car behind her turned right, also.

Which meant she had just one option. She stepped on the gas and drove straight for the police station, a few blocks away. As soon as she turned left into the parking lot, the car behind her sped off. It was dark that night, not much of a moon and no bright lights in front of the building.

But Alicia was almost sure she recognized the car. It looked like something Jack Renton had driven back when they were dating.

A shiver of fear splashed icy cold through Alicia's veins. She pulled into a parking spot and sat in the car trembling. No need to go in if the car wasn't there, right? Nothing to report. She waited five minutes, until she was sure the car following her was gone.

Then she drove to the other side of the parking lot and exited by way of another street. *Don't be afraid, Alicia. Don't be afraid.*

She went out of her way to take the longest possible route home, until she was certain no one was tailing her.

God, please help me not to be afraid. She turned onto her street. From a good distance she could see there was no car in front of her house. No one waiting for her.

I am with you, My child. You are not alone.

Yes. Alicia felt herself relax. That was truth. God was with her now and always. She pulled into her garage and clicked the remote to shut the heavy door before getting out of her car. No need to call Wendell or the police or anyone else. God was with her.

The whole thing was probably nothing more than her imagination.

20

Other than the usual armed guards, Luke Baxter was the first person in the courtroom that day. The judge had given permission for the media to be present, and already network vans and trucks were setting up outside, getting their cameras and reporters ready for the start of the trial.

Luke was looking through his notes, going over his opening statement when the courtroom door opened. He glanced that way and saw the one person he'd truly hoped would be here today. The man who had been there for him ever since Luke was a little boy.

His father, John Baxter.

"Son." His dad smiled and came closer. "I thought you could use a little support."

"Dad." Luke went to him and the two hugged. "You have no idea."

"I can't do much." His father put his hands on Luke's shoulders and looked into his eyes. "But I'll be sitting in that back corner praying." He smiled. "I won't stop."

Luke was touched to his core. "I can't believe you drove all this way."

"One of my kids needs me, I'm there." John winked at him. "That's the Baxter way."

"Yes, it is." Luke motioned to the chair beside him. "Sit for a minute. We have time."

The two faced each other and his dad looked at the stack of notes in front of Luke. "So . . . how are you going to win this thing?"

They hadn't talked much about it since that first day, when Luke got the call that Wendell Quinn needed him. This would be good, explaining things to his father. Just the practice run-through Luke needed.

Luke opened the folder of notes in front of him. "Well . . . religious freedom cases are all about precedent. As you know." He turned to the first page, the one that detailed his opening statement. "In this case precedent doesn't work in our favor. So things will be a little unconventional."

"I like it." His dad smiled, even though his eyes remained serious, engaged. "The Baxters have always been a little unconventional."

"True." Luke laughed. Already he felt better about the drama ahead. Thirty minutes later, after he'd gone through his strategy for the day, Luke was more ready than ever. All because his dad loved him that much.

Cameramen were arriving, setting up and creating a buzz around them. Luke and his dad stood and hugged before his dad took his place in the back corner of the court-room. Luke watched him go. His father looked great for his age. Fit and tanned, proof of the miles of walks he and Elaine took every day. His dad turned and held his hands together, raising them up a bit. Then he mouthed the words Luke knew he could count on. "I'll be praying."

An hour later the courtroom was packed. Wendell was seated next to Luke, and across the aisle Eli Landsford sat beside Andy Nelson. The man looked terrible. Gray complexion, his hair long and stringy, hang-ing in his face. Back stooped. Whatever private battle he'd been going through, Andy was losing.

Two minutes before the trial was set to begin, Luke heard the courtroom door open again. Wendell turned and smiled, and Luke followed his gaze. A pretty black woman entered the courtroom. Whatever her rela-tionship with Wendell, Luke was certain about this much: Wendell was thrilled to see her. She took one of the last seats and Judge Wells used her gavel to bring the courtroom to order.

Landsford gave his opening statement first, since he represented the plaintiff. He was dressed like a catalog model or a mafia pit boss. Luke saw him more as the latter. Pin-striped suit, shiny leather shoes, hair neatly styled. Just enough facial shadow to give off a dashing air as he strutted in front of the jury.

"This is a First Amendment case. Open and shut, really. Because the truth is, religious freedom cases are not difficult in today's political landscape." He smiled at the jurors like he was the best friend they never knew they had. "Certainly you all know that. And for that reason I apologize for wasting your time."

Luke was on the edge of his seat. If Landsford pushed too far he would object. Luke didn't want the jury's first impression of him to be antagonistic. But if that was what it took, so be it. He would only let his opponent go so far before something would have to be done.

Landsford stopped pacing and smiled again. "What you absolutely must not do is let your emotions get the better of you in this case." He looked over his shoulder at

Wendell Quinn, then back to the jury. "Principal Quinn is a good man. A man intent on helping students, whatever that looks like."

Great, Luke thought. *He's using my exact words.*

"But you must not form an emotional connection with the matter at hand. The Constitution of the United States is not an emotional text, and neither is the First Amendment. This is a black-and-white document intent on protecting the freedoms allotted to each and every citizen." He smiled. "So let's not trivialize it by letting our sentiments rule our decisions. There's too much at stake for that."

The jury was hanging on every word. They might as well have been applauding Landsford. They were that caught up in what he was saying, that much in agreement. Luke could tell by the looks on their faces.

Landsford's remarks took only a few minutes. He told them the trial shouldn't take long. Open and shut. Find Wendell guilty. Close down the ridiculous after-school Bible study and they could all get on with more important matters.

Before he sat down, Landsford flashed his best smile at each of the jurors. "Thank you for your time." He glanced at the clock on the wall. "I promise not to take up too much of it. For the sake of all of us."

Luke gave a quick glance to his father as he stood. His dad didn't say anything, didn't flash any signals. He didn't have to. His eyes said it all. He believed in Luke, and no one else in all the world could handle what was ahead the way Luke could. The look gave him strength.

With a greater determination than before, Luke faced the jury and stepped forward. "My name is Luke Baxter. Attorney for Wendell Quinn."

He spoke deliberately, willing his words to come unrushed. Luke motioned to Landsford. "My esteemed colleague has already thanked you for your time. But let me reiterate that." He looked at each of them, individually. "Your involvement in this case is priceless." He paused. "Look at each other, at the people on either side of you."

The jurors did as he asked.

"You are the reason we live in a free country. Justice looks like the group of you. People who love America. People this court believes in." Luke pointed to the judge. "Long before you were chosen as jurors, Judge Wells could've decided this case. That was within her right." He looked at Landsford. "If this case was as easy as Mr. Landsford makes it seem, then you wouldn't be here." He smiled. "The simple truth is we need you."

Luke watched the jurors relax a little. A few of them leaned back in their seats. They were important. They were needed. Luke felt a surge of hope. *So far, so good.* "Mr. Landsford told you not to make an emotional decision in this case. I would agree with him. There is nothing emotional or flighty about defending the U.S. Constitution. About defending the First Amendment." He took a step closer and dropped his voice a notch. "This is one of the most serious things you will ever do. Your decision in this trial will become part of history. A way to defend the groundwork of the founding fathers of this country . . . or a way to tear it down."

In the corner of his eye he saw Landsford start to stand to object. But whatever protest was on the tip of his tongue, he must've changed his mind because he sat back down. Luke smiled at the jury. "So, thank you. Truly."

He went on to explain that his client, the defendant in this case, was the much-loved principal at Hamilton High. "You might not be familiar with Hamilton High." Luke needed this part to make an impact on the jury. "Hamilton is a school where things were so bad, the district considered shutting the place down. Shuttling kids across town by bus to avoid the carnage happening year in and year out."

Luke went on to explain exactly how bad things were. In a few sentences he told the jurors about the murder rate and the gang violence and the low test scores. How Wendell Quinn did what he could. He brought in counselors and created Individualized Education Programs for the most at-risk students. And he tried new curriculum and kindness initiatives.

"But nothing worked." Luke was pushing his luck here. The history of failed efforts at Hamilton was not truly part of the scope of the case. Religious freedom cases were typically cut and dried. No mention of motive was generally allowed.

But Landsford didn't object, so Luke continued. "You can understand how Principal Quinn had reached the end of his options. How he was at a loss when it came to helping his students.

"And so Wendell Quinn started a voluntary program called Raise the Bar." Luke smiled at the jurors again. "What a great idea, right? Take these students who were failing at every level and raise the bar.

Something you or I might do to help high school kids."

A few of the jurors nodded.

"Only instead of kind words or special academic considerations, the club involved reading the Bible and praying." Luke didn't want to spend much time on the fact. This was Wendell's alleged crime, after all. "And wouldn't you know it . . . Principal Quinn's program worked." Luke walked back to his table. "I have a folder here with all the ways the Raise the Bar club has helped the students at Hamilton High." He opened the folder. "For instance —"

"Objection." Landsford was on his feet. His smile remained, but his tone was ice cold. "Your Honor, Mr. Baxter knows better than to present evidence during his opening statement. We all have things to do, places to be. Mr. Baxter is merely dragging out the inevitable."

Judge Wells clearly agreed. She cast Luke a look of disdain. "Sustained. Wrap it up, Mr. Baxter."

Luke was fine with the reprimand. It was enough that the jury had seen the presentation folder, that they were aware facts supported the very real truth: Hamilton High was a better place because of the Bible study program. He nodded at the judge. "Thank you, Your Honor."

Luke went on to talk about the establishment clause. He didn't dwell on the details. Didn't want to give the jury a reason to lose the emotion of his opening statement. Details would come later. Rather he summed it up by reminding the jury that the founding fathers never meant to have freedom *from* religion. But freedom *of* religion. Freedom to practice religion where it was so desired.

The way it was at Hamilton High.

Finally Luke turned again to the jury. "I have to tell you something, friends. Mr. Landsford is wrong about one thing. This trial won't be quick." Luke paused. "The truth is this trial might take more than a few days of your time." Luke allowed a sense of indignation in his tone. A passion that hadn't been there before. "Men and women have fought and died for the privilege we enjoy today, the privilege of meeting in this courtroom and deciding the fate of a man like Principal Quinn.

"Today, here in this courthouse, *you,* my friends, are the heroes. Not because you stormed a beach or were deployed to the Middle East. But because you gave up your very valuable time in the quest for freedom." Luke looked each of the jurors in the eyes once more. A few of them were nodding along. "Thank you for that. Thank you."

Luke took his seat and waited. Never had he expected his opening statement to be so well received. His heart was beating out of his chest, but he couldn't show it.

Landsford rose and called his first witness. Head of the Indianapolis Public Schools board, James Black. Again Landsford seemed intent on rushing through his questions. His attitude screamed indifference. As if he were merely going through the motions so he could get his friends, the jurors, home as soon as possible.

"Mr. Black, do you have a school policy prohibiting teachers or administrators from leading after-school Bible study programs?" Landsford glanced at the jury, as if the answer were painfully obvious.

But this time the answer seemed anything but obvious to James Black. The man hesitated and squirmed in his seat on the witness stand. He shot a quick look at Wendell Quinn and then back at Landsford. "No, sir. We . . . uh, we don't have anything specifically written out."

Landsford was as good an actor as any lawyer, but even he couldn't hide his surprise. He checked the notes on his desk, clearly scrambling for a way to rebound. He tried again. "Okay, so you have nothing in writing, but would you say it's against the intentions of the school board members for a teacher or administrator to lead an after-school Bible study group?"

Luke was on his feet. "Objection, Your Honor. Innuendo." Luke kept his tone pleasant. He gave a slight nod toward the judge. "Mr. Landsford couldn't possibly speak for every single school board member."

Luke could tell Judge Wells didn't like the way this was going, but it seemed she had no choice here. The way Landsford had worded his question, Luke was well within his right to object. Landsford had set himself up to fail.

The judge cleared her throat. "Sustained." She cast a disapproving look at Luke's opponent. "The prosecution will limit questions to the scope of the witness's knowledge."

Luke sat down. Again Landsford looked horrified. He didn't address the judge. Instead he faced the witness once more. "Would you consider it a violation of duties for a teacher or administrator to lead an after-school Bible study on campus at one of your schools?"

"Would I consider it a violation?" James

Black squinted, as if he was more confused now than before. "Yes. But we go by the book at our district. And there is no explicit law on the books prohibiting such an action by anyone on our staff."

"Are you disappointed that Mr. Quinn took such an action?" Landsford clearly had no choice but to change the direction of the questioning. He could've mentioned precedent cases here, asking James Black if he was familiar with a whole list of cases.

But he didn't. Luke could only silently thank God for the fact.

Black looked at Wendell. "Yes. I'm very disappointed. None of us wanted this media circus."

Landsford looked satisfied. "No further questions."

It was Luke's turn. His opponent had unwittingly given him a gift. By the nervous look on Landsford's face, the man clearly knew what was coming. Luke stood in front of the witness and forced himself to feel relaxed. "You told this court there is no policy prohibiting one of your teachers or administrators from leading an after-school Bible study, is that right?"

"There will be after this."

"Stick to the question, please, Mr. Black. Is there such a rule or not?"

"No." Black breathed in sharp through his nose. "The Indianapolis Public Schools district has no such rule."

"Very well." Luke looked at the jury for a moment, letting the reality sink in. Then he turned to the witness once more. "Are you aware, Mr. Black, that after one year of the Raise the Bar club, the homicide rate at Hamilton High is down?"

Black's face screamed disdain for the question. "Yes, I'm aware of that."

"And are you aware that after a year of this club's meeting every week, test scores for Hamilton High students are at an all-time high?"

Landsford slammed his hand on the table in front of him. He jerked his chair back and stood. "Objection. Mr. Baxter must limit his questions to the scope of the direct testimony."

Luke didn't give the judge a chance to respond. "That's what I'm doing, Your Honor." He looked at the court reporter. "If the court could please repeat the witness's testimony beginning with Mr. Landsford's question that reads 'Are you disappointed that Mr. Quinn took such an action?' "

Judge Wells sighed. "Very well. Go ahead. Read the testimony."

The court reporter did as she was asked. She read Landsford's question again and then the answer from James Black, stating that yes, he was very disappointed. Luke turned to the judge. "When Counsel suggested that the witness had a reason to be disappointed, it allowed the introduction of information that might not make him disappointed." Luke paused. "What's brought up in the direct is permissible in the cross. As you know, Your Honor."

She raised her eyebrows halfway up her forehead. "Be careful, Mr. Baxter. You're walking a thin line here."

Actually, Luke was working within the law. But he had won this point, so he smiled. "Yes, ma'am."

Luke waited until Landsford returned to his seat. Then he shifted his attention to the witness once more. He asked James Black again if he was aware of the increased test scores. And if he was also aware of the improved attendance records at Hamilton High, the decreased gang activity and the reduction in teen pregnancies. To each of these questions, Black responded that yes, he was aware.

"And are you disappointed in these improvements, Mr. Black?" Luke refused to allow even a hint of sarcasm in his tone.

"Of course I'm not disappointed." The witness looked at Wendell and his expression eased a little. "I'm very happy with the changes at Hamilton."

Luke had to be very careful with his next question. "And would you agree that the time frame for these positive changes at Hamilton High coincides with the existence of the Raise the Bar Bible study club?"

There was only one way for Black to answer. This wasn't his opinion now, it was fact. "Yes." He gave a slow nod. "The dates do coincide."

Another small victory.

Black left the stand and as the morning wore on, the plaintiff called several other witnesses. Among them was a police officer — Aspyn Jones — who had been at the scene when Dwayne Brown was shot and killed.

There was something ethereal about her, something Luke couldn't quite pinpoint. But he was sure of one thing. The woman was a Christian. Her eyes, her demeanor, the kindness in her voice. Her faith was as clear as the name on her badge.

Again Landsford let his arrogance get the best of him. Once Aspyn was on the stand, Landsford established her name and position, and the fact that she had tended to

Dwayne in his final minutes.

Then Landsford looked at the jury. "The defendant in this case, Mr. Quinn, likes to say that his Bible study group has changed lives, that the students are better off because of it. If that's true" — he turned to Aspyn — "then maybe you could tell us whether Dwayne Brown was a member of the Raise the Bar club?"

"Yes, as far as I know he was in the Bible study club." Aspyn kept her calm.

Luke could've objected, since knowledge of attendance at the Bible study was beyond Aspyn's scope. But he remained quiet. Again Landsford was giving him an opportunity. One Luke was certain to use later.

"And was Dwayne at a gang fight at the time of his death?" Landsford sneered at Wendell Quinn. His look said the principal was a fool if he thought some Bible study could ever change a student like Dwayne.

Aspyn agreed that yes, Dwayne had been killed in a gang fight.

It was Luke's turn. The policewoman wouldn't know the answer to his next questions, but Luke had the right to ask. They were things Luke had only found out when he read Cami's report. "Did you know that Dwayne was baptized a few weeks before he was killed in the gang fight? Or that he had plans to live a life for God? That the Raise the Bar club had changed his mind-set on a number of issues?"

Aspyn hesitated. Then with the sweetest, clearest eyes she looked straight at Luke. "Yes, I knew all of that."

Luke had to work to hide his surprise. The woman might as well have been an angel. Luke took a step closer to the witness stand. "How did you know that?"

"I spoke with Dwayne before his death." Aspyn nodded slowly. "I was aware of his baptism. His time at that gang fight was a bad decision. Not something that reflected his newfound character."

Luke's heart was racing. "And so you think the Raise the Bar club actually was beneficial for Dwayne?"

"Oh, definitely." Aspyn smiled. "He was a different person because of the club." She paused. "He's in heaven today because of it."

There was no way of understanding how this officer could know these things. Unless she really was an angel. But it didn't matter. Her testimony was stunning, and from the corner of his eye Luke could see the jury taking in every word.

For the most part, the first day was going better than Luke could've imagined. Answered prayers, for sure.

Cami Nelson was called to the stand last. She was asked by her father's attorney to state how very much she'd been against Christianity prior to attending the Raise the Bar club.

"You were against the idea of the Raise the Bar club when it first started, is that right, Ms. Nelson?" Landsford paced in front of the witness stand, never looking at her.

"I was. Yes, sir." She sat a little straighter, clearly trying to stay strong.

"And who swayed you into thinking the club was a good thing?" He stopped and stared at her. As if this was the point where he would catch her in some great admission.

Instead, Cami shook her head. "No one. Kids make up their own minds." She hesitated. "God was the One who changed my mind."

Several whispers came from across the courtroom. Judge Wells slammed her gavel on her desk. "Order."

The whispers died off. But the point was clear. Landsford had inadvertently led Cami to score points for Luke's side. He might as well have grabbed a gun and shot himself in the foot.

The whole time she talked, Cami's father stared at his hands, his shoulders shaking. Again, Luke wondered what was going on inside the man. He looked tortured. Like he hated himself for putting his daughter through such a thing.

When it was his turn, Luke asked her questions about her newfound faith and did his best to undo any damage done by Landsford. Still, in the end, Cami's testimony remained a victory for the defense.

In the battle for clarity on the First Amendment, the conversion of students once hostile to Christianity was not seen as a positive, it was seen as coercion.

Luke watched Wendell's son Jordy comfort the girl once she was off the witness stand. She couldn't know how damaging her testimony had been. How it had scored points for the prosecution. None of this was her fault.

The trial was adjourned until the following morning, and Luke's father was at his side first. "You've got this, Son. You were brilliant." His dad hugged him. "I'll be back tomorrow."

The support of family meant everything to Luke. He grinned at the man, always an older version of himself. "Love you, Dad."

"Love you, too."

When his father was gone, Luke turned and shook Wendell's hand. The principal searched Luke's face for some kind of assessment. "How did it go?"

"Not terrible. I have some ideas for later this week."

"Good." Wendell smiled, ever the optimist. "God's going to use you, Luke Baxter."

The pretty black woman from the spectator section joined Wendell and slipped her arm around his waist. She introduced herself to Luke. Alicia Harris. "I wasn't going to come today." She looked at Wendell and back at Luke. "But I had to be here. I had to see for myself. You know why?"

"No, ma'am." Luke liked her. She had spunk.

"Because." Alicia smiled. "You're the one who will win this case . . . because you're not up there by yourself." She looked at Wendell and then back at Luke. "The Lord is with you."

While they were talking, Andy Nelson slithered from his seat toward the door and out of the courtroom. There was no one at his side, no one to comfort him. No matter how things turned out, Luke hoped he might get the chance to talk to the man. Pray with him, even.

Because when it was all said and done,

Andy Nelson still needed his daughter.

And Cami still needed her father.

Andy still couldn't believe he was alive. When he woke up the morning after taking the pills, his body shaking, he'd assumed he was dead. It had taken only a few minutes to realize he was in neither heaven nor hell.

He was in his bedroom.

Still alive. Still facing a trial he didn't want. Even now, three days later, his head throbbed and his body ached. He felt like a zombie as he sat through the testimonies. His only relief was when the judge adjourned for the day.

He pushed his way down the hallway and out the courthouse doors. As he did he bumped into a man who looked familiar. The guy had a rich-looking coat and designer pants and shoes.

Andy could be wrong, but the guy seemed to be fumbling with his belt. Almost as if he were hiding a gun. Or maybe Andy was just paranoid. Either way, when the guy spotted Andy, he brushed his hands together and uttered a strange-sounding laugh. "Excuse me."

"Yeah." Andy looked at the man for a long moment. Where had he seen him before? On TV maybe . . . he ran some citywide charity. Yes, that was it. Last night. The guy had been on the news. Jack something.

So why was he armed and heading toward the courthouse?

Probably Andy's imagination. His mind wasn't exactly thinking clearly. He dismissed the thought and moved past the man into the parking lot. Andy's body ached and his heart was broken in half. There were still moments when he wished he would've died, but less so after seeing Cami today.

His daughter had been brave and poised. Answering questions that caused her pain. All while showing great confidence for her age. Andy couldn't help but feel proud of her.

She might hate him for now, but maybe it wasn't too late to change that. Andy had an idea, something that had hit him halfway through her excruciating testimony. He had no way of knowing whether it would work or how it might change things, but it was something he could do.

Andy got in his car and headed to the only place that could help him.

The tattoo parlor.

21

Wendell did his best to stay positive as the second day of the trial dragged out — just the way Luke had promised. Every few witnesses, Wendell's attorney thanked the jurors. Assured them that their time was not being wasted.

The quest for freedom was worth every minute.

No question Luke's demeanor was far more enjoyable than his opponent's. The jury liked Luke Baxter better. Wendell could tell. But even that didn't mean they'd get a victory.

Earlier that day the court had heard from parents who were furious with Wendell's decision to host an after-school Bible study. Voluntary or not. These were witnesses for the plaintiff; of course they were mad. Even still, Wendell was constantly whispering to Luke, telling him that the parents on the stand no longer had students at Hamilton, or had never raised a complaint before.

It didn't matter, according to Luke.

Parents had a right to send their children to a public school without threat that their students would be proselytized to by a school official. Period. Never mind that the jury seemed to like Luke and maybe they even liked Wendell. A few of them had taken to smiling at him at the end of the day, or so it seemed that way.

The only thing that mattered, Luke told him, was the interpretation of the establishment clause. No school official could act in a way that would establish a religion at a public school. And based on the comments by the parents Andy Nelson's attorney had scrounged up, Wendell was all but sunk.

Even so, there was good news. Luke was yet to call his witnesses. Something that would happen when Landsford was finished. But for now Wendell could only wait.

Finally, Landsford called Wendell to the witness stand. His last witness, he told the court.

Wendell had known this moment was coming. He had prayed about it and given it to God. Alicia was there in the courtroom again, and she was praying, too. A few times recently she'd told him she thought someone was following her home. But nothing had come of it.

Wendell smiled. No matter how fear tried to creep back into her life, Alicia was here. Wendell loved her for that. She sat in the back of the room near Luke Baxter's father. Members of the media were still in full force, but the spectators had dwindled. Wendell noticed the open rows of seats as he moved to the witness stand.

His heart pounded, but he felt his courage surge. Still, no matter how ready he was for his chance to testify, Wendell was not prepared for what happened next. The back doors of the courtroom opened and in came Jordy and Cami, followed by a stream of Hamilton High students.

Tears stung the corners of Wendell's eyes as he settled into his seat on the stand and watched the scene play out. The students filled the empty rows and then the back of the courtroom and the sides until there wasn't a spot left.

Judge Wells rapped her gavel. "Order. Order in the court."

The students weren't being loud. They weren't saying a word. Just trying to get seated.

"What's happening here?" Judge Wells stood and looked to one of the bailiffs. "Who are these people?"

"Students." The bailiff looked guilty. "We got word earlier that they were coming. These are Principal Quinn's students. Kids from Hamilton High."

The jurors were straining now, looking toward the door to see how many teens were still in the hallway. Wendell glanced at Luke. His attorney was stifling a grin. At the back of the courtroom, Alicia's smile filled her face. Luke's father, too.

Judge Wells huffed. "How many students are here?"

Again the bailiff looked embarrassed. "Nearly eighty."

"What?" Judge Wells waved her hand. "That's impossible. They won't fit."

Landsford was on his feet, too. But there was nothing any of them could do. The students kept filing in.

Wendell smiled at the group of them packed into every available space in the room. He couldn't have been more proud of their diligence and effort. The way they had come here to support him.

Never mind that all eighty students couldn't get a seat in the courtroom. They didn't need one. Their presence had already been felt by the judge, the spectators and yes, the jury.

Judge Wells was still on her feet. "Keep

them outside," she yelled to a bailiff standing near the back door. "No more in the courtroom. They can stay in the hall."

Finally the commotion settled down. The students in the room linked arms and only then did Wendell realize what they were wearing. Each of them had a blue shirt with white lettering that read HAMILTON HIGH — RAISE THE BAR.

They might not get a chance to testify, but their message was clear. The club was theirs. They didn't want anyone to take it away. Wendell blinked back tears and he saw a few jurors do the same.

"Order!" Judge Wells sat down. She was clearly furious over the loss of control. "All right, then. Mr. Landsford, proceed."

The prosecuting attorney looked cornered. He dusted off his suit jacket and shrugged in the direction of the jury. Then he turned to Wendell. "Did you brainwash all of these students to join your Christian faith, Mr. Quinn?"

"Objection." Luke couldn't stand fast enough. "Antagonistic." Luke seemed hurt by Landsford's harsh wording. Wendell assumed Luke's reaction was one way to counter the severity of the question.

"Sustained." Judge Wells looked at Landsford.

Luke sat down. He must've known that Landsford was showboating. A desperate move, for sure. Landsford's question went against previous testimony by James Black. It was the attorney's attempt to impact the jury. And it was wrong.

The judge leaned forward, definitely bothered. "Stick to direct questions, Counsel."

"Yes, Your Honor." He glared at Wendell. "Did you ask these students to come today?"

"No, sir." Wendell smiled at the students. "It was a surprise."

The attorney didn't seem to like that answer. He checked his notes and changed the direction of his questioning. "Did you know it was unconstitutional to start a Bible study at Hamilton High?"

It was the first in a long list of questions meant to get at Wendell's motive. For every question, Wendell answered truthfully. Starting the Raise the Bar club was the only way he knew to do his job.

"And violating the Constitution was the only way you could think to do your job?"

Wendell didn't blink. "My research tells me I did not violate the Constitution. Again, I was just trying to do the job I agreed to do."

"I see." Landsford nodded, his tone sarcastic. "And your job was to teach students the Christian faith?" The lawyer's tone mocked Wendell.

Luke stayed in his seat, so Wendell responded. This was his chance. The one he'd been waiting for. The attorney had asked, so Wendell took a quick breath. "No, sir. My job was to establish a schoolwide vision of commitment to high standards and ensure the success of all students."

The definition seemed to take Landsford by surprise. "That sounds memorized. Is it memorized, Mr. Quinn?"

"Yes, sir. It's the job duties I agreed to as spelled out in my contract with Hamilton High." Wendell looked at Jordy and his classmates. "And the students are better for it. You can see for yourself. They're here. They will tell you themselves their lives have improved. Their grades are better. They are in class more regularly. Their lives are changed."

Wendell could feel the presence of God beside him, within him.

Landsford looked exasperated, like he couldn't be bothered putting each kid on the witness stand. It would take too much time, time he'd promised the jurors he wouldn't waste. Wendell could feel the tide turning.

Landsford stumbled through a few more questions. "Surely as an educator you can see the good that comes with separation of church and state, Mr. Quinn." The attorney lost some of his sarcasm and found a modicum of the charm he'd had at the beginning of the trial. "You do see that, right?"

"Well, yes." Wendell nodded. "If I forced religion on my students, it wouldn't be their own. It wouldn't be real." He smiled, polite to the core. "The reason you see change in the students at Hamilton High is because no one forced them. They chose Christianity all on their own."

Landsford looked like he was deflating. His shoulders sank and he stared at Wendell. Finally he shook his head and handed Wendell off to Luke Baxter. Luke was smiling before he stood up.

He had a copy of Wendell's contract and once Wendell established that the document was indeed his employment contract, Luke read the definition of Wendell's job duties once more. Straight from the document. Luke's questions moved to Wendell's discouragement when things were in a dire state at Hamilton High, and then to the research Wendell had done that summer.

"I needed to find a way to do my job,"

Wendell said. "There was nothing in our district's policy prohibiting me from starting a voluntary Bible study. So I decided to give it a try."

The next set of questions dealt with the success of the program. Overall, Wendell was sure his testimony couldn't have gone better if he'd put the students, themselves, on the stand. And the fact that eighty of them had arrived just before he took his testimony was more than Wendell could take in.

When he returned to his seat, he couldn't stop the tears. Wendell wiped at them and tried to find his composure once more. Before court was adjourned for the day, Landsford rested his case. Tomorrow Luke would have his chance.

"I have a surprise for everyone." Luke patted Wendell on the shoulder. "Today was perfect, Wendell. Absolutely perfect."

"Only God could've worked things out the way they went today."

"I agree." Luke chuckled. "I have a feeling we'll say the same thing tomorrow."

Cami and Jordy and dozens of students were lined up behind the railing waiting to talk to Wendell. Alicia was waiting, too. But before Wendell could thank Luke again and move on, Andy Nelson approached the two of them.

By then, Landsford was gone. He had packed up his things and exited the courtroom without talking to the media. Andy, though, had remained at the plaintiff's table and now, as he approached, Wendell could see tears on the man's face.

"I'm sorry, Mr. Quinn. I never . . . I never meant to hurt you or . . . the students at Hamilton."

Luke's eyes grew wide, but he didn't say anything. Wendell took the cue. "Well . . . I appreciate that. I'm sorry about you and your daughter. What's happened between you."

"I have a lot of work to do." Andy pressed his lips together, obviously emotional. He looked at Luke. "But I'm making changes for the better." He paused. "I assume you'll call me as a witness tomorrow. When you present your defense."

The look on Luke's face told Wendell that his attorney was scrambling. "I . . . uh, yes. I'm planning on it."

"Good." Andy nodded at Luke and then Wendell. "Again . . . I'm sorry."

With that he turned and left the courtroom. He avoided Cami and the other students and ignored the shouts from the reporters. Wendell watched him leave and then turned to Luke. "What in the world?"

"Exactly." Luke looked dazed. Andy had testified on the first day of the trial. Landsford had kept his questions brief and functional. Establishing only that yes, Andy had filed the lawsuit. That left Luke no chance to cross-examine the man beyond those questions. "I thought Landsford didn't ask enough questions the first time around. Maybe he knew that Andy had become a liability to the case."

Wendell nodded. "I guess we'll find out tomorrow."

"I can hardly wait." Luke smiled at Wendell as he gathered his paperwork. "Go greet your fans. They won the game for us today."

"We serve a very good God, Luke." Wendell patted his attorney on the shoulder.

"Yes." Luke's eyes softened. "Win or lose. That much will always be true."

It took an hour for Wendell to greet the students. Alicia stayed by his side the whole time, saying hello to students she hadn't seen in more than a year. Out in the parking lot there were two buses that had brought the students. A decision made by Wendell's assistant principal.

Before the students took off, Jordy and Cami came up to Wendell and Alicia. His son hugged him and then looked straight into his eyes. "Dad . . . this idea was Cami's and mine. I thought you should know."

"I wondered." Alicia gave Cami a hug. "What a wonderful thing to organize."

"She got the booster club to make us the shirts a few days ago." Jordy smiled at the girl. He was clearly proud of her.

"Wow . . . that's . . . that's amazing." Wendell thought about the unkind things he'd said about her and her father the other night. He smiled at the girl. "Thank you, Cami. Jordy tells me the two of you have gotten very close."

A slight blush worked its way across Cami's cheeks. "We have. Yes, sir."

Jordy took hold of Cami's hand. He had never looked happier.

"Well, then." Wendell smiled from Cami to Jordy. "When all this is over, I hope you'll join us for dinner."

Cami beamed. "I will. Thank you, sir." Her smile faded some. "I'm sorry again. About all this."

"It's not your fault." He patted the girl's shoulder. "Besides, Jordy reminded me a few days ago. God's got it."

Wendell walked Alicia to her car just as a dark SUV sped out of the far side of the parking lot. She stopped and shaded her eyes, watching the vehicle leave. "There it is."

"What?" Wendell followed her gaze. "Is that the car? The one you've seen following you?"

"I think so." She sighed and turned to Wendell. "I never see it in the daylight. Sometimes I think it's all in my mind." She wrapped her arms around Wendell and hugged him. "Tell me it's all in my mind."

Wendell ran his hand along the back of her head. "It's all in your mind." He wanted desperately to believe that. "Who do you think it could be?"

She lifted her pretty eyes to his. "Who else?"

"Jack? But he's married." Wendell hadn't considered for a minute that Jack Renton might be the one following Alicia. "You said he was out of your life."

"He was. It's just . . . Only Jack would do something like that." Her eyes told him she was fighting the fear, trying to keep it from rising up within her once more. "It has to be my imagination."

"Why don't you come over for dinner? We're getting takeout. Jordy's picking it up on the way home."

"Really?" Her fear eased a little. Alicia smiled at him. "I'd love that."

"Okay, then." He stepped back. They were still taking things one day at a time. For now, anyway. "See you there."

It wasn't until Wendell backed out of his parking space that he saw something that made him wonder if Alicia was right. Maybe someone was watching her, following her. Parked thirty yards away from the exit was a familiar car, one very much like the car that had sped out of the lot a few minutes earlier.

A dark SUV.

Before Wendell could pull up beside the SUV, the driver raced off. Wendell thought about chasing the vehicle or calling the police, but then he stopped himself. What could he say? And what would the police be able to do?

Crazy people hung out at courthouses. There were trials taking place in every courtroom. No one was following Alicia. Jack Renton was married. He hadn't called her in months. Wendell waited at the next light. He and Alicia were about to have a fun evening together. Nothing to worry about.

End of story.

Ashley Baxter Blake was working in Janessa's classroom that day, the way she always did on Thursday afternoons. It was story hour, time for the kids to read books they'd brought from home. Students could read either quietly to themselves or aloud with their classmates.

Today Ms. Jenkins wanted the kids to read aloud.

Janessa ran with the other children toward the cubbies lined up on one side of the classroom. Ashley watched her daughter pull a large book from her backpack and then carry it to her desk. Ashley was organizing puzzles on the other side of the room, but she was curious about the book.

The other kids were still getting situated, so Ashley walked over to Janessa and only then did she see what her daughter had brought today. It was her pink Bible, the one Ashley and Landon had given her last Christmas.

This ought to be interesting, Ashley thought. She knelt beside her daughter's desk. "You brought your Bible?" She smiled into the girl's blue eyes. "What made you choose that one, honey?"

Janessa rubbed the leather cover, her expression completely free of guile. "Ms. Jenkins said to bring our favorite book." She smiled at the Bible. "This is my favorite."

"Perfect, honey. That's perfect." She

kissed Janessa's cheek and returned to her organizing. *All right, then.* Ashley kept her trepidations to herself and waited.

Ms. Jenkins took volunteers. The first little girl read a selection from *Junie B. Jones.* "That's my favorite book," the child said sweetly.

Janessa's hand was up next.

"Go ahead, Janessa." Ms. Jenkins was a young teacher, in her mid-twenties. The students were crazy about her. She smiled at Janessa. "Tell us about your book."

Like her classmate before her, Janessa stood and held up her book. "I brought the Bible. My favorite part is the Twenty-Third Psalm because —"

"Oh, honey, no." Ms. Jenkins approached Janessa quickly and reached for her book. "You can't bring a Bible to school. That's against the rules."

"Hold on, boys and girls." Ashley couldn't stop herself. She smiled at the students, all of whom were turning to hear her. "I need to have a little talk with Ms. Jenkins." Ashley pointed to a few of the students. "Read your books quietly until we're finished."

Ms. Jenkins looked shocked. But given the situation she didn't seem to have any choice, so she followed Ashley to a back corner of the room. "Mrs. Blake . . . what's this about? I'm the teacher here."

"I realize that." Ashley had to make her point quickly. "I'm very sorry. No offense intended." She hesitated. It was important for the teacher to understand the full weight of what she was about to say. "My brother is a lawyer, Ms. Jenkins. He takes on religious freedom cases. And I assure you that what you just did was a violation of Janessa's First Amendment rights."

"What?" The young teacher looked confused. "I thought Bibles were against the law?"

Ashley couldn't believe what she was hearing. "You thought — Never mind. Ms. Jenkins, I assure you Bibles are not against the law. It would be a violation of church and state if you forced the students to read the Bible. But you cannot deny any child the right to read his or her own Bible." She straightened herself. "I'm glad I was here to clear things up for you."

"Yes." Ms. Jenkins looked bewildered. "I'm . . . I'm glad, too. I'll have to check with my principal. But for now . . ."

"Ms. Jenkins." Ashley smiled. "For now and for always . . . any child may read the Bible during reading time." She nodded, her voice kind. "And no one can stop them. That's the law."

Ms. Jenkins nodded. "Thank you. I meant . . . no harm."

"I know." Ashley patted the woman's hand. "Sorry about the interruption."

"Right." The teacher still looked bewildered. She returned to the front of the class. "Okay, boys and girls. We'll resume reading now." She turned her attention to Ashley's daughter. "Janessa. You may read whatever part of the Bible you'd like."

Janessa looked uncertain. She glanced at Ashley.

"It's okay, honey." Ashley whispered her encouragement. "Go ahead."

For a second Janessa seemed unsure. Then she opened the cover of her pink Bible and turned to the Twenty-Third Psalm. In a shaky voice she began, "The Lord is my Shepherd, I shall not want . . ."

Janessa's voice grew stronger as she read. Ashley fought back tears as she listened. Did the other children understand the weight of what was happening? How Janessa's sweet young voice was the voice of religious freedom? Ashley felt sick about what would've happened if she hadn't been here today.

Janessa would've been told that her Bible was illegal. Prohibited from school grounds like drugs or guns. Ashley was devastated at the thought. This was how a nation was losing its freedoms. One teacher at a time, one classroom at a time.

Ashley leaned against the back wall and listened to Janessa finish the Twenty-Third Psalm.

". . . and I will dwell in the house of the Lord . . . forever."

Forever. Which was how long Ashley and the others in her family needed to stand up for religious freedom in the United States.

The whole ordeal reminded Ashley to pray for her brother. Luke's case would wrap up in the next day or so. That night she told Landon what had happened at Janessa's school. And how important it was to pray for Luke. Especially now.

Landon held her in his arms, and he prayed the most beautiful prayer. That Luke would be helped by God, Himself, in the days to come, and that America might continue to be a place where people could openly worship the Lord.

So that Janessa's children wouldn't grow up in a world where Bibles really would be illegal. So that the name of God never had to be whispered. But rather shouted from on high.

The way He deserved.

22

Luke's surprise witness was Rosie Carter, mother of Rasha Carter.

Rasha had been a promising sophomore when she was gunned down a few years ago in the parking lot of Hamilton High. Caught in the crossfire of two rival gangs.

A week ago, Wendell had brought a video to his meeting with Luke. A video he had showed students when he first presented the idea of the Raise the Bar club.

That day in his office, Luke had watched the short film through teary eyes. Rasha had been everything right about youth today. And now she was gone. Still, Luke had figured the video wasn't going to be any help in the trial. He told Wendell as much.

Luke had no permissible reason to show the emotional footage. Rasha had passed before Wendell's Raise the Bar club was even founded. Therefore the video didn't pertain to the case, and so Judge Wells would never allow it. But on the first day of testimony, God had given Luke a gift.

Something he'd held on to until now.

When court was in session, Luke stood and looked at Judge Wells. "I would like permission to show a brief video to the jury. It's only a few minutes long."

Landsford slid to the edge of his seat. Beside him, Andy Nelson hung his head. He still appeared so very troubled. But now there was hope around the edges of his soul. There had to be. He had cut his hair and his eyes were more alert. He looked presentable.

"What would this video contain, Mr. Baxter?" Judge Wells practically rolled her eyes.

"It's footage of a female Hamilton student who was killed in the parking lot a few years ago. Caught in the crossfire of two rival gangs."

Now Landsford couldn't scramble to his feet fast enough. "Objection. Irrelevant. Mr. Baxter must only introduce evidence and witnesses that pertain directly to the defense in regards to the complaint." He glared at Luke. "Counsel should know better."

"It does pertain to the case, Your Honor. As we've said, what's brought up in the direct is permissible in the cross. That goes for the introduction of evidence." Luke kept his voice humble, free of any of Landsford's disdain. Luke was merely stating facts here. Trying to keep things in order.

The judge called a five-minute recess and ordered both attorneys to a meeting at her bench. "Mr. Baxter." She looked at him with eyes that could pierce a piece of metal. "You will not make a mockery of this court. If you seek permission to show this video, you need a reason."

"I have one." Luke directed his next statement to the court stenographer. "If the court would please review Mr. Landsford's comments from the first day of trial. The witness on the stand was policewoman Aspyn Jones."

Landsford's face was red. "This is ridiculous."

"Proceed." Judge Wells shot a look at Landsford. "If your comment opens the door for the video, we need to review it." She motioned to the stenographer.

The stenographer found the spot in the record and read it out loud. "Mr. Landsford said, 'The defendant in this case, Mr. Quinn, likes to say that his Bible study group has changed lives, that the students are better off because of it.' "

"That's all." Luke thanked the woman and turned to Judge Wells. "Since Mr.

Landsford called into question whether students are better off because of the Raise the Bar program, the defense has the right to explore that issue. The condition of students prior to the club. The video will do just that."

For a long time Judge Wells only stared at Luke. Then she breathed deep and nodded. "Permission granted."

"Your Honor, I can't believe this court is going to —" Landsford looked furious.

"Permission granted." She rapped her gavel on the bench. "Court will resume. Everyone take their seats."

Luke could finally breathe again. He could hardly believe how things had worked out, that Landsford had slipped up and allowed him a chance to have the video shown in court. He had the equipment in place and a remote at his table. A bailiff dimmed the lights and the video began to play.

Wendell's work on the brief film was spectacular. It began with a burst of sad, dismal statistics. Then a slide that read: *Those are the statistics. These are the stories.*

The next part of the film was a more personal look at the losses from the previous year. Rasha Carter, a sophomore. Killed in an exchange of gunfire between two rival gangs. In the school's own parking lot.

Rasha had been a journalism student, so Wendell's friend Alicia had given the footage to Wendell for the film. With Lecrae's "Don't Waste Your Life" playing in the background, the video showed Rasha getting set up in front of the camera, giggling as her microphone struggled to stay in place, and then finally staring into the lens.

"My name is Rasha Carter. One day I'm going to be President of the United States. But first I'm going to finish school with straight As and go to Harvard University." She grinned into the camera. "At least that's my dream."

The next clip contained the devastating imagery of Rasha's family gathered around an open hole at the cemetery. Her mother breaking down, falling over the casket as they lowered it into the ground. "Not my baby . . . not my Rasha!"

A few sniffles came from the jury box.

The film ended with photos of other Hamilton students who had been killed and those were followed by a montage of news headlines featuring Hamilton High's worst criminal element. The final image was the quote from Alexander Hamilton. *Those who stand for nothing . . . will fall for anything.*

When the lights came up, Luke looked at his notes. "The defense would like to call

Rosie Carter."

A sad, small woman — the one from the video — stood at the back of the courtroom and made her way toward the front. As she approached she stopped at Wendell's chair and put her hand on his shoulder. "Thank you." She wiped at the tears on her cheeks. "Thank you."

Then she took the witness stand.

For the next ten minutes Luke gently asked Rosie one question after another. He established that Rosie was still grieving the loss of her precious Rasha and that life at Hamilton High had previously been dangerous and deeply discouraging.

Then came the surprise.

Rosie was one of the parent volunteers involved in bringing free food to the students in the Raise the Bar club. "Have you seen a change in the students at Hamilton High, Mrs. Carter?" Luke allowed more emotion in his tone. This woman deserved her say.

"Yes." Rosie Carter looked at the jury. At every member on the panel. "Don't you let that Mr. Landsford tell you there hasn't been a difference. We lost Dwayne. But so many other kids have been saved. So many. And even Dwayne was saved, because today he's in heaven. Safe for all eternity. All because Principal Quinn was brave enough to start an after-school Bible study."

"Objection." Landsford didn't yell out the word this time. He smiled at Rosie and then at the judge. "Beyond the scope of the question."

Judge Wells thought for a long moment. "Overruled." She nodded to Rosie Carter. "The witness may continue."

And Rosie did just that. Luke had to work to contain his smile as Rosie told about one student after another who had changed for the better because of the club. Then her eyes welled up. "Principal Quinn couldn't stand by and let these kids kill themselves. So he started the club. Just for the kids who wanted it." She paused, her tone feverish. "In that way . . . Rasha's death wasn't in vain."

When it came time for her cross-examination, Landsford passed.

There was nothing he could ask her that would undo the impression she'd made on the jury. Luke could've danced on the ceiling he was so happy.

This was where he'd planned to rest his case. But the comment from Andy Nelson yesterday had changed his mind. What Luke was about to do was risky. Cami's father could've been setting him up to fail here.

But if so, Luke would know soon enough.

"The defense calls one final witness. Andy Nelson, please take the stand."

A murmur rose from the spectators and even the jurors. Judge Wells rapped her gavel on the bench. "Order. Silence in the courtroom, please."

The noise settled down and slowly, under the glare of his own attorney, Andy took the stand. He looked shaky, more nervous than the first time he'd been called.

"I'd like to make it clear to the jury" — Luke looked at each of them — "that Andy Nelson is testifying today on behalf of the defense." He paused. "Although Mr. Nelson brought this case against Principal Quinn, today he will testify on the principal's behalf."

Landsford dropped his pen and leaned back in his seat. Clearly he had not expected this.

Luke formed his first question with great care. *Help me here, God.* He was glad his dad was still there, still praying from the back row. "Mr. Nelson, it's come to my attention that you've gone through some personal changes since filing suit against Wendell Quinn. Is that right?"

"Yes, sir." Andy wore a long-sleeve white cotton shirt and light blue jeans. He had cut his hair for the occasion, and though he still looked nervous, his eyes were brighter than they'd been all trial.

"Okay, and could you tell the jury about those changes? In your own words?"

Andy's eyes filled with tears. He looked to the first row of spectators, where Cami and Jordy sat with a small group of Hamilton High students. The man wiped at his eyes and looked at the jury. "I made a mistake when I sued Principal Quinn. There were . . . personal reasons why I didn't want my daughter reading the Bible." He looked at her and his tears came harder. He shook his head and whispered, "I'm sorry, baby. I never meant for this to . . . I'm sorry."

Landsford looked like he might object, but instead he only crossed his arms and stared at the table in front of him.

"Mr. Nelson, if you could please stick to the question." Luke used his most gentle tone. He loved the exchange between Andy and his daughter. But this wasn't the place for it, and he wanted the jurors to hear the reason Andy had changed his mind.

"Yes. Sorry." Andy blinked a few times, like he was trying to see through his tears. He turned to the jury once more. "I seen the difference this club has made in my daughter. God is . . . He's her best friend now. She used to be angry and now . . . she has peace. The only problem in her life today is . . . well, it's me."

"And have you changed your mind about the importance of a club like Raise the Bar, Mr. Nelson?" Luke took a step forward, his voice quiet.

"I've changed my mind about a lot of things regarding God. When I filed the lawsuit . . . I was so angry at God and Cami and Principal Quinn, I went and got a tattoo on my arm. It said 'NO GOD.' Because that's how I felt . . . like there was no God. Like He wasn't real."

Luke walked back to his table, giving the jurors plenty of time to let Andy's testimony hit them. On his way he noticed that Cami was crying. Jordy put his arm around her as they listened. Luke faced Andy once more. "And now, Mr. Nelson? How do you feel now?"

"I tried to kill myself before the trial started. But God . . . He wouldn't let me die. So I went back to the tattoo parlor." Andy sniffed, fresh tears filling his eyes. He struggled to pull up the sleeve of his shirt. And there on his bicep was the tattoo he'd mentioned a minute ago. But something was different. He'd had a few letters added.

"See?" Andy held up his arm. "Now it says

'KNOW GOD.' Because He alone can help us. Me and Cami. The students at Hamilton High." He looked at Wendell. "And you, Principal Quinn. We all need God. I believe that now."

Judge Wells sat back in her chair and grabbed on to the arms. Like she'd never seen anything so unexpected in all her days on the bench. Landsford, too. If he could've tunneled his way out of the courtroom with his pen, he would've.

At least by the expression on his face.

Luke nodded. "Thank you, Mr. Nelson. No further questions. The defense rests, Your Honor."

"No further questions." Landsford didn't bother to look up from his notes.

"Very well. The jury will now hear closing arguments."

Landsford went first. He was hardly compelling. His client had turned against him. Of all the cases the man would win against Christians, this no longer appeared to be one of them.

He was going into a halfhearted spiel about precedent cases and the prior determination that a school official absolutely could not lead a Bible study on campus — voluntary or not — when Andy Nelson walked across the courtroom to his daughter.

Cami stayed on her side of the railing, but the two hugged like their lives depended on it. Luke couldn't have written a better script for how these final moments might play out. Most of the jurors were crying, dabbing at their eyes.

"Order." Judge Wells stood, beyond frustrated. "Mr. Nelson, your attorney is making his closing arguments. The least you could do is sit and listen."

Only then did Andy seem to realize how rude he'd been. Luke covered his smile with his hand as Andy apologized and returned to his seat.

"The jury will not allow that scene between Mr. Nelson and his daughter to influence its decision." The judge looked at the jury. "Is that understood?"

Each of them nodded. As if anything could erase the touching moment they'd just witnessed. Landsford finished his closing statement and sat down.

It was Luke's turn. Anything he could say at this point would be superfluous. Rosie Carter, Andy Nelson, the hug the man had shared with his daughter. All of that had said more than Luke could ever say.

But still he had to drive home one final

point. The reason the jury could feel good about the legalities of deciding in favor of Wendell Quinn. The point Tommy had first brought up after the musical that night. Luke wasn't sure if it would help, but it couldn't hurt. Not at this point. And both Wendell and Tommy were right — whether it was a proven defense in a case like this or not.

Wendell really was just doing his job.

Luke stepped in front of the jury and looked at them. Each one of them. "First, thank you again for your time. I told you it would take a while, and it has. But freedom is always worth the time. Always."

Luke came closer to the jury box. These were no longer Landsford's friends. They were Luke's. "I want you to take two truths with you into that deliberation room. Two truths that will make your decision that much easier." Luke paused. "First, there was nothing in the school district handbook prohibiting Principal Quinn from leading a voluntary after-school Bible study. You heard James Black testify to that on the first day of trial."

Luke smiled at the jurors and then he turned and looked at Wendell. Looked at him long enough that every one of the jurors could do nothing but follow his lead.

After several seconds, Luke turned his attention back to the jury. "Second, Wendell Quinn started the Raise the Bar club for one reason." Luke nodded. "Yes, because it was his job."

One more trip back to his table and Luke picked up a piece of paper. "When Wendell Quinn signed his contract as principal of Hamilton High he promised this: To establish a schoolwide vision of commitment to high standards . . . and ensure the success of all students."

Luke set the piece of paper down and smiled at the jury. "Friends, when a man like Wendell Quinn does whatever it takes . . . when he risks his reputation and his job to carry out the duties of his position on behalf of his students, we don't find him guilty. We drop the charges and we give him a standing ovation."

The sentiment hung in the air for a long moment, and then Luke thanked the jury one more time and returned to his seat.

He'd done all he could. He had prayed and so had his family. Now the decision was in the hands of the jury. And of God Almighty, who had brought them this far.

An hour later it was no surprise to anyone in the room when the jury returned with a verdict of not guilty. After the foreman read their decision he did something Luke had never seen, not in all his years of practicing law.

The man began to clap.

His fellow jurors joined in and all of them rose to their feet. So that Wendell Quinn finally had what he deserved.

A standing ovation.

23

The jury's verdict, their applause, was still fresh in Wendell's heart when Judge Wells lit into him.

"Mr. Quinn, you need to know that the verdict today does not mean your troubles are over."

Next to him, Luke whispered. "Just hear her out. You're fine, Wendell."

He kept his eyes on the judge, respectful. Listening. "Yes, Your Honor."

"What I'm saying is anyone, anytime could bring a lawsuit much like the one Mr. Nelson brought. As long as you run your Bible study club, you're placing yourself and your school in jeopardy."

Wendell nodded.

"Ultimately, the landscape of religious freedom is changing in this nation." Judge Wells raised her brow. "A person has to be either very brave or very foolish to continue such a club."

"Yes, ma'am." Wendell smiled. "I'm probably a little of both."

Wendell heard Luke chuckle quietly. "Thank you, Judge Wells. If Your Honor is finished, my client has places to be."

She gave Luke a wary look. "Very well." She waved her hand like she'd done before. "I expect I'll see you again. But for now, you may go. Both of you."

Wendell and Luke stood at the same time and as Luke moved to shake his hand, Wendell went straight for the hug. "I had the best lawyer in the business."

"I couldn't have planned half of what happened here." Luke patted Wendell on the back. "God alone gave us this victory. Never should've happened."

Alicia walked up to them. She hugged Wendell and then shook Luke's hand. "Thank you. Wendell was right about you."

"He tell you I cry easy at sad videos?" Luke grinned at Wendell and shook his head. "Twice, in this case."

"No." Alicia's eyes were soft. Full of gratitude. "He told me there was no lawyer better. That jury loved you."

Wendell watched as Luke looked across the room to the place where his father was still waiting for him. A kind expression filled Luke's face. "My dad told me a long time

417

ago that the best way to win an argument was with gentle words and honesty. Worked as a kid. Still works now."

Luke patted Wendell on the back once more. "I'll be in touch. I want our families to get together soon. After Christmas, maybe."

"Definitely." Wendell would remember Luke Baxter's kindness all his life. He watched as the young attorney headed toward his dad. And maybe today God had given his old coach Les Green a window. Wendell lifted his face. *Lord, tell Les it worked. Good was done here today. In this moment.* With a full heart, Wendell turned to Alicia. "You ready to go?"

"Dinner at your house?"

"Absolutely. I texted Jordy after the verdict." He chuckled. "Seems I got a houseful of kids ready to celebrate."

It was only three in the afternoon, so the courthouse was still busy, action and drama filling just about every room. But for Wendell, the excitement was over. For now, anyway. Like Judge Wells had said.

He put his arm around Alicia's shoulders and walked with her to the front of the building. They were barely out the doors when Wendell saw the commotion twenty yards away.

Suddenly there was a series of popping sounds. People all around them screamed and dropped to the ground, covering their heads and hiding behind walls and cars. Wendell did the only thing that mattered.

He grabbed Alicia and shielded her with his body. If it was the last thing he did on earth, he was going to protect her. And if God gave him the chance, he would keep her safe the rest of her life.

The shooting was over as quickly as it began.

Alicia moved closer to him. "What is it, Wendell? Was someone . . . did someone . . . ?"

"I don't know." Whatever had happened it looked serious. But it also looked like the incident was over.

Wendell and Alicia stayed in their spot for what felt like an hour. They didn't move or talk again until an officer approached them. He had a photograph in his hand and seemed to be comparing it to the people leaving the courthouse. Only then did Wendell make out what the man was saying.

"Alicia Harris? Anyone here by the name of Alicia Harris?"

She must've heard him, too, because Wendell felt Alicia gasp. Her arm tight around Wendell, she spoke up. "Here. I'm . . . Alicia."

The officer approached her. "Mrs. Harris. We need to talk with you." He motioned for Alicia and Wendell to follow him to the far side of the steps. Wendell watched four different officers begin escorting people into the parking lot, away from the scene.

When they were removed from the rest of the crowd, the officer looked straight at Alicia. "Mrs. Harris, has anyone been stalking you lately? To your knowledge?"

Wendell felt Alicia's knees grow weak. Her breathing became slightly irregular. "Yes. I thought someone might've been following me. It happened . . . several times."

The man nodded, deeply serious. "You wouldn't know his name, would you?"

Nothing was making sense. Wendell couldn't believe the direction of the conversation. He turned to Alicia. "Tell them about Jack."

"Yes." Alicia looked like she might drop to the ground from the shock. But she clung to Wendell instead. "I was stalked for a long time by a man named Jack Renton. But . . . he got married. I thought things were different."

"Well, looks like he didn't change." The officer clenched his jaw. "I'm afraid Jack

Renton followed you to the courthouse. He tried to enter the building with a loaded gun, but our guards stopped him." The man hesitated. "That's when Jack aimed his weapon at the officers." Wendell looked toward an ambulance being loaded with a body bag. "One of our own fired and killed him."

Wendell couldn't believe what he was hearing. Jack Renton had been following Alicia all this time? So his was the car they'd seen leaving the parking lot the day before and he was the one she thought had followed her home? A terrible queasy feeling worked its way through Wendell.

What if . . . what if Jack Renton had made his way into the courthouse?

Alicia wasn't talking. She turned her face toward Wendell's chest and clung to him. The officer was still standing there, patient, waiting. Wendell held up his hand. "Just give her a minute. This is . . . it's a lot for her."

"No problem." The officer had a notepad. "What's your name, sir?"

"Wendell Quinn. I'm . . . Ms. Harris and I are friends."

The officer nodded. "Do you know anything about Jack Renton?"

Did he know anything? Wendell had no idea where to begin, but he was about to start with the slashed tire when Alicia straightened. She looked at the officer. "I'll tell you. Jack and I used to date, but he got very controlling."

It took her five minutes to explain the entire situation. Then she was quiet for a moment before asking the question that was clearly on her mind. "Do you think . . . he came here to kill me?"

The officer frowned. "I think there's a good chance." He looked over his shoulder. "I can say this much. Jack Renton won't bother you ever again."

"If it's okay, we need to get going." Wendell thanked the police officer. He and Alicia both gave the man their contact information and then they were free to leave.

All the way to the car, neither Wendell nor Alicia said anything.

Not until they were inside with the doors shut and locked did Alicia fall into his arms and cry. But her tears didn't last long. After a few minutes she looked at Wendell. "I knew he would kill me." She searched his eyes. "He would've killed you, too."

Wendell had a feeling Alicia was right. If Jack had made it all the way to the courtroom he would've killed them both. Why else bring a gun here? He had to know he'd be caught or shot immediately. He must've been intent on going down in a big blaze of gunfire.

"I felt it, the panic attack. It was taking over, and then I whispered the name 'Jesus.' " She wiped her tears. "And instantly I wasn't afraid. That's why I could talk to that officer." She managed the slightest smile. "Thank you, Wendell." Her eyes locked on to his. "For protecting me."

"Thank you . . . for being here." He had never wanted to kiss her more than right now. But Wendell knew better. The time would come, he was almost certain. But not now. There was too much to process.

Over the next few days Wendell and Alicia would learn that Jack's marriage had fallen apart only weeks after it had started. And that in the past month or so his obsession with Alicia had gotten so great, he no longer went to work.

The man was certifiably insane.

Wendell prayed with Alicia about the matter, and they both felt peace. And while it would take some time for Alicia to stop looking over her shoulder, Jack would never threaten her again. Those days were behind them. It was time to move on, time to stop thinking about the past.

And start dreaming about the future.

■ ■ ■ ■

Luke couldn't believe the drama that had played out in front of the courthouse moments after he left the building. If the timing had been different, anything might've happened.

It didn't take long for the media to report with near certainty that Jack Renton had been headed for the courtroom. Based on notes they'd found on his computer, he intended to kill both Alicia Harris and her male friend. Luke's client. Wendell Quinn.

Crazy world, Luke told himself more than once. If not for God's protection, anything could've happened.

Especially if the man had gotten that far with his loaded gun. Luke had been in the courtroom, too, after all. He and his father. Reagan had struggled to fall asleep the first few nights after learning what had happened. Any threat by Jack Renton was obviously behind them.

Still, it made Luke grateful that he'd been spending more time at home. If the gunman had made it into the courtroom, he could've died. But he would've died knowing he'd made the right decision.

Putting Reagan and the kids first. The way

he would do forevermore.

Of course, Luke's resolve didn't stop the mountain of cases that wound up on his desk Monday following the verdict. Luke was inundated with offers to defend every sort of religious freedom violation he could imagine.

A football player who had always pointed to the sky after a touchdown, now being asked by his athletic director to no longer make the motion. A school where a teacher was being sued for having a Christmas tree in the corner of her room, and a school with a pending lawsuit over the existence of a memorial rock. The rock had been placed on one side of the football field in memory of a teacher who had been killed in a car accident.

But the rock had a cross on it.

Now an atheist group in Ohio wanted it gone, or else.

So many cases, more than Luke could ever fight alone. And the good news was, he never would. God would go before him.

The way he had with Wendell Quinn.

Reagan could barely breathe as she and Luke and the kids walked up the steps to Landon and Ashley's house the Sunday afternoon after Thanksgiving. Tommy knew what was happening, but the other kids had no idea.

Tommy shared a smile with Reagan as Luke rang the doorbell.

Shadows moved beyond the glass on either side of the front door, but Luke missed it. The door opened and they were hit by the loudest, most joyous chorus of voices ever.

"Surprise!" Lights flew on and standing there just inside the house were all the people who loved Luke.

Not just the entire Baxter family, all his siblings and their kids, and John and Elaine, of course. But their friends the Flanigans, along with former basketball and baseball coaches who still knew Luke. Friends from high school and the church youth group.

More than seventy people filled the house.

Luke stood there, looking stunned, taking it in. For a minute or so he kept muttering. "What? I can't believe this." Then he turned and looked at Reagan.

At the same moment the entire group began to sing. "Happy birthday to you . . . happy birthday to you . . ."

The voices of the adults and children blended together in the most beautiful song. Even before they were finished, Luke came to his wife and took her in his arms. In a whisper only Reagan could hear, he spoke straight to her heart. "You did this . . . all of this?"

"I did." She felt tears in her eyes. "I love you, Luke. I wanted you to know."

He kissed her then. The sort of kiss that took her breath and made everyone break into cheers and applause. He looked at her again, the moment still theirs alone. "You are God's greatest gift, Reagan. I love you with all my life."

They kissed again and in that moment every minute of planning, every delayed concern about his work hours, every time she had taken the situation to God instead of complaining to Luke paid off completely.

Because Luke's expression wasn't just one of surprise or gratitude. It was one of love.

Beautiful, unconditional, forever and ever love.

Luke was still taking it all in, trying to get his mind around the fact that Reagan had planned this surprise party for him. All the work and time and effort. The way his entire family had come together.

How was it God loved him so much, that He would give him a wife like Reagan? Someone who stood by him even when his hours at work had been completely unreasonable? Luke stepped back from his precious Reagan, his arm still around her. As he did, his dad and Elaine and then the others started calling out. "Speech, speech, speech!"

Luke chuckled, blinking back tears. "Okay, first . . ." He looked around the room at the people he loved so much. "This is incredible." He turned to Reagan. "I never had a clue."

"Well . . . I had a lot of help." Reagan grinned at Ashley and Kari and Brooke.

"Still . . ." Luke felt his smile fade. "I've been really busy lately. Too busy." He paused. "I've let the late hours become a habit." He drew Reagan gently to his side. Then he looked at Tommy and Malin and Johnny. "At the expense of my family."

The looks on the faces of his family were a mix of compassion and understanding. Luke pressed on. "I know better now. This" — he looked at each of them — "all of you. You're the reason I'm here. God wants me to balance my time better." He turned to Reagan. "And I will. From now on." He kissed her again. "I promise."

Another round of cheers and applause came from his family and friends.

Luke wanted to freeze how he felt right now, memorize it. Because in this moment, here and now, he could feel God's grace. This wasn't the response he deserved from the people he loved. But starting with Reagan, they had cared enough to stand beside him. To love him through the busiest season of his life.

Which maybe shouldn't have surprised him, after all. Because like his dad said, standing by each other was what the Baxter family did. Whatever the situation.

Now and always.

After the guests had left and it was just the Baxters at the house, the conversation shifted to Luke's cases.

"People are running scared." Luke set his fork down and leaned his forearms on the table. "They truly believe it's against the law to be a Christian except behind closed doors."

His dad sat at the head of the table with Elaine on one side and Brooke and Peter on the other. A sad look crossed his dad's face. "Which is the opposite of how Jesus tells us to live. Sharing our faith and making it a light to everyone."

Landon nodded. "Exactly."

Next to Landon, Cole — Ashley and Landon's older son — seemed to pay particular attention. He shot a look at Tommy, in the chair beside Luke. "Tommy and I have a plan." Cole smiled at his cousin. "Sure we're only in high school now. But in a few years we'll be in college and then law school." Cole looked at his dad and then at Luke. "We want to work for your law firm. So we can do what you do."

Luke smiled. "I'll look forward to it." He put his arm around Tommy's shoulders. "Couldn't have won the Wendell Quinn case without God's providence and a lot of help from this guy."

A grin flashed across Tommy's face. "That's what I told Cole."

The conversation continued; talk of how it was harder this past year for Brooke to renew her operating license at the crisis pregnancy center she ran in town. Something she did in addition to being a doctor. All of them agreed it was becoming more difficult to be a Christian. More difficult to live out their faith.

"We have to love people." Kari looked at her husband, Ryan, and then at the others. "But we have to protect the truth, too. The Gospel deserves defending. That's our calling."

"Hard times are promised to people who believe." Dayne set his napkin beside his plate and glanced at Katy. Luke's older brother reminded them how he had struggled to find support for his faith-based films. "But now we have a good story for the investor. The one looking for a religious freedom tale." He winked at Luke. "Inspired by a very real story."

Katy smiled. "The day before we flew home, the team at Hobby Lobby agreed to help us with funding." She looked at Luke and then the others around the table. "There will be hard times, but God is over it all. And we have to remember, this is just earth. That's what my dad used to say."

Luke listened as the conversation shifted to Ryan's coaching and how the whole family planned to be at his football playoff game next weekend. Then the next afternoon everyone was going to help paint the crisis pregnancy center in Bloomington. Even the kids were excited about that.

The sounds of his family around him filled Luke's soul. This night was just what he needed. No one was like the Baxters, which was always how it had been. It was why he and Reagan came here so often. They wanted their kids to know the love of this group of people, too.

Luke thought again about the many people that would need his legal help in the months to come. None of it felt overwhelming. Not with the support of his family. Whatever case he took on, he would not fight it alone. He would have his dad in the back of the courtroom . . . his family behind him all the way and God at his side.

What more could he ask for?

24

It was early February, the spring semester well under way. Finally the media circus surrounding Wendell's lawsuit and Bible study club had waned. Sure, he was still contacted to do interviews for magazines or newspapers.

But the tone of the articles was different now. TRAILBLAZER STANDS BY HIS FAITH, a recent headline read. Or HAMILTON WOULD HAVE BEEN PROUD OF HAMILTON HIGH. Wendell had smiled at that one. In the most recent story, a reporter referred to him as a champion for his students.

Wendell looked at a stack of articles on his office desk. He didn't pay much heed to what reporters said about him. Not then and not now. It was nice to be off the public's most-hated list, but all of it was temporary.

Like Judge Wells said, he was always just one lawsuit away from losing the right to talk about Jesus here at Hamilton. Wendell stood and walked to the window. No matter what happened, no one could take away his faith. And no one could take away the faith of the students here.

The ones whose lives had been changed.

Wendell smiled. God was with them all. Wendell could feel the Spirit deep within him. And because of that, he would never be reliant on happy circumstances or held captive by difficult ones.

This world was not his home.

A wave of anticipation came over him. Heaven was waiting for him, but he hoped not for a very long time. Especially in light of what this day held. The day he'd been looking forward to for what felt like a life-time.

Wendell put his hand in his pocket and felt the small velvet box.

Today was the day.

Inside was the most beautiful diamond ring Wendell had ever seen. It was the same one Alicia had remarked about more than a year ago, when they were at the mall. She hadn't meant her comment to serve as a hint, still Wendell had made a note to himself. A note he remembered.

It had taken him most of the last month to find the ring again.

He checked the clock on his wall. Just a few more minutes. He sucked in a quick breath. *Lord, please let her say yes. I can't imagine my life without her. My kids and I . . . we need her.*

Alicia was teaching here again. The last transfer she ever wanted, she had told him. Wendell's joy knew no bounds as he headed to work each day knowing she was here. Knowing they'd be together.

Which was how it had been since the trial.

Alicia joined them at the house for dinner most nights, and the kids had come to love her dearly. It was Jordy who had pulled him aside after Christmas. He and Cami had made their dating relationship official by then. Cami and her sisters had moved back home. Jordy spent time there, too, now, and he and Cami's dad were finding a friendship.

"Dad, you're moving pretty slow here." Jordy had grinned at him. "I thought you'd get her a ring for Christmas."

Marrying Alicia was all Wendell could think about, but he hadn't talked to the kids yet. After Jordy's comment, Wendell waited a few days and then held a family meeting before bedtime.

"I'm thinking . . . about asking Alicia to marry me." He told the four of them. Before he could ask them what they thought about the idea, Leah and Alexandria were in his arms.

"Oh, Daddy, please ask her . . . please!" Alexandria hugged his neck so hard Wendell could barely breathe. "Everything's better when she's here."

"Yeah." Darrell danced around and pumped his fists in the air. "We love her, Dad!"

When the merriment settled down a bit, Leah cuddled up next to Wendell and lifted her sweet eyes to his. "If we can't have Mom, then we want Alicia." She smiled. "I think Mom would want that, too."

From a few feet away, Jordy grinned and shrugged. "What did I tell you?"

Wendell loved Alicia more every day. Just last night after dinner when the kids were in bed, Alicia sat beside him on the sofa and shared the most intimate thoughts of her heart. The way she often did.

The conversation this time was about belief in God. "With faith, I never had any reason to fear for my job and walk around terrified of Jack Renton," Alicia told him. "The Bible says not to worry about those who can kill the body. Because nothing can ever kill the soul."

Wendell listened, amazed. One of the

reasons he had been drawn to Alicia in the first place was that she needed him. She felt safe with him. That would always be true. But this new Alicia, the one with a belief in God as strong as his own . . . this was a woman he was falling more in love with every day.

He glanced at his office door just as Alicia appeared. Her smile lit up his heart. *Here I go, Lord . . . give me the words.*

Classes were out for the day, and the Raise the Bar club meeting had already wrapped up. An unusually warm couple days had melted the snow on the ground so Wendell could ask her the way he had planned.

In the place on campus that belonged to them.

He joined her in the hall and gave her a quick hug. Which was all he'd done since she'd been back in his life. She needed to know he valued her friendship, her character, her faith. The way she loved his children.

And so every time he longed to kiss her, Wendell had waited.

"Hey." He smiled into her eyes. "How was your day?"

Alicia took a deep breath and looked at the wall, the one with Hamilton's quote. "This is where I belong." She turned to him. "You'll never know how thankful I am that you made this move happen."

He slipped his hand in his pocket again and felt the box. "You'll never know how thankful I am that you're *here.*"

They talked about her third-period English class as they walked across campus. Wendell could barely concentrate, barely respond. All he could think about was the ring and the question. It felt like every minute of the past two years had led up to this moment.

"We're going to the baseball field, right?" Her eyes sparkled.

"Right." He realized he hadn't told her where they were going. He had just asked her to meet him at his office after school so they could talk. He grinned at her. "Where else?"

Her coat hung unbuttoned. It was warm enough that neither of them really needed more than a sweater. *Perfect weather,* Wendell thought. He glanced at the blue sky overhead. *Thanks, God. You've got every detail here. Now, please . . . just let her say yes.*

They reached the bleachers and Wendell led her to a spot somewhere in the middle. He turned and faced her and without saying a word he took her hands in his.

"Wendell . . ." Her eyes looked surprised.

"Your fingers are freezing!"

He chuckled. "You're right." Alicia would understand why soon enough.

"So . . ." She searched his eyes. Her easy expression told him she had no idea what was coming. "We're here." Her smile had never looked more beautiful. "What did you want to talk about?"

"Alicia . . . I've loved you for a very long time now." He ran his thumbs softly over her knuckles. "I loved you before you left and I loved you every day while you were gone."

"Me, too." Happy tears filled her eyes. "I used to dream I was still teaching here. That we could still see each other." Her smile faded. "I'd wake up and have to feel . . . the hurt of losing you all over again."

Wendell nodded. He let her words hang in the air between them for a few seconds. Then he felt his smile fill his face. "Those days are behind us. And now . . . every night when you're at our dinner table, I find myself thinking just one thing."

Understanding started to dawn in her expression. She waited, almost as if she were holding her breath.

"I don't ever want you to leave again." He released one of her hands and worked his fingers gently along the side of her face. "I love you, Alicia."

"I love you, too."

Then, in a move he had imagined himself making a thousand times, Wendell dropped down to one knee. Not easy on the bleachers, but Wendell was still able to pull it off.

When she seemed to fully realize what was happening, Alicia brought her hands to her face and gasped. Her eyes lit up and tears spilled onto her cheeks. She whispered his name in a way he would remember forever. "Wendell! What are you . . ."

He pulled the velvet box from his pants pocket and slowly opened the lid. "Alicia, I want you to come for dinner and never go home. I want to live with you and wake up with you and raise my children with you." Tears welled up in his eyes, too. "I want to serve God with you all the days of my life."

She was already nodding, crying and laughing and grinning. "I want that, too."

"So, Alicia Maria Harris" — he held the ring up to her — "will you make me the most grateful man in the world? Will you marry me?"

"Yes!" She bounced up and down a few times, shaking the bleachers with joy. Then she took the box from him, staring at the ring and then back at Wendell. "Yes, Wendell Quinn. I'd marry you today if I could!"

He was on his feet now, pulling her into his arms and holding her the way he had longed to hold her since he saw her outside his office. Alicia Harris was going to be his wife! Wendell looked at the sky and wondered what he'd ever done for God to bless him so fully.

Then he did something he'd refrained from doing until now. He put his hands alongside her face and let himself get lost in her eyes. Then slowly he erased the distance between them and he kissed her.

Nothing had ever felt so good.

And suddenly they were both laughing and crying and staring at each other. "We're getting married!" Alicia looked at the ring in her hand.

"Here. I'll help you." Wendell's cold hands shook, but it didn't matter. The ring was a perfect fit.

As soon as it was on her finger, they heard cheering in the distance and they looked up to see Jordy and Leah, Alexandria and Darrell running their way. This was the part Wendell had worked out with his oldest son. After class got out, Jordy and Leah went to the middle school and picked up their younger siblings.

All so they could hide near the trees and film Wendell's proposal.

Now Darrell led the way as his four children ran into the bleachers and piled into a group hug. The joy of the moment was so great Wendell teared up again. He grinned at his kids. "She said yes!"

"We know!" Alexandria hugged Alicia. "You're going to be our mom, now!"

Alicia smiled through her tears and kissed the young girl's cheek. "I can't wait, Alexandria." She glanced at Wendell and her happy expression deepened. "Truly . . . I cannot wait."

Jordy hugged his father. "Way to go, Dad."

"Thanks." Wendell winked at him. "And thanks for the encouragement at Christmastime."

"No problem." Jordy smiled at Alicia. "I thought he should've done this a long time ago."

They all laughed and hugged again.

Wendell held on to every moment, every word. He wanted to remember this as long as he lived. The way it felt to be so loved, so happy.

Wendell kept his arms wrapped around the people he loved most. God had done this. God, his mighty Father and Savior, who Wendell would forever praise and whose truth Wendell would always share with whoever wanted a second chance at life. The One Wendell would trust with his children and his career and his future. And Alicia Harris. The woman he was going to marry.

God had given him all of this. And Wendell would defend Him until his final breath.

Whatever the cost.

ACKNOWLEDGMENTS

No book comes together without a great deal of teamwork, passion and determination. That was definitely true for *In This Moment*!

First, a special thanks to my amazing publisher, Judith Curr, and the team at Atria Books and Howard Books. Judith, at the Simon & Schuster offices, you're known as the Rainmaker. How blessed I am to be working with you and your passionate team. You clearly desire to raise the bar at every turn. Thank you for that and for everything!

A similar thanks to Carolyn Reidy and my family at Simon & Schuster. I think often of our times together in New York and the way your collective creative brilliance always becomes a game changer. Thank you for lending your influence in so many ways. It's an honor to work with you!

This book is so very special because of the incredible talents of my editor, Becky

Nesbitt. Becky, you have known me since my kids were little. Since the Baxters began. How many authors actually look forward to the editing process? With you, it is a dream. And always you find ways to make my book better. Over and over and over again. Thank you for that! I am the most blessed author for the privilege of working with you.

Also thanks to my design team — Kyle and Kelsey Kupecky — whose unmatched talent in the industry is recognized from Los Angeles to New York. Very simply you are the best in the business! My website, social media, video trailers and newsletter, along with so many other aspects of my touring and writing, are what they are because of you two. Thank you for working your own dreams around mine. I love you and I thank God for you every single day.

A huge thanks to my sisters, Tricia and Susan, along with my mom, who give their whole hearts to helping me love my readers. Tricia as my executive assistant for the past decade, and Susan, for many years, as the head of my Facebook Online Book Club and Team KK. And Mom, thank you for being Queen of the Readers. Anyone who has ever sent me an email and received a response from you is blessed indeed. All three of you are so special to me. I love you and I thank God for each of you!

Thanks also to Tyler for joining with me to write screenplays and future books that — for now — the readers don't even know about. You are such a gifted writer, Ty. I can't wait to see your work on the shelves and on the big screen. Maybe one day soon! Love you so much!

Also, thank you to my office assistant, Aurora Galvin. You create space for me to write! This storytelling wouldn't be possible without you.

I'm grateful also to my Team KK members, who use social media to tell the world about my upcoming releases and who hang out on my Facebook page answering reader questions. I appreciate each of you so much. May God bless you for your service to the work of Life-Changing Fiction™.

There is a final stage in writing a book. The galley pages come to me, and I send them to a team of five of my closest, most special reader friends. My niece Shannon Fairley, Hope Painter, Donna Keene, Renette Steele and Zac Weikal. You are wonderful! It always amazes me the things you catch at the final hour. Thank you for loving my work, and thanks for your availability to read my books first and fast.

Also, my books only happen with the help

of my family, especially my amazing husband, Donald. Honey, thank you for your spiritual wisdom and leadership in our home, and thanks for talking through books like this one from the outline to the editing. The countless ways you help me when I'm on deadline make all the difference. I love you!

And over all this, there is a man who has believed in my career for two decades — my amazing agent, Rick Christian of Alive Literary Agency. From the beginning, Rick, you've told me to dream big, set my sights high. Movies, TV series, worldwide reach. You imagined it all, you prayed for it to be. You believed. While I write, you work behind the scenes on film projects and my work with Liberty University, the Baxter family TV series and details regarding every book I've ever written. You are brilliant and driven, compassionate and dedicated. I used to dream of having you as my agent. Now I'm the only author who does. God is amazing. Thank you, Rick, and thank you for praying for me and my family. That most of all.

Finally, my greatest thanks to God Almighty, who is First and Last and all things in between. I write for You, through You and because of You. Thank you with my whole being.

Dear Reader Friend,

I stapled together the pages of my first book when I was five years old, when I wrote a story titled *The Horse.* I never stopped writing, but there was a time, back when I was in college, that I considered becoming a lawyer.

I gave the idea careful consideration. That same semester a writing professor called me to the front of the room after class. He had just finished reading one of my assignments.

"Two things," he told me. "First, you will never stop writing. And second, you are on the newspaper staff. Report to my office in the morning."

With those words I put aside my thoughts of a legal career. I was supposed to be a writer. A good decision, for sure.

But over time — every now and then

— I think about the very real stories of religious persecution in the United States and I know that if I'd gone into law, I'd be out there on the front lines. Standing up for religious freedom the way Luke Baxter did in Wendell Quinn's case.

It's a fine line — the balance between freedom of religion, and freedom "from" religion. We need lawyers working these cases to be sure that the intent of our founding fathers is preserved.

And so it was with a full, sometimes racing heart that I had the pleasure of writing this story. It feels very real to me. Very timely. I hope you learned things from it, truth you can take into your own world and situations as you live freely the faith you have.

As with my other books in this new Baxter Family collection, this book and the ones to come will allow us the chance to live with the Baxters. We will see what matters to them, and how their work and family lives affect the people and culture around them.

The next Baxter book — *To the Moon and Back* — is another of those! I know you'll love it! These are among the most favorite books I've ever written. I'm grateful you're sharing in the journey!

Being back with the Baxter family has been the greatest gift. Always when people ask me, "How are the Baxters?" I have an answer. I honestly do. I can see them at work and play, holding close conversations, and looking for new horizons. Participating in never-seen-before adventures.

You've probably heard by now that the Baxter family is coming to TV. The series is expected to become one of the most beloved of all time. I know you'll be watching. You can find out more details about that and how to connect with me on social media at my website — Karen Kingsbury.com.

But in the meantime, I'll see you in the spring with my next book, *To the Moon and Back.*

Because the Baxter family isn't just my family. They're your family.

And with them at the middle of our lives, we are all family.

Until next time . . . thanks for being part of the family.

Love you all!

THE BAXTER FAMILY: YESTERDAY AND TODAY

For some of you, this is your first time with the Baxter family. Yes, you could go back and read twenty-some books on these most-loved characters. The list of Baxter titles — in order — is at the beginning of this book. But you don't have to read those to read this one. In fact, there will be other Baxter books coming in the next few years. These books are a collection, not a series. They can be read in any order.

If you wish, you can begin right here.

Whether you've known the Baxters for years or are meeting them for the first time, here's a quick summary of the family, their kids and their ages. Also, because these characters are fictional, I've taken some liberty with their ages. Let's just assume this is how old everyone is today.

Now, let me introduce you to — or remind you of — the Baxter family.

The Baxters began in Bloomington, Indiana, and most of the family still lives there today.

The Baxter house is on ten acres outside of town, with a winding creek that runs through the backyard. It has a wraparound porch and a pretty view and the memories of a lifetime. The house was purchased by John and Elizabeth Baxter when their children were young. They raised their family here. Today it is owned by one of their daughters — Ashley — and her husband, Landon Blake. It is still the place where the extended Baxter family gathers for special celebrations.

John Baxter: John is the patriarch of the Baxter family. Formerly an emergency room doctor and professor of medicine at Indiana University, he's now retired. John's first wife, Elizabeth, died ten years ago from a recurrence of cancer. Years later, John remarried Elaine, and the two live in Bloomington.

Dayne Matthews, 42: Dayne is the oldest son of John and Elizabeth. Dayne was born out of wedlock and — against his parents' wishes — given up for adoption at birth. His adoptive parents died in a small plane crash when he was 18. Sometime later, Dayne became a very visible and popular movie star. At age 30, he hired an attorney to find his birth parents — John and Elizabeth Baxter — which led to a moment with Elizabeth in the hospital before she died. In time, he connected with the rest of his biological family. Dayne is married to Katy, 40. The couple has three children: Sophie, 7; Egan, 5; and Blaise, 3. They are very much part of the Baxter family, and they split time between Los Angeles and Bloomington.

Brooke Baxter West, 40: Brooke is a pediatrician in Bloomington, married to Peter West, 40, also a doctor. The couple has two daughters: Maddie, 19, and Hayley, 16. The family experienced a tragedy when Hayley suffered a drowning accident at age 3. She recovered miraculously, but still has disabilities caused by the incident.

Kari Baxter Taylor, 38: Kari is a designer, married to Ryan Taylor, 40, football coach at Clear Creek High School. The couple has three children: Jessie, 16; RJ, 10; and Annie, 7. Kari had a crush on Ryan when the two were in middle school. They dated through college, and then broke up over a misunderstanding. Kari married a man she met in college, Professor Tim Jacobs, but some years into their marriage he had an affair. The infidelity resulted in his murder at the hands of a stalker. The tragedy devastated Kari, who was pregnant at the time with their first child (Jessie). Ryan came back into her life around the same time, and years later he and Kari married. They live in Bloomington.

Ashley Baxter Blake, 36: Ashley is the former black sheep of the Baxter family, married to Landon Blake, 36, who works for the Bloomington Fire Department. The couple has four children: Cole, 16; Amy, 11; Devin, 9; and Janessa, 5. As a young single mom, Ashley was jaded against God and her family when she reconnected with her firefighter friend Landon, who had secretly always loved her. Eventually Ashley and Landon married and Landon adopted Cole. Together, the couple had two more children — Devin and Janessa. Between those children, they lost a baby girl, Sarah Marie, at birth to anencephaly. Amy, Ashley's niece, came to live with them a few years ago after Amy's parents, Erin Baxter Hogan and Sam Hogan, and Amy's three sisters, were killed in a horrific car accident. Amy was the only survivor. Ashley and Landon and their family live in Bloomington, in the old Baxter house, where Ashley and her siblings were raised. Ashley paints and is successful in selling her work in local boutiques.

Luke Baxter, 34: Luke is a lawyer, married to Reagan Baxter, 34, a blogger. The couple has three children: Tommy, 14; Malin, 9; and Johnny, 5. Luke met Reagan in college. They experienced a major separation early on, after having Tommy out of wedlock. Eventually the two married, though they could not have more children. Malin and Johnny are both adopted.

In addition to the Baxters, this book revisits the Flanigan family. The Flanigans have been friends with the Baxters for many years. So much so that I previously wrote five books about their oldest daughter — Bailey Flanigan. Those books are part of the twenty-some Baxter family books. For the purpose of this book and those that follow, here are the names and ages of the Flanigans:

Jim and Jenny Flanigan, both 45. Jim is a football coach for the Indianapolis Colts, and Jenny is a freelance writer who works from home. Bailey, 23, is married to Brandon Paul, 26. Bailey and Brandon were once actors in Hollywood — Brandon, very well known. Today they run the Christian Kids Theater in downtown Bloomington and they are the parents of baby Hannah

Jennifer. Bailey's brothers are Connor, 20 — a student at Liberty University; Shawn and Justin — both age 17 and juniors at Clear Creek High; BJ, 16, a sophomore; and Ricky, 14, an eighth grader.

ONE CHANCE FOUNDATION

The Kingsbury family is passionate about seeing orphans all over the world brought home to their forever families. As a result, Karen created a charitable group called the One Chance Foundation.

This foundation was inspired by the memory of her father, Ted C. Kingsbury. Ted always said, "Life is not a dress rehearsal. We have one chance to love, one chance to truly live!"

Karen often tells her reader friends that they have "one chance to write the story of their lives!"™ Now, with Karen's One Chance Foundation, readers can join her in the belief that all of us have one chance to make a difference in the lives of orphans.

In the Bible, James 1:27 says people with pure and genuine religion care for orphans. The One Chance Foundation was created with that truth in mind.

If you are interested in giving to Karen's

One Chance Foundation and having your dedication printed in one of Karen's upcoming novels, visit www.KarenKingsbury .com. Below are dedications from some of Karen's reader friends who have contributed to the One Chance Foundation:

- To Jennifer, The love of my life! My artist muse! Thank you for every day. Love Brett
- Love our great kids, Steve, Mike & Patty, & 7 gr-kids! Mom E (Sharon Evers)
- To the One Chance Foundation — Randy Collins
- To our incredible children and grand-children — Jim and Peggy Peterson
- In memory of AJ my sweet son in Heaven, my love for you is forever. Love mom (Cynthia Tuttle)
- To Ron Brudi, my loving husband of 58 years. Love, Lois. Psalm 91:14–16
- Don, "Pops" — Your legacy lives on in our children. You are forever in our hearts. Our bond is eternal. Love Ya! Loretta, Zach & Meghan, Taylor, Jacob & Alex
- To My Beloved Wesley, I miss you more than words can express. I love you the most. Always! Thank you for

loving me unconditionally for the short time we had together. — Amy

- For Sherry, my God-given mother. He could not have chosen better. Love, Kristy
- In memory of my mom, Huldah Coltrane, who taught me about Jesus. Miss you, Mom! Susan
- To my mom and Theresa for introducing me to life changing books. Love, Pam
- Kyle & Lexi, Julie, Paul, & Carlin . . . 3 John 1:4 . . . Love & Blessings, Mom & Dad
- To Joe & our children & grandchildren: Crystal, Rob, Staci, Joe, T, Megan, Ryan, CJ, Ray, Riley, Rowdy, Brody, Cole & Hunter — All my love, Jackie Holson
- To my sisters Sarah & Becca. I love you! Love, Amy
- Richard Shawback — Your faith inspired so many! We love & miss you! Psalm 27:1. Love, Leslie Kelley
- I'm thankful for you, Mom! Love, Lynette Fryling
- My Mom, Ruth Jones — Finally Home with Jesus! We love & miss you. Joy for us all
- Maeva Kaye 12-30-16 — You were

wanted and loved beyond words! Forever in our hearts

- Grammie, Before I was born, God knew how much I would need you. I love you! Amber
- Lisa Cromwell — "IN THIS MOMENT" God will sustain you. Love Tina, Tracy & Sylvia
- To the One Chance Foundation — Fonda Baker
- Zuzu, I am blessed God chose you to be my Mom. You are my inspiration! Love, Kayla
- Anna Marie, The Lord joined us, and you changed my life, my forever love. Your Nick
- To Reba: Mother, You are all I ever aspire to be. I love you always, Erin
- In memory of my sister, Christine Adair Delano.
- We miss you so much. You are always in our hearts. Love Jenny
- In memory of our baby boy, Amos Steven Frei. 8.18.16–2.15.17 Love, Mommy and Daddy
- Remembering Art . . . who lived well, loved well, and laughed much! — Kurt & Sheila Holman
- Hi Mommy! You have been such an example of Christ for me. I love you

so much! Love, Jennifer

- In Memory of Jody Mathis — Mom, you taught us how to love, have courage & faith when the world seems out of control. You shared your life, stories & love with us each day! We love & miss your smile & encouraging words each day! Love Forever, Your Family
- In Memory of Norma Green — Mom, you shared your servant's heart with us & everyone you came in contact with. You were an inspiration, encourager, cheerleader & a biblical example of what a Christian should be. You taught us to love Jesus & others. We love & miss you! Your Family
- In Memory of Mavis Hussey — Gate, Gram, Nana, Mum. We all love and miss you. Love, Jon & Kristy Hatch
- Betty Hoadley — 4 yrs. ago GOD took you home. Miss & Love You Mom. Kathy Raymond
- To my wonderful children, Ashley Lauren and Trey Alexander. Love forever, Mom, Cindy Vestal
- Baby Girl — I loved you before I even saw you! Love Mom (Meghan Clark, June 2017)
- To my beautiful daughter and Mommy, we miss you so very much.

You'll always be in our hearts. Erika Ann Louise West, 01/22/1975 to 09/09/2015

- Mom, Thank you for all that you do and all that you've made us! Love, Shelby and Kennedy
- 2016, Evette finding us, larger family. Praise God. Love to all my children, Mom
- In loving memory of Mom & Dad — forever in our hearts. Love Julie, Dave, Alan & Andrea
- Jeramiah wasn't a bullfrog, but a very special person to many friends & loved ones. His smile, hugs & jokes could turn anyone's day from dark to light. We lost a piece of our hearts when we lost you. This isn't goodbye but see you later alligator. — Love Mom, Dad, Sis, Dave & your love bug Mia. (Jeramiah J. Truckey 1983–2016)
- To Mary Arnholt, Thanks for being our prayer warrior mom! Love, Staci & Becci
- Deb Garber: To Mom, Shirley Van Gilst, I love you. XOXO
- For Larry Fox: Daddy, We will always remember for you. Love, Lisa, Donna & Rich
- Mom, thanks for teaching me to love,

live, and to always trust God. I love you! Jessica Glasscock

- Kylie + Caroline: You make us so proud. Never forget you're priceless! Love, Mama
- Susie Lewis — forever in our hearts. Love, Wendy, Rhonda, Victoria & Angela
- Thank you Mom for showing us what true love is! Love, Chris, Ben and Jess
- Sarah; I love being your Nana Fia, Love Sophia Smither
- In loving memory of Velma Resseguie. Thank you for all the happiness you brought your family & friends. Love, Judy Resley
- Maria Gardner: Without you none of these moments would be possible. Love, your six monkey kids!
- Mom, The ribbons are packed away, but thanks for the awesome memories! Love, Julie
- In honor of Rachel Maurer, Nicole Farr, Sarah Nicolai. I love you always, Mom, Chris Vroman
- To Dr. Vicky Arcadi & Jackie Padgette-Baird: Both of you use your God given gifts & have blessed my life & countless others by patiently teaching and supporting through FYF4Good. Thank

you for always being there. I'm one of God's miracles in the making because of both of you. Love, Jan Kukkola-Miller

- Remembering Adella Grace & John Max Sellers — Always in our hearts and thoughts!
- In honor of the One Chance Foundation! Love, Claudina Masura
- One Chance Foundation — Thank you for all you do! Love, Shannon Bush
- In loving memory of Papa & Granny, Big Will & Meme! In out hearts forever!
- To Jeri, you inspired my love of reading and of life! Love you, mom! ~Melinda
- Team KK, You are the BEST team around!! It's an honor to work with you all! Love, Susan
- In memory of an amazing Mom & Mamaw who is now with her Lord. Her favorite hobby was reading Karen Kingsbury. We miss you, Nora Francis Sackman (Feb. 24, 1921–Mar. 2, 2017). We hope you are enjoying your new eternal home. Love, Christy & Jackie

READING GROUP GUIDE: IN THIS MOMENT

KAREN KINGSBURY

1. What are your thoughts on Wendell Quinn as a principal? What sort of man was he?

2. Do you think it was wrong or right for Wendell to begin the Raise the Bar club? Explain your thoughts.

3. What do you think of Wendell's claim that he was merely trying to do his job by starting the club?

4. Would you be willing to defend Wendell Quinn in a court of law? Why or why not?

5. What have you noticed about religious freedom in the United States or in your country? Give examples.

6. How do you think the founding fathers

intended us to view religious freedom?

7. Have you ever felt afraid to talk about your faith in public? Share your feelings or stories about that.

8. What is one way you can help preserve religious freedom in this country or in the nation where you live?

9. Why is it important that we have religious freedom? What are the risks if those freedoms and rights are taken away?

10. Alicia lived much of her life consumed by fear. Explain her fears and whether you feel they were rational or not.

11. When have you been deeply afraid? How did you come through that time?

12. Luke Baxter has a very supportive family. Still, his work hours were out of control. Has work ever consumed you or someone you love?

13. What did you think about Reagan's determination to love Luke despite her husband's excessive work?

14. Reagan's Bible study taught her that marriage requires 100 percent from both people, every day. What does this mean to you? Do you agree?

15. Another lesson from Reagan's Bible study was the idea of loving your spouse because such an action is mandated by God — whether the spouse deserves the love or not. How can this truth help you or someone you love?

16. The Raise the Bar club made tremendous changes in the lives of the students at Hamilton High. When have you seen God work in a transformational way in your life or in the life of someone you know?

17. Cami and her father were jaded toward God because of a hurtful past experience. Have you or has someone you know ever blamed God for something another person has done? Why or why not? How did that situation work out and what did you learn?

18. What were some of the key reasons Luke was able to successfully defend Wendell Quinn? Discuss this.

19. Reagan's surprise party for Luke was her way of loving him, even when his actions frustrated her. Talk about a time when you or someone you know loved unconditionally. What was the result? How did it feel to love that way?

20. What do you think about the lawsuits that are often filed against schools and sports teams because of long-standing traditions that involve God and religion? Are there cases that have come to your attention? What are your thoughts?

ABOUT THE AUTHOR

Karen Kingsbury, #1 *New York Times* bestselling novelist, is America's favorite inspirational storyteller, with more than twenty-five million copies of her award-winning books in print. Her last dozen titles have topped bestseller lists, and many of her novels are under development as TV movies and major motion pictures. Her many Baxter books will be the subject of a TV series — *The Baxter Family* — in conjunction with Roma Downey, Mark Burnett, and MGM Studios. Karen is also an adjunct professor of writing at Liberty University. She lives in Tennessee with her husband, Don, and their five sons, three of whom are adopted from Haiti. Their actress daughter, Kelsey, lives nearby and is married to Christian recording artist Kyle Kupecky. The couple has one child, Hudson.